Check into the Pennyfoot Hotel . . .
for delightful tales of detection!

Room with a Clue
The view from the Pennyfoot's roof garden is lovely—
but for Lady Eleanor Danbury, it was the last thing she
ever saw. Now Cecily must find out who sent the
snobbish society matron falling to her death . . .

Do Not Disturb
Mr. Bickley answered the door knocker and ended up
dead. Cecily must capture the culprit—before murder
darkens another doorstep . . .

Service for Two
Dr. McDuff's funeral became a fiasco when the mourners
found a stranger's body in the casket. Now Cecily must
close the case—for at the Pennyfoot, murder is a most
unwelcome guest . . .

Eat, Drink, and Be Buried
April showers bring May flowers—when one of the guests
is found strangled with a maypole ribbon. Soon the May
Day celebration turns into a hotel investigation—and
Cecily fears it's a merry month . . . for murder.

Check-Out Time
Life at the Pennyfoot hangs in the balance one sweltering
summer when a distinguished guest plunges to his death
from his top-floor balcony. Was it the heat . . . or
cold-blooded murder?

Grounds for Murder
The Pennyfoot was abuzz when a young gypsy was
hacked to death in the woods near Badgers End. And
now it's up to Cecily to find out who at the Pennyfoot has
a deadly axe to grind . . .

MORE MYSTERIES FROM THE
BERKLEY PUBLISHING GROUP . . .

SISTER FREVISSE MYSTERIES: Medieval mystery in the tradition of
Ellis Peters . . .

by Margaret Frazer

PENNYFOOT HOTEL MYSTERIES: In Edwardian England, death
takes a seaside holiday . . .

by Kate Kingsbury

GLYNIS TRYON MYSTERIES: The highly acclaimed series set in the
early days of the women's rights movement . . . "Historically accurate
and telling."   —Sara Paretsky

by Miriam Grace Monfredo

PAY THE PIPER

KATE KINGSBURY

BERKLEY PRIME CRIME, NEW YORK

PAY THE PIPER

A Berkley Prime Crime Book / published by arrangement with
the author

PRINTING HISTORY
Berkley Prime Crime edition / March 1996

The Putnam Berkley World Wide Web site address is
http://www.berkley.com

ISBN: 0-425-15231-6

Berkley Prime Crime Books are published
by The Berkley Publishing Group,
200 Madison Avenue, New York, NY 10016.
The name BERKLEY PRIME CRIME and the BERKLEY PRIME CRIME
design are trademarks belonging to Berkley Publishing Corporation.

PRINTED IN THE UNITED STATES OF AMERICA

10 9 8 7 6 5 4 3 2 1

CHAPTER

❈ 1 ❈

The first three months of the year in Badgers End were fairly predictable as far as the weather was concerned. The dark, damp, dreary days seemed to limp by, one after the other, with nothing to relieve the depressing monotony of dull gray skies and empty windswept streets. Little disturbed the silence of the cold, lonely beaches, except perhaps the harsh cries of ravenous sea gulls and the frothy breakers slapping the shore.

Even the Pennyfoot Hotel, normally a splendid sight with its white walls glittering in the summer sun, seemed drab as it faced the fury of the raw east wind screaming in from the North Sea, tossing aside everything in its path that wasn't anchored down.

Samuel Rawlins was forced to hang on to his cap as he

drove the trap into town early that morning. This was the time of year he despised. He couldn't wait for the warmer days of spring to thaw out his bones.

For once, however, there was something to brighten the dismal days of January in that year of 1909. For the very first time, the Scots were coming to town.

In honor of Robert Burns, the celebrated poet, whose birthday fell upon 25 January, the civic leaders in Wellercombe were holding a massive celebration. Visitors, and more importantly the shillings and pence they brought with them, were scarce on the coast that early in the year. The town council hoped to lure not only the citizens of nearby London, but also those from the north where the weather was even more miserable.

Samuel was eager to discuss the upcoming events with Tom Abbittson, the local butcher. The hotel's stable manager had been sent to pick up the chef's meat order, and he was looking forward to chatting with Tom. He liked the butcher, a big, jovial man with a belly laugh that could always bring a smile to Samuel's face, no matter how miserable he was feeling.

This morning in particular, Samuel needed cheering up. He loved his job at the Pennyfoot, even if it did mean taking on added duties when business was slow. Cecily Sinclair, the widowed owner of the hotel, took on extra staff for the summer months, but in the winter the regular staff took care of everything.

The problem wasn't with his job, Samuel thought, as the chestnut clipped at a steady pace along the deserted Esplanade. His problem was with Doris, the new kitchen maid. Doris and her twin Daisy had been hired less than three months ago, and right away Samuel had taken a fancy to the shy, rosy-cheeked young girl.

They would get along together perfectly, if it wasn't for Doris's ambition to become a singer. Not yet fifteen, she had already made up her mind that she was going to marry a toff, and had decided that the way to meet one was to sing in the Variety Halls. Nothing Samuel could say or do would change her mind.

Just thinking about it gave Samuel an ache in his belly. He could still feel the pain of it when he left the chestnut tied up at the curb in the High Street and walked into the butcher's shop.

Sawdust swirled in front of his feet as the wind followed him through the door. The smell of raw meat greeted him, and he wrinkled his nose, trying vainly to rub some warmth into his frozen hands. He just wanted to get out of this cold drafty shop and back to the warmth of the stables.

Tom stood at the block, hacking at a slab of meat with a wicked-looking chopper. The muscle in his thick arm knotted above the elastic that banded the sleeve of his white shirt.

Catching sight of Samuel, he winked and called out a greeting without breaking the strong, steady rhythm of the chopper as it sliced cleanly through the bone.

A woman stood near the counter, clutching a shawl about her skinny shoulders as she waited for her order. Samuel nodded to her and lifted his cap, then called out to Tom.

"I've come for the Pennyfoot's order. Michel said he dropped it off to you last night before you went down the pub."

"Right." Tom paused, wiping a hand down his blood-smeared, blue-striped apron. "I've got most of it, but he wants a side of beef. Get you downstairs, there's a good lad, and pick one out for me, will you? I've got to take care of this order here for Lord Withersgill, and it'll take me a while."

Samuel nodded and touched his cap again at the woman before heading for the steps to the cellar.

If there was one thing he hated, he thought as he slowly descended the narrow wooden staircase, it was having to go down in that stinking cellar. He wasn't partial to the smell of a butcher's shop anyway, but it was a whole lot better than the stench that awaited him in the cold, dark shadows below.

This was where the carcasses hung, until Tom could get them cut up into the various joints—great huge slabs of red raw meat, swinging side by side from the racks overhead, dripping blood everywhere. It was enough to make Samuel bring up his breakfast.

As he reached the foot of the steps he could see the chickens swinging upside down with their ruffled feathers waiting to be plucked. Their beady eyes stared at him from their dead faces, which hung limply from twisted yellow necks.

The sooner he got out of there the better, Samuel told himself, trying to avoid the sticky puddles that even the sawdust and straw couldn't disguise.

At the back of the cellar, in the darkest corner, the long rack ran across the rafters, bearing its grisly weight of raw beef. Samuel shivered in the cool, moist air. He wouldn't be a butcher if they paid him a hundred pounds a month.

He crept forward, squinting in the dim light that filtered through the dusty window high above his head. He should have brought a lamp with him, he thought, as he spread out his hands in front of him. Though how in the heck he was supposed to know a good side of beef from a bad one, he had no idea.

The choice was easy. Take the first one he laid hands on. That was the worst part—grabbing hold of that cold, lifeless lump of flesh wrapped in its gauze stocking.

His hands touched a carcass, and he clutched at it, bracing himself to take the weight as he lifted it off the hook. The beef came off easily, and he grunted under the heavy burden as he balanced it on his shoulder. He was about to turn away when something caught his eye.

He looked. And looked again. That wasn't a side of beef he was looking at, his mind assured him. It was a man . . . hanging from a hook next to the swaying beef, with his chin on his chest and his face as white as chalk, as a man only can look with every drop of blood drained out of him.

* * *

"I do believe that this will be our finest effort ever," Phoebe Carter-Holmes declared. "I am most excited at the prospect."

"It doesn't take very much to excite you," a languid voice answered.

Cecily Sinclair, seated at the head of the long, Jacobean table in the library of the Pennyfoot Hotel, viewed the other two women with the futile hope that for once they would not get into another of their spiteful spats.

Phoebe, as always, looked as if she'd stepped from the pages of the *Tatler*. A French lace ruffle at her throat peeked out from the jacket of her navy blue suit, and her hat tilted at a provocative angle under the weight of several pink silk roses.

No one would ever know, Cecily mused, that Phoebe made do with clothes that had seen far more light of day than she cared to admit. No longer enjoying the support of her dead husband, Phoebe still struggled to keep up appearances, and was a dab hand at attaching or removing whatever trimmings were fashionable at the time.

At the moment, Phoebe was glaring at Madeline Pengrath, who lounged unbecomingly on her chair, one arm flung over the velvet padded back. Madeline's long, black silky hair flowed over her shoulders, spilling down the bodice of her mauve cotton frock, and her eyes, dark and brooding, rested on Phoebe's outraged face.

"I'll thank you to keep a civil tongue in your head," Phoebe snapped. "Unless I am mistaken, we are here to discuss the plans for the Tartan Ball on Saturday, not to exchange insults with one another."

"I agree," Cecily said, lifting her pen from the inkwell. She shook the excess ink from the nib, then poised it over the sheet of paper on the table in front of her. "Perhaps you will begin, Phoebe? Were you successful in persuading the bagpipers to play for us?"

Phoebe beamed, smoothing out the creases in her elbow-length gloves with a triumphant flourish. "I was indeed. How fortunate we are that the civic leaders in Wellercombe decided to hold a contest for the pipers. There must be several hundred of them in town for the event."

"I'm not surprised," Madeline said, hiding a yawn behind her long fingers. "There are some very lucrative prizes. I do believe the Grand Prize affords the opportunity to perform in front of the king, no less."

"Not only that," Phoebe said, her voice rising in excitement, "but the winner of the Grand Prize will also be invited to audition for the Sandringham pipers at the king's retreat in Norfolk. Can you imagine what an honor that would be? Why, it could change a man's life forever. Imagine, being part of the royal court."

"Imagine," Madeline murmured, her voice heavy with sarcasm.

Ignoring her, Phoebe rattled on. "There are ten pipers in all staying here at the hotel. I talked to Mr. McPherson, who appears to be their spokesman, and every one of them has agreed to band together and give us a short presentation. They were all most charming, I must say."

"Heaven help us," Madeline said, rolling her eyes up at the ceiling. "Even one set of those dreadful wailing pipes is enough to raise the dead. Can you imagine ten of them?"

"I think it will be most stirring," Phoebe said huffily. "Why, at times the music from the pipes brings tears to my eyes."

"I agree, the noise is enough to make a grown man cry," Madeline murmured.

"Ladies, please!" Cecily glanced at the clock on the mantelpiece above the marble fireplace. In spite of the red glow of the coals in the grate, she felt uncommonly cold for some reason. "I have a hundred tasks to get through today. I would like to close this meeting as quickly as possible."

"Well, perhaps if Madeline would refrain from questioning my every remark, we could conduct our business with more expedience." Phoebe raised her hands and gave the brim of her hat an unnecessary tug.

Cecily sent a pleading look to Madeline, who merely shrugged.

"In any case," Phoebe went on, "I have yet to report on the second part of the entertainment. Since we are presenting the Tartan Ball in conjunction with the Scottish celebrations in Wellercombe, I thought it would be only fitting if we employed my little troupe of dancers to perform two of Scotland's most famous dances, the Highland Fling and the Sword Dance. That's if they can manage it without cutting off their toes."

Cecily nodded, doing her best to look enthusiastic. "That's a wonderful idea, Phoebe," she said valiantly.

Madeline muttered something under her breath that was mercifully inaudible.

"Yes, I thought so." Phoebe preened for a second or two. "In any case, Mr. McPherson kindly offered to assist me in teaching the girls the steps. He's also offered to play the bagpipes for the rehearsals. So much better than asking Lydia to play the piano. I'm not certain she'd be able to play the Scottish tunes."

"I'm not certain that Lydia knows how to play any tune all the way through," Madeline said, earning a frown of reproof from Cecily.

"That is most kind of Mr. McPherson." Cecily scribbled a few notes, then dipped the pen into the inkwell. "But will he have time to manage all that work? I understand the pipers will be rehearsing for the contest in the church hall."

"Yes, they are." Phoebe nodded, sending the roses on her hat trembling for their safety. "We will be rehearsing in the village hall. But Alec . . . Mr. McPherson has assured me he will be able to fit everything in. He told me it will be extra practice for him. He seems quite determined to win that contest."

"Alec?"

Cecily sighed. She might have known Madeline wouldn't

let that reference pass without comment. The slender woman leaned forward, her expressive eyes gleaming with mischief.

"Why, Phoebe dear, don't tell me you have acquired a possible suitor? He is certainly a fast worker. On intimate terms, are we? Using Christian names already?"

Phoebe's cheeks took on a rosy hue. "Mr. McPherson treats me with the utmost respect. I warned him that he might have taken on a formidable task in teaching my girls the steps in such a short space of time, and he suggested that we use our first names to present a united front, so to speak. There are times when my ladies are inclined to disregard my instructions."

Madeline nodded slowly, looking pleased at the prospect of taking Phoebe down a peg or two.

Cecily closed her eyes for a brief moment. Sometimes she wondered if these meetings were really worth the time spent on them. If she didn't know that deep down Madeline and Phoebe had a real affection for each other, she'd suggest meeting them separately.

If she did that, however, she'd no doubt offend the two of them, and hurt them dreadfully. Cecily had a feeling that the two of them actually enjoyed sparring in this inelegant manner.

"So," Madeline was saying in her low, melodic voice, "Alec is helping you teach your young ladies to perform two of Scotland's most famous dances. I wonder if he truly knows what he is facing."

Phoebe sniffed. "As I said, I explained the inadequacies of my troupe. They do try, however, and that's the important thing."

"Well, my dear, I have only one thing to say." Madeline yawned, stretching her arms above her head and managing to look like a beautiful, sultry cat. "If you want to keep your sanity, beware of any man who wears a skirt."

Even Cecily had to hide a smile at that.

Phoebe straightened her back with a loud huff of breath.

"I can assure you, Madeline, that there are some men in this world to be trusted. For your information, in order to take part in the contest, every man has to have an impeccable background. They don't allow just anybody to audition for Sandringham, you know."

"I'm sure they don't," Madeline purred, looking unimpressed.

"Why, just yesterday, Alec . . . Mr. McPherson was kind enough to miss his second day of practice in order to give the first dancing lesson. I thought that was terribly gallant of him."

"Really! He must, indeed, be confident if he can afford to miss a practice."

"He can afford to be confident," Phoebe retorted. "I have heard him play, and his expertise on the bagpipes is most impressive. He fully expects to win the contest."

"Ladies!" Her patience finally giving out, Cecily tapped the polished surface of the table with her fingernails. "I must ask you to continue this conversation elsewhere. I need to know what arrangements you have in mind for the ballroom, Madeline."

"Red and gold," Madeline said promptly, apparently recognizing her friend's authoritative tone. "Chrysanthemums for the most part, I think. They do so well this time of year. And lots of greenery. Perhaps your gardener can help me there?"

Cecily nodded. "I'm sure John will be happy to provide you with whatever you need."

"I thought I would use some wide Scottish-plaid ribbon in various tartans, since the pipers belong to different clans, and their kilts will be varied."

"That sounds wonderful, Madeline." Cecily put down her pen. "This has been a most productive meeting. Thank you, ladies. We will—" She broke off as a sharp tap sounded on the door. "Come in!"

The door opened, and Baxter's face appeared in the opening. Cecily could tell at once by her manager's expression that he had disturbing news for her. As always, her first thoughts flew to her son Michael. He owned the local village inn, the George and Dragon, and one never knew when someone might cause trouble under the influence of too much ale.

"If you will excuse me, madam," Baxter murmured, "I would like a word with you when you are finished with your business here."

"We are finished, Baxter." Cecily rose to her feet. "The ladies were just leaving."

"Oh, my, yes," Phoebe exclaimed, clutching the brim of her hat as she rose. "I had no idea it was so late. My girls will be expecting me very shortly."

Hurrying across the thick carpet, she threw her farewells over her shoulder, managing a simpering smile for Baxter at the same time as he stood holding the door open for her.

Baxter inclined his head, then waited for Madeline, who remained at the table staring at him with an odd, still expression on her face.

Cecily looked from her friend to Baxter, her uneasiness growing. Very slowly, Madeline got to her feet. She crossed the room, her skirt swishing gently about her ankles. Baxter's face looked wary as she paused in front of him.

"Whoever he was," she said softly, "may God rest his soul." With that, she passed through the doorway and disappeared.

CHAPTER

2

"Bloody 'ell, Doris, look where you're bleeding going, will you?" Gertie's piercing voice carried above the crashing of Michel's saucepans as he expertly tossed the soft roes in the sizzling hot fat, stirred the oatmeal, and lifted a lid to peer at the scrambled eggs seemingly all at the same time.

Doris, a scrawny young girl wearing a white pinafore apron that seemed to swamp her thin body, almost tripped over the hem of her long gray skirt as she scurried across the stone floor. The sack of potatoes she carried looked bigger than she was. "I'm sorry, Miss Brown," she said, her voice barely raised above a whisper.

"You're always bleeding sorry. That's the third time you've stepped on my blinking foot today. I'll be a bloody cripple by the time you've finished." Gertie stood in the center of the floor, her fists dug into her wide hips, and glared at the hapless girl.

"I'll watch it, Miss Brown, honest I will." Doris heaved the sack onto the edge of the sink and opened the neck. Potatoes tumbled out into the sink, making a thunderous noise that prompted Michel to throw back his head.

"*Sacre bleu!* What with ze crying babies, housemaids who scream, and a housekeeper who does not stop jabbering all day, it is no wonder I 'ave the coddlewillies."

"Collywobbles," Gertie murmured. She didn't know why she bothered to keep correcting the irritable chef. He bloody knew as well as she did what the word was. Him and that stupid French accent. He soon forgot it when he tipped the brandy bottle once too often, that was for bleeding sure.

"And just who is it who makes all the noise in here, then?" demanded yet another strident voice.

Gertie shoved a stray lump of her dark hair under her cap, hoping it was on straight. When Mrs. Chubb was on the bleeding warpath, no one escaped her wrath. Although Gertie towered over the Pennyfoot's matronly housekeeper, she still jumped when the woman started yelling.

Michel glared at Mrs. Chubb and crashed a saucepan lid onto the stove, causing Doris to utter a startled yelp. "Does not anyone here have ze respect for my talent?" he yelled. "I cannot concentrate with all this racket going on."

"Then I suggest you refrain from creating so much noise yourself," Mrs. Chubb said tartly. "You'll wake up the babies if you keep this up. Then you'll really have something to complain about."

"Cor blimey, Michel, you'd better not do that," Gertie said with feeling. "I've never seen so much blinking noise come out of such little bodies. If I'd known I was going to have bleeding twins I'd have drowned meself."

"Hush, child, don't say such a thing." Mrs. Chubb looked at the kitchen door as if she expected the babies to come walking in at any minute. "Talk like that can do untold damage to tiny ears."

Gertie rattled the silverware she was sorting on a tray. She knew the housekeeper meant well, but she wished Mrs. Chubb would give up telling her how to take care of her babies. That's all she heard all day long, *don't do this, don't do that*. It was enough to make her blinking scream at times.

"Well, I just hope they behave theirselves at the christening next week," she muttered. "I don't need the both of them screeching in the vicar's ear. He might bleeding drop them, knowing him."

"The Reverend Algie Carter-Holmes might look awkward at times," Mrs. Chubb said, frowning as one more of Michel's pans hit the edge of the stove, "but he is well used to handling babies. I'm quite sure that James and Lillian will be safe in his hands."

Gertie watched the housekeeper reach up to the high ledge above the enormous fireplace. Mrs. Chubb lifted up one of the china spaniels and took down the slip of paper that served as Michel's menu for the week. After quickly scanning it, she put it back again.

"Did Samuel get the order from Abbittson's this morning?" she asked the sullen chef as he threw bacon into the sizzling pan. The gorgeous smell of frying bacon made Gertie's tummy rumble loud enough for everyone to hear it.

Michel gave an expansive shrug, lifting his hands in the air. "I sent him, but I have not seen hide nor hair of him. I will need ze beef for the midday meal, so I 'ope and pray he get here soon."

"Where's Doris?" Mrs. Chubb demanded.

"You're bleeding staring at her." Gertie held up a fork and shook her head. "Look at this. Still got bloody egg on it."

The housekeeper stared at Doris's back. "That's Doris? Then where's Daisy?"

"Looking after the babies. It's her morning off, remember?"

Mrs. Chubb huffed in irritation, glaring at Doris as if it was her fault she hadn't recognized her. "I'll never be able to tell you two apart. What with twin housemaids and now your twins, Gertie, I'm beginning to think I'm seeing double everywhere I look. Thank goodness you had a girl and a boy. At least we'll be able to tell the difference between them when they get older."

"If they get bloody older," Gertie muttered darkly. "They blinking keep me up at night much longer, I might be tempted to drop the little buggers in the sea."

"Gertie Brown! For heaven's sake, child, how can you say such a terrible thing? They're not yet three months old, poor little mites. You must not be giving them enough milk, that's all I can say. Anyway, there's not a peep out of them now."

"That's because Daisy's looking after them. They seem to have taken to her." Gertie stared thoughtfully at the fork in her hand. "She's a strange one, that Daisy. She might look exactly like you, Doris, but she bloody ain't like you in manner."

Doris sent a nervous glance over her shoulder. "Daisy always was the strong one. She took care of me when we lived with our aunt. She was always the one what took the hidings, 'cause she said I was too weak and our aunt would kill me."

"Strewth," Gertie muttered, her respect for Daisy deepening. "It's no bloody wonder she never smiles."

"Our Daisy doesn't care much for people," Doris said, turning back to her task of peeling the potatoes. "She likes animals better, because she says they can't stick up for themselves and need protecting."

"Like babies," Gertie said softly. At first she couldn't think why the belligerent scullery maid would be so obliging about watching over her twins. Now she was beginning to understand.

"Well, I'm looking forward to the christening," Mrs. Chubb said, crossing over to the pantry. "And I think it was very nice indeed of madam to give you a reception afterward in the ballroom."

"It was really nice of her." The silverware finally sorted,

Gertie picked up the heavy tray. "I just hope everyone can come. I invited everyone."

"You did not invite me," Michel declared, waving his wooden spoon at her.

"I bloody did, too. You—" Gertie never finished the sentence for at that moment the door burst open, and Samuel charged into the kitchen, his cap clutched in both his hands and his eyes wide and staring, as if he'd seen a ghost.

"Blimey," Gertie said as Samuel stared wildly around the room, "What's the bleeding matter with you, then?"

"It was horrible," Samuel said, his teeth chattering. "It was bloody awful."

"Samuel!" Mrs. Chubb shook her finger at him. "You're beginning to sound like Gertie. I've given up trying to make her wash out her mouth, but you should know better." Sending a scathing glance at Gertie, she added, "Though I hope to heaven you don't say those filthy words in front of your babies, Gertie Brown. Little ones pick up so fast, they'll both be talking like guttersnipes before they're old enough to think for themselves."

For once Gertie let the criticism pass over her head. Samuel looked as if he was about to chuck up his breakfast. "What was bloody awful?" she demanded, not sure she wanted to know.

"He was hanging on a hook in Tom's cellar," Samuel said, staggering to a chair at the large scrubbed table. "He was white as a sheet of paper, he was. Not a drop of blood left in him."

Gertie promptly lost her appetite.

Mrs. Chubb stood staring at Samuel, while Doris leaned weakly against the sink, her eyes fixed on Samuel's face. Even Michel had paused, one hand still holding the lid of a frying pan.

"Who was?" Gertie whispered.

"One of the Scots pipers, that's who." Samuel buried his face in his hands, as if trying to shut out the grisly sight. "His throat was cut with a butcher knife, as clean as a whistle. Whoever did it hung him up next to the beef carcasses on the rack and left him to bleed all over the floor."

"Oh, my." Mrs. Chubb clutched her throat. "Was it one of the pipers who was staying here at the hotel?"

Samuel nodded, then lowered his hands. He looked straight at Doris and said quietly, "It was Peter Stewart."

Gertie carefully lowered the tray to the table, just as Doris gave a little moan and slid to the floor.

Cecily watched Baxter cross the floor toward her, his face set in an expression she knew well. "What is it?" she said as he paused a few feet away. "What's happened now?"

"I'm afraid there's been a death, madam."

She waited for a few seconds, knowing that, as always, she would have to prompt him for further information. She had difficulty forming the question. "Family?"

He shook his head, looking distressed. "Oh, no, madam. A guest at the hotel."

Concern followed her relief almost immediately. "Was it an accidental death?"

That was too much to hope for, of course. She wasn't too surprised when Baxter said quietly, "I'm sorry, madam. I'm afraid it was murder."

"Oh, dear, no. Who is it?"

"One of the pipers. Peter Stewart."

Cecily closed her eyes. "Such a nice young man."

"Yes, madam. Samuel discovered the body."

Cecily sat down rather heavily in her chair. "Samuel? Found him here in the hotel? Where?"

"Oh, no, not here in the hotel."

"Then where, Baxter?"

"At Tom Abbittson's shop, madam."

Baxter's maddening habit of giving only one piece of information at a time could drive her insane. "Baxter, would you kindly tell me everything you know?"

"I don't have too much to tell." Baxter lifted his chin,

looking affronted. "Samuel arrived back from the shop a short time ago and informed me that he had found Peter Stewart hanging on the rack with the beef in Tom Abbittson's cellar."

"Good Lord." She stared into the fireplace for a second or two to gather her thoughts. "Has the constable been informed?"

"I believe the butcher sent for him."

"The poor man was hanged, you said?"

"Not exactly, madam."

Cecily gave him a meaningful look.

Baxter clasped his hands behind his back and added stiffly, "His throat was cut. I wasn't sure you would care to hear the details."

"No doubt I shall hear them all in due course," Cecily said dryly.

"I do believe Police Constable Northcott intends to question Samuel more thoroughly here at the hotel after he has finished his investigation at the shop." Baxter's tone suggested that the procedure would be a complete waste of time.

Cecily knew that her manager's adverse opinion of the constable was due largely to the fact that many years ago Stan Northcott had stolen away Baxter's only true love. Even so, she was inclined to agree with his low estimation of the policeman's capabilities.

P.C. Northcott was, at best, a pretentious boor who lived in awe of his superior, Inspector Cranshaw. The vast majority of the constable's actions and decisions were aimed at pleasing the inspector, rather than performing his job with any degree of proficiency.

"I would like a word with the constable after he has talked to Samuel." Cecily leaned back in her chair with a sigh. "When is this ever going to end, Baxter? It seems we get over one crisis, only to be faced with another. I don't suppose you know who might have committed the murder, or why?"

Baxter's gray eyes softened with sympathy. "I'm sorry, madam. Can I get you anything? A pot of tea, perhaps?"

She smiled at him, feeling a sudden warmth. "Thank you, Baxter, but I'll wait awhile. I haven't long had breakfast." She looked up at him from under her lashes. "As a matter of fact, though, I would adore one of your little cigars."

"I would prefer to bring you the pot of tea." Nevertheless, he reached in his top coat pocket and pulled out the slim package of cigars.

Cecily allowed him to light the end for her, and drew in the welcome fragrance. She enjoyed watching the smoke curl in front of her and found it most relaxing. "I suppose all we can hope for in this instance is that the constable solves this murder as quickly as possible. With all the festivities planned for this weekend, we do not need to be disrupted by a murder investigation."

"It is really not all that surprising," Baxter said, retreating to his position at the end of the table. "I have heard tales of some nasty brawls taking place at the George and Dragon. Apparently the Scots do not care too much for our British government. They still resent being ruled by an English king. Their attitude tends to incite the local farmers."

"Yes, I'm sure it does." Cecily gazed moodily at the glowing end of her cigar. "Why can't people get along, Baxter? The world is in such turmoil. Even the New Women's Movement is becoming more violent in their protests, though I can't say I blame them. I would have thought Churchill might have been willing to help their cause, now that he has a new wife."

"Mr. Churchill has stated that he will not lift a finger to help as long as the protesters physically attack the politicians."

"So I have heard." Cecily glanced up at the portrait of her late husband, which hung above the fireplace. James had been dead three years now. There were times when she found it difficult to remember his face. The fact no longer unsettled her the way it used to.

Had it not been for James's untimely death, she would not have inherited the Pennyfoot Hotel. Even with all the trials and tribulations of struggling to maintain quality service, and despite the enormous debts James had left, Cecily adored her life and would not have it any other way. Except, perhaps, for one or two exceptions.

"Then there's all this talk of potential war between England and Germany," she added, tapping the ash from her cigar into the silver ashtray. "I wish I could think it was merely pessimism on the part of the prime minister, but I have to admit, Baxter, the rumors worry me."

Baxter's face was grave as he looked down at her. "Might I suggest that you try to forget the problems of the world and concentrate on the immediate problem at hand?"

She smiled up at him. "What would I do without you, Baxter? Of course you are right. The problems of the world I can do nothing about. I can only hope that this latest murder does not directly involve the hotel or any of its staff."

"And that," Baxter said heavily, "is a trust with which I can heartily agree."

Shortly after her conversation with Baxter, Cecily was accosted in the hallway by Colonel Fortescue, who for once appeared to be quite sober—a state he no doubt would make haste to rectify before lunch was served in the dining room.

"Ah, Mrs. Sinclair! Topping day, what? What?" The elderly gentleman twirled his luxuriant mustache with a flourish. "Can't imagine why anyone would want to stay inside on a day like this."

"It's a little too cold for most people," Cecily pointed out, glancing hopefully toward the lobby for an avenue of escape.

"Poppycock!" The colonel's booming voice echoed down the passageway. "This bracing air is just what the doctor ordered. Give's one a healthy appetite, by George. In my opinion, people tend to mollycoddle themselves nowadays. Going about all wrapped up in mufflers and those fur thingummies . . . one needs to get the air to one's body. Good for the soul, you know."

Fortescue slapped his protruding belly with such gusto he coughed, gasping for breath.

"I'm sure it is, Colonel," Cecily murmured, doing her best to edge past him.

"Mind you, I don't approve of baring the skin altogether, of course," the colonel said, recovering his breath. "Not like those damn natives in India. Why, I remember once—"

"If you'll excuse me, Colonel," Cecily said desperately. "I really must be going."

Colonel Fortescue looked disappointed. "Oh, of course, old bean. Wouldn't want to keep you. Must be busy with all these Scottish chappies running around. Now there's a barbaric sight if ever I saw one."

The murder of Peter Stewart still on her mind, Cecily reacted without thinking. "I beg your pardon? What sight would that be, Colonel?"

He tilted forward and dropped his voice to a loud whisper. "All those bare knees, madam. In front of women, mind you. Shocking, if you ask me. Wouldn't be so bad if the men kept their dashed knees together when they sit down. Downright wicked, I call it. 'Pon my word, those hot-tempered heathens are worse than the natives."

"It is their uniform, Colonel. Scotsmen have been wearing the kilt for centuries."

"They can call it what they like, madam. But a skirt is a skirt. And a damn short one at that. They should be horsewhipped. Every last one of them. Not a gentleman among them." Still muttering and grumbling, the colonel wandered off, his head moving from side to side like a tired walrus looking for something to eat.

Cecily's relief was short-lived, however, when Doris timidly approached her in the lobby. The skinny girl dropped an awkward curtsey, then said in her breathless voice, "Mr. Baxter says as how you wanted to speak with P.C. Northcott, mum."

Cecily gave the nervous girl a smile of encouragement. "Yes, I would like a word with the constable, Doris." She peered closer. "It is Doris, isn't it?"

A glimpse of white teeth reassured her. "Yes, mum. It's Daisy's morning off."

Doris had seemed surprised that Cecily had recognized her right away, though in Cecily's opinion, anyone who knew the girls would never confuse Daisy's rebellious, belligerent attitude with her sister's meek and mild manner.

Studying the girl, Cecily noticed with concern her ashen cheeks. "Are you feeling all right, Doris? You look a little pale this morning."

"Yes, mum, thank you, mum. It was just the shock and all. I was just talking to Peter yesterday, you see."

Surprised, Cecily said quietly, "I'm sorry, Doris. I know how very upsetting these things can be. Has the constable finished with Samuel?" She glanced at the grandfather clock in the corner of the lobby. The morning seemed to be passing much too quickly.

"Yes, mum. He wanted to know where you wanted to receive him, mum."

Cecily sighed, giving up for now her intention of a few quiet moments alone in the roof garden. The secluded area created between the sloping roofs of the hotel had been James's idea—a refuge from the hectic turmoil of the guests and their constant demands, and the numerous crises engendered by the unpredictable staff.

Cecily had often escaped there when she needed time to rest, or to ponder on a dilemma, which seemed to happen at frequent intervals at the Pennyfoot.

This latest news of a murder in the town had unsettled her a great deal. The fact that the victim had been a guest at the hotel was enough to implicate the Pennyfoot, something Cecily could ill afford.

The hotel was a favorite hideaway for the aristocrats who

preferred to alleviate their boredom in more imaginative ways than was considered entirely proper. Secluded as it was on the quiet southeast coast, the village of Badgers End afforded a privacy that could not be found in the city, or in any town of some size.

In the bowels of the Pennyfoot the affluent society could pursue card games and other forms of gambling without fear of being observed, and in the lush scented boudoirs one could dally with a lover without risk of tattling tongues.

For it was the policy, and a strict one, that all who worked at the hotel did so with the knowledge that one word of gossip escaping from the realm of belowstairs meant instant dismissal.

It was therefore imperative that any contact with the authorities in town be kept to an absolute minimum. The appearance of a uniformed policeman on the premises would not be likely to instill the trust that brought the majority of the Pennyfoot's customers flocking from London on a regular basis.

Then again, finding a guest of the hotel hanging in a butcher's shop with his throat cut wasn't exactly the kind of publicity Cecily needed either.

"Mum?" Doris said tentatively, jolting Cecily out of her worried thoughts.

"Oh, I'm sorry, Doris. I'm afraid I was wool-gathering. Please ask the constable to meet me in the drawing room. It is unlikely there will be any guests in there at this time of day."

"Yes, mum." Again Doris dropped a curtsey, then rushed off to the kitchen stairs, leaving Cecily ruefully wishing it had been warm enough to meet P.C. Northcott outside the hotel. Preferably on the beach, where no one would be likely to notice him.

She needed to know as much about the murder as Northcott was willing to tell her, however. As long as there was the slightest chance of the hotel being involved in an investigation, Cecily wanted all the information she could get.

She retraced her steps and headed for the drawing room, trying to ignore the little voice of foreboding that usually preceded yet another calamity at the Pennyfoot.

CHAPTER

❀ 3 ❀

Having dispatched the constable to the drawing room, Doris took the opportunity of a spare moment to look in on Daisy. Upon opening the door to Gertie's room, she was greeted with a fierce "Hush!"

Daisy sat in the rocking chair with a pile of pale blue fabric on her lap, her needle poised ready to strike. Across the room a large cradle took up most of the corner space between a small wardrobe and the three-legged bedside table.

"They're asleep," Daisy whispered, jerking her head at the cradle.

Doris nodded and crept across the floor to take a look. The babies lay on their side facing each other. Each head was barely covered by a fuzz of hair the color of coal, and one tiny fist seemed to threaten anyone who disturbed them.

"I bet that's the boy," Doris whispered, looking at the fist.

"That's James on the right," Daisy said softly. "I just changed their nappies so I know."

Pleased with her guess, Doris trod carefully back to the rocking chair. "I'd hate to change nappies. They must smell awful."

Daisy shrugged. "No more than mucking out stables or cleaning pigpens, and I don't mind that."

"Well, you always did like messing about with animals. Thank goodness Aunt Beatrice never knew it was you taking my turn with the chickens and pigs. She'd have made me do it, and you know how I hated it."

"Well, you did my share of the needlework." Daisy swore and stuck a finger in her mouth. After sucking on it for a moment, she withdrew it and examined the tiny spot of blood that appeared on the rounded tip of the finger. "See what I mean? I'm hopeless at this sewing lark."

"Leave it, then," Doris said warmly, remembering how many times her sister had come to her rescue. "I'll do it when I get off this evening."

Daisy peered up at her twin. "You feeling better now? Mrs. Chubb said you took a nasty turn when you heard about Peter Stewart."

"I'm all right." Doris patted her waistline. "I've still got a queasy feeling in my stomach, though. Fancy him being done in like that. Who do you think could have done it?"

"I dunno. I didn't know him like you did."

Doris felt her cheeks grow warm. "I only spoke to him a couple of times. He heard me singing and was really nice about it. Said as how I could make it on the stage. He even promised to help me."

Daisy's green eyes fastened intently on her sister's face. "You'd better watch what you're doing, Doris Hoggins. You're so blinking wrapped up in that dream of yours, it will get you into trouble one day, you mark my words."

"I only talked to him, I did. What's wrong with that? He

might have helped me get on the stage. Then you'd be saying as what a nice gentleman he was."

"He couldn't have been such a nice gentleman if someone wanted to bump him orf," Daisy retorted. "You talk too easily to strangers, that you do. You're not yet fifteen, and you know what happens to young girls what talk to strange men. You heard it often enough from Aunt Beatrice."

Doris tossed her head, resenting the fact that deep down she knew Daisy was right. "Peter Stewart wasn't like that. He was a nice man. I'm careful who I talk to, I am."

"Yeah? Well, Samuel didn't think you was being too careful. I heard him yelling at you for talking to the pipers."

"Samuel thinks he can tell me what to do. He doesn't own me, and nor do you. Just because you hate men doesn't mean that they're all bad. I only want to find someone to help me get on the stage, that's all."

"Well, you'd better watch your step, or you'll find yourself hanging in the butcher's shop like Peter Stewart."

Doris clutched her stomach. "Just shut up, Daisy. You make me sick, you do."

A loud yell made both girls jump. The howl was immediately joined by another lusty voice. Daisy leapt to her feet and rushed across to the cradle. "Now look what you've gone and done. Woke up the babies, you did. It took me forever to get them to sleep."

Ashamed of her outburst, Doris hastily left the room, her sister's warning still ringing in her ears. Daisy just didn't understand, that was all, she thought as she hurried back to the kitchen.

She wouldn't take no funny business off any man, and Daisy should know that. And so should Samuel. He had no business telling her off like that, just because he saw her laughing with Peter Stewart in the courtyard.

Her stomach did another strange little dance. Peter Stewart weren't going to do no more laughing, that was for sure. The thought gave her the cold shivers.

*   *   *

"Yes ma'am, that h'is what I said." Police Constable Stan Northcott rocked back and forth on his heels in front of the fireplace in the quiet drawing room. "Tom Abbittson 'as been taken into custody for the murder of Peter Stewart. I took him down to the station meself."

Cecily regarded the constable, inclined to be skeptical. "I must say, Constable, you seem to have solved this murder with the utmost alacrity. I must commend you."

"Thank you, Mrs. Sinclair. H'I do appreciate your compliment. I must say, I'm rather pleased with the way things have turned out, as a matter of fact."

"I'm sure Inspector Cranshaw will be pleased as well," Cecily said carefully. "It was quite clever of you to get a confession from Mr. Abbittson."

"Oh, no, ma'am, I didn't get no confession. No, just the opposite, h'in fact." The constable tucked his helmet more securely under his arm. The buttonholes on his uniform stained across his bulging belly as he puffed out his chest. "The butcher 'ollered all the way down to the station that he didn't do it. Course, I knew he had. He had guilt written all over his face, that he did."

"I see," Cecily murmured. She waved a hand at her best blue velvet padded Queen Anne chair. "Won't you have a seat, Constable? You must be tired after your busy morning. A cup of tea, perhaps?"

"Oh, well, thank you, ma'am. Very kind of you, I'm sure." The constable stopped preening long enough to seat himself on the chair.

Cecily crossed the room to the doorway and pulled the bell rope. "It should be no more than a few minutes. Pull that chair closer to the fire, if you like. It's quite chilly in here this morning."

It was uncommonly cold in the room, she thought, drawing closer to the fire herself. In fact, she'd been decidedly chilled all morning. She hoped she wasn't coming down with something.

"Ah, well, don't mind if I do." The constable bumped the chair across the carpet, moving it a few inches closer to the fireplace. "It were cold in that butcher's shop, all right. 'Specially down in that there cellar. I don't mind telling you, Mrs. Sinclair, when I saw that body hanging there, all white and shriveled, like, I thought I would freeze to the spot."

"It must have been quite a sight." Cecily seated herself on the ottoman, wondering what Baxter would have said if he'd seen Northcott sit down without waiting for her to take a seat.

"It were, ma'am, that's the truth of it. What with the poor sod's feet dangling like that above the ground and that dirty great butcher's knife lying there . . ." Northcott wagged a fat finger at her. "Well, it told the h'entire story, didn't it. Not to mention the bloodstained butcher's apron all crumpled up, like someone had thrown it off in a hurry."

"You could tell it was Tom Abbittson right away, then," Cecily said, watching the constable's face. His bushy brown hair had begun to thin above his forehead, and had been carefully combed to disguise the fact that he had more growth on his chin than on the top of his head.

It never failed to astonish her that any woman could have preferred this pompous, incompetent oaf to her forceful, efficient manager. Baxter had more intelligence, more charm, more integrity, and certainly more pleasing looks than P.C. Northcott could ever hope to imagine.

"Well, not right away, no, ma'am," Northcott said in answer to her question. "It were the key, you see."

Cecily clasped her hands in her lap in an effort to warm them. In spite of the heavy cotton blouse she wore with her long black skirt, her arms felt as if they had been buried in snow. "The key?" she asked politely.

"Yes, ma'am." The constable's beady eyes gleamed with pride. "It h'occurred to me that had it been someone else what cut the young man's throat and hung him up like a side of beef in the butcher's cellar, that someone else would've had a key to let himself in, like. Otherwise, the door would have been broken in, which it weren't."

"It weren't . . . ?" Cecily shook her head. ". . . Wasn't?"

"No, ma'am, h'it definitely was not. Examined it meself, I did—" Northcott broke off as a light tap sounded on the door.

Impatiently Cecily turned her head to see her housemaid standing in the doorway. "A pot of tea, Gertie, please, and a slice of Mrs. Chubb's Dundee cake."

Gertie bobbed her knees. "Yes, mum."

"And put your cap on straight, Gertie. I can hardly see your eyes."

"Yes, mum."

Cecily turned back to look at the constable, who sat rubbing his hands in gleeful anticipation. "Dundee cake. Oh, yes. My favorite. Much obliged, I'm sure, ma'am."

"Not at all, Constable. You were saying about the key?"

"Oh, yes, the key. Well, like I said, someone 'ad to have a key to get inside the shop. But when I asked Tom Abbittson h'if there was another key to the shop, he told me there was only one. Had the lock made special, he did, and there weren't another one like it to his knowledge. He had the only key right there in his pocket. He showed it to me."

"How strange," Cecily murmured.

"Very," the constable said, obviously unaware with what he was agreeing. "That's what I thought. The butcher reckons he don't remember coming home from the pub. Drunk, he was, as per usual. He says as how he woke up lying in the road in front of the shop with his wife, Elsie, bending over him."

"How absolutely fascinating." Cecily leaned forward, knowing that Northcott would not be able to resist recounting his cleverness in minute detail. "Do go on."

"Yes, well, Elsie says she helped him up to their flat above the shop. They have to go through the shop to get to the flat, since it don't have no outside entrance, so to speak.

"So Tom didn't have to use his key."

The constable blinked. "I beg your pardon?"

Cecily shook her head. "No matter. I'm sorry, Constable. Do go on."

"Well, Elsie swears they went straight to bed, and neither of them moved out of it until the next morning. Abbittson says he didn't have time to go down into the cellar, so he didn't know the body was there until Samuel comes screeching up the stairs, hollering blue murder."

Making a mental note to talk to Samuel as soon as possible, Cecily said brightly, "But you knew Tom was lying, of course."

"Well, after he said as how there was only one key, stands to reason, doesn't it? I mean, he was the only one what could have got inside the shop, and the Scotsman's throat was cut, clean as a whistle with a butcher's knife."

The constable looked up as a sharp tap on the door heralded the arrival of the tea.

Cecily waited until Northcott had devoured a large portion of the cake before saying, "So what do you think really happened, then, Constable?"

The policeman's throat worked at the cake as he swallowed it. "Well, ma'am," he said, his words muffled while he swiped at his mouth with his serviette, "I reckon it happened like this. I found out from Samuel that Abbittson was engaged in fisticuffs with the victim at the pub last night. Course, according to Samuel, just about everyone down there was 'aving a go at each other, but there was no doubt that h'Abbittson and Peter Stewart was mixing it up, like."

A lump of coal shifted in the grate, sending sparks up the chimney. Cecily watched the greedy flames lick at the shiny black nugget. "Both men were seen leaving the pub?" she asked quietly.

"Oh, yes. Samuel was sure about that, right enough." Northcott gulped down the rest of his tea and clattered the cup back in the saucer. "He told me that the Scotsman got the worst of the fight. He left right away apparently. I reckon he waited outside the pub until the butcher left, then followed him back to the shop to have his revenge, like."

"You think Peter Stewart followed Tom into the shop?"

"That's right. They got into it again, and this time Abbittson finished him off. Big muscles in his arms, that butcher's got. One good punch would do it. Then he grabs the knife and slits his throat. Ties an apron around hisself so's not to make a mess on his clothes, then humps him up onto the rack to hide the body until he can get rid of it later."

"And leaves the knife and the apron on the floor."

"Well, no one but him goes down there, do they? All he had to do was wait for the chance to dispose of the h'evidence later."

"Except that Samuel did go down there."

"Yes, well, h'as they say, it's the unexpected what always trips 'em up." The constable rubbed his hands and held them out to the fire. "Oh, yes, I do believe that h'Inspector Cranshaw will be most 'appy with me this time. Saved him a lot of grief, I did. Put this one away all by meself. Should be good for a spot of promotion, I daresay."

Cecily rose, intending to put an end to the conversation. "Congratulations, Constable. Well-deserved, I should say."

Northcott looked up. "Oh, thank you, ma'am. Much appreciated, yes." Finally remembering his manners, he scrambled to his feet. "Well, I best be getting along. I've got to make out my report and send it to Wellercombe right away. The inspector will want to know all the details, no doubt."

"No doubt," Cecily echoed, leading the way to the door. "You can find your own way out, Constable? I have an errand to take care of."

"Oh, certainly, madam. Certainly. And thank you for the cake. Good cook, that Mrs. Chubb. Wouldn't mind having one like her meself. Though as I always says, too many cooks spoil the broth." Laughing uproariously at his obscure joke, the stout policeman made his way down the hall.

Cecily shook her head, then once more tugged on the bell pull. This time Doris answered her summons. "Find Samuel for me, please, Doris," Cecily said, noting that the girl had more color now, "and tell him I would like to see him right away."

"Yes, mum." A shy smile flickered across the girl's face, then she turned and scurried down the passageway.

In no time at all, it seemed, Samuel stood in the doorway of the drawing room, twisting his cap around in his hands. "You wanted to see me, mum?"

"Yes, come in, Samuel, and close that door. I can't seem to get warm today."

"Yes, mum."

Samuel shot a nervous glance down the hallway as if afraid he was doing something bad. What was wrong with these men, Cecily thought irritably, that they were afraid to be in a closed room with a woman? When were they ever going to be rid of Victorian thinking and come to terms with the new age?

Samuel stood just inside the door, looking as if he was ready to bolt at the merest excuse.

"I want you to tell me everything that happened at the pub last night," Cecily said, taking care to keep her place at the fireside. "I would also like to know exactly how you found Peter Stewart's body this morning."

Samuel looked ready to lose his breakfast. "It weren't a pretty sight, mum. I don't know as I should be telling you all the gory details."

Cecily suppressed a shudder. "You don't have to be explicit about how the body looked, Samuel. Just tell me how you found it."

"Yes, mum."

She listened carefully as the stable manager stumbled through his version of the previous night at the pub and his grisly discovery in the butcher's cellar.

"What I don't understand, mum," Samuel said, coming to the end of his story, "is why Tom Abbittson would send me down to the cellar, knowing full well that the dead body was hanging right next to the beef I was supposed to fetch up for him. It was like he wanted to be caught out, weren't it?"

It was a good question. And one that made Cecily very curious about the answer.

CHAPTER

❖ 4 ❖

Gertie picked up the tray from the small round table in the drawing room. She loved the pale blue velvets and blue-and-silver brocades of her favorite room in the hotel. Long ago she'd made up her mind that when she had a house of her own, she would use those very same colors in her own drawing room.

With a last longing look at the warm fireplace, Gertie carried the tray out into the hallway and headed for the kitchen. She was halfway across the lobby when a deep masculine voice called out from the staircase.

"Excuse me, miss. Can ye no' tell me where I can find the housekeeper?"

Swiveling her head around, Gertie saw a burly Scotsman leaning over the banisters, a cheeky grin spread all over his rugged face. He had thick dark hair beginning to go gray at the temples and hazel eyes that twinkled at her as if he was laughing at her.

"She's probably in the kitchen, sir. Can I give her a message?"

The grin widened as the piper descended the rest of the stairs. "Oh, and it's sir, is it? Such a pleasure to be called sir, especially by a bonny lass such as yeself."

Gertie's jaw dropped. The saucy bugger was actually flirting with her. It had been a while since anyone had done that. Not since she'd got married to Ian, in fact. Or thought she was married to him. Until he'd told her about the wife he'd left behind in London.

Of course, she'd been pregnant after Ian had left, and as big as a blinking house. It had been quite a relief not to have to worry about a playful hotel guest giving her a slap on the bottom, or a painful pinch on the tits.

Eyeing the Scotsman, she sized him up. He was a big chap. She was tall for a woman, but he towered over her. Had the bloody shoulders of an ox. He was one of the few pipers she'd seen who managed to look masculine in a kilt. She'd have bleeding trouble with that one, she decided, if he tried to lay his hands on her.

To her immense surprise, the prospect didn't seem all that unpleasant. Rattled by her unexpected response, she said tartly, "I'll tell Mrs. Chubb you are looking for her, sir." She made a smart turn, swishing her skirt around her ankles. She waited for the heavy cloth to settle before stepping out once more across the lobby.

"Wait a minute!" The piper caught up with her, though he didn't touch her. Keeping pace with her brisk stride, he said cheerfully, "What's your hurry, lass? I'll just come along with you to the kitchen, if that's all right with you?"

Gertie shrugged. "Suit your bleeding self." She saw his bushy eyebrows rise and added quickly, "Sir."

"Aha! A feisty lass if I ever saw one. Must have some Scottish blood in your veins, I'll be bound."

"Nope." Gertie kept her chin in the air as she swept toward the stairs.

"Can I carry your tray for you, then?" the Scotsman persisted. "I don't like to see a wee lass carry such a heavy load when I have two big brawny arms doing nothing."

"It's me job," Gertie said, trying to still the odd flutter in the region of her stomach. "I'll catch bloody merry hell from Mrs. Chubb if I let you carry this into the kitchen, that I will."

"Not if I tell Mrs. Chubb that I insisted."

Gertie gasped as the tray was whisked out of her hands. Before she could recover her breath, the Scotsman clicked his heels and inclined his head.

"Pardon me, madam, but we havena been properly introduced. "My name is Ross McBride, and I have the very great pleasure of making your acquaintance."

Fascinated by the way the piper rolled his *r*'s, Gertie forgot to be indignant. Besides, the man had called her madam. Nobody in the entire nineteen years of Gertie's life had ever called her madam.

"Gertie Brown," she murmured, and bobbed her knees. Too late she remembered she should have offered him her fingers. But then, she wasn't wearing gloves. That wouldn't have been proper, either. Besides, he could hardly kiss her hand if he had his own bloody hands full with the tray.

The very thought of his lips touching her fingers made her feel faint. She hadn't felt like this since . . . she didn't know when.

A strident voice bellowed up the stairs, shattering her delicious bubble. "Gertie! What are you doing up there, girl? You're supposed to be down here sorting out the silverware for lunch. Doris is waiting to lay the tables."

Mortified by the harsh summons in front of this fascinating stranger, Gertie yelled back without thinking. "Keep yer bloody hair on, I'm bleeding coming."

Ross McBride grinned. "That's my lassie."

"I'll get bleeding lassie when I get down there," Gertie

muttered, seizing hold of the tray again. "You wait there. I'll send her majesty up to you." Before he could utter a protest, she scrambled down the stairs and into the kitchen.

A cloud of steam rose from the stove, almost obscuring the gaunt figure of the chef in his tall bobbing hat. The clash of saucepan lids on the iron surface warned Gertie that Michel was throwing one of his tantrums again.

Doris looked at her nervously from the sink, her arms covered in soap bubbles, while Mrs. Chubb stood in the middle of the kitchen, arms folded across her abundant breasts.

"How many times do I have to tell you, my girl," the housekeeper demanded, "that time wasted is time lost? You have been here long enough to know that once we get behind we can never catch up. The midday meal will be served in less than an hour, and the tables are not yet laid."

Gertie dumped the tray on the table in a gesture of defiance. Before she could say anything, a deep voice spoke from the doorway. "Dinna get onto the lass. I kept her gabbing, and she was just being polite to a guest, that's all."

Mrs. Chubb's hand fluttered at her breast. "Oh, good morning, sir. I didn't see you standing there. Is there something we can do for you?"

Ross McBride thoroughly flustered Gertie by giving her a broad wink. "Aye, there is, if ye'll be so kind. I was wondering if I might have an extra blanket for my bed."

"Oh, certainly, sir. I'll have one sent up to your room as soon as possible, if you'll give me the number?"

"It's room number nine. I'll be much obliged . . . Mrs. Chubb, is it?"

"It is indeed," the housekeeper said, beaming at the piper's smiling face.

"Ross McBride." Again the Scotsman clicked his heels and bowed his head.

Gertie felt a small spasm of resentment as Mrs. Chubb clutched her throat with a lilting laugh. "I could have a bigger fire made up in the fireplace if you're feeling the cold," she said in a voice that made Gertie feel sick.

"Oh, no, I dinna need the fire. The blanket will do just fine. But thank you for the kind thought."

"Oh, not at all," Mrs. Chubb murmured, apparently forgetting all about the rush to get the silverware sorted. "Anything we can do for a guest here at the Pennyfoot . . . you only have to ask."

"I'll keep that in mind." Ross McBride sent a bold look at Gertie that made her knees tremble. "I'll get out of your way now. I can see you're all busy."

The kitchen seemed suddenly empty after the sturdy Scotsman left. Gertie noisily clattered at the silverware, hoping to drown out the singing in her ears. She was being bloody stupid, she told herself, slamming a knife down on the pile already sorted.

She'd made up her mind once and for all that she was never going to get mixed up with a bleeding man again. Not that any man would have her. Even if Ross McBride was interested, which was a laugh for a start, once he found out she was lumbered with two tiny babies, he'd run so fast in the other direction she wouldn't see his arse for dust.

Still, she thought wistfully, it had been awfully nice to be treated like a lady for once, instead of a bleeding slave. For one very brief moment, Gertie wished that things could've been different. Then she thought of James and Lillian sleeping in her room down the hall, and knew she wouldn't be without her babies no matter what might have been.

When Gertie announced that Elsie Abbittson had asked to see Mrs. Sinclair early that afternoon, Cecily had a strong inkling of the reason for the unexpected visit. She asked Gertie to show the butcher's wife into the library, and a few minutes later she joined her there.

Elsie Abbittson wore a perpetual frown and constantly chewed on her nails. Although in her early thirties, she had managed to retain a somewhat faded country-fresh beauty, assisted by a luxurious mane of strawberry-blond curls caught in a knot on top of her head.

Her clothes were less than fashionable, but her figure was still firm enough to turn a man's eye. She seemed self-conscious of her appearance in front of Cecily, however, and persisted in smoothing out a fold in her blue serge skirt, or fingering a pleat in her cotton blouse, accompanied by an occasional pat to her hair.

Doing her best to put the woman at ease, Cecily invited her to sit on the comfortable green velvet armchair by the fireplace, while she herself perched on the end of the chaise lounge.

"Can I offer you some tea?" she asked as Elsie's gaze darted about the room.

The butcher's wife shook her head, snatching her gloved finger away from her mouth. In an apparent attempt to prevent her hand from straying back, seemingly of its own accord, she clasped it firmly and buried her fingers in her lap.

"I suppose you've heard that the police have taken Tom in for the murder of that poor man," she said with a trace of belligerence.

"Yes," Cecily said carefully. "P.C. Northcott was here this morning to question Samuel."

Elsie nodded. "I thought as much, seeing as how it was Samuel who found the body. Must have been a shock for the lad."

"Indeed it was." Cecily paused for a moment. "And for you, no doubt."

"Could have knocked me down with a feather." Elsie raised her hand, then shoved it back into her lap. "He didn't do it. I know he didn't. I know my Tom, and he wouldn't do something like that."

"I understand he was fighting with the victim at the pub last night," Cecily said, feeling sorry for the butcher's wife. Elsie was obviously distraught. Nevertheless, Cecily had to admire the woman's loyalty.

"Well, I'm not saying my Tom's a saint, mind you. He has his faults like everyone else. And he's been known to use his fists now and again when he's drunk. Which is most of the time lately, I'm afraid to say."

"Your husband told the constable that he woke up lying in front of the shop and saw you bending over him."

"Yes, that's right. He did." Leaning forward in her chair, Elsie looked earnestly into Cecily's eyes. "He didn't do it, Mrs. Sinclair. It were the knife, you see. He would never have left it lying on the ground like that. My Tom would have cleaned it up and put it back where it belonged. Real particular about his tools of the trade, he is. Won't let no one touch them but himself."

"I see," Cecily said, wondering when Elsie was going to get to the point.

"Anyhow, I came here because I knew if anyone could help me, you could." Elsie nibbled on a nail for a moment, then once more dragged her hand away from her mouth. "When you have a shop in the High Street, everyone talks, you see. I know as how you've helped other people, like that Madeline Pengrath, when the police thought she'd murdered someone."

"Madeline is a good friend of mine," Cecily said quietly.

"Yes, I know. But you see, Mrs. Sinclair, Tom doesn't have anyone else who can help him. Not clever like, the way you are. The police have already decided he's guilty, and unless someone helps him, he could end up in prison, or worse—"

Elsie gulped and searched in her pocket for a handkerchief.

Cecily waited a minute while the woman loudly blew her nose. When Elsie seemed composed again, she said gently, "I can recommend a very good lawyer in Wellercombe—"

She broke off as Elsie violently shook her head. "Oh, I couldn't afford a lawyer, Mrs. Sinclair. I really couldn't. Besides, I don't trust those buggers, excusing my language.

I've had dealings with the likes of them before, I have. No, thank you."

Cecily sighed. "Why don't you tell me your version of what happened."

Sniffing, Elsie tucked the handkerchief back in her sleeve. "Well, Tom was down the pub as usual. I knew he would be home late. He always is lately. And I was tired of sitting around, doing nothing, so I went to bed early. I fell asleep, and then something woke me up. I looked out of the window and saw Tom staggering up the road."

"He was alone?"

"Oh, yes. I never saw no one with him, anyhow. I watched him, I did, cursing at him under me breath. I mean, there he was, out in the street, stumbling all over the road, looking like a proper fool."

"So you went down to bring him inside."

"No, I didn't. Not right then, any rate. I saw him fall down, right outside the shop, and I thought, let him stay there, silly bugger. I was getting right fed up with him, I was, always getting drunk night after night. So I decided to let him sleep it off right there in the road."

"What time was that?" Cecily asked, as Elsie paused to nibble once more on a nail.

"I dunno, I never looked at the clock. I just went back to bed. But it must have been late. Tom never came home until they turned him out of the pub at eleven, and then he had to walk home."

"So you left Tom out there in the street."

"Not for long." Elsie sighed. "Proper soft, I am. I knew it was cold out there, and I couldn't go back to sleep knowing my husband was lying out there on the hard ground. So after a while I went down to get him. He was coming around when I got to him. Opened his eyes, he did."

Elsie paused, shaking her head at the memory. "He said, 'Hello, luv,' just like it was normal to wake up lying in the road. I helped him to bed, and the two of us never moved again until this morning. The next thing I knew, Samuel was hollering up the stairs that there'd been a murder."

The clock on the mantelpiece ticked unevenly as Cecily watched Elsie gnawing on her gloves. "P.C. Northcott mentioned that your husband had the only key to the shop, and that it was still in his possession this morning."

"That's right." Elsie glanced up at the clock. "Oh, my, look at the time." She rose awkwardly to her feet. "I had best be going, Mrs. Sinclair. They'll be looking for me in the shop. And I expect you're busy with all these pipers in town."

Her face changed, and for a moment it seemed as if she would cry. Then she appeared to compose herself. "I don't know how I'm going to manage now Tom's gone. I'll have to ask his brother to come in and cut the meat, I suppose. Bert used to be a butcher before he took up farming."

Filled with compassion, Cecily patted the woman's slender shoulders. "Try not to worry, Elsie. I'll see what I can do, though I'm afraid I can't promise anything. The police do not look kindly on me interfering in their business."

"Oh, I know, Mrs. Sinclair, and I wouldn't ask you if I wasn't desperate. But, please, do try and help my Tom. I know if anyone can get him off, you can. I just feel so awful knowing he's locked up down there for something he didn't do. He has a terrible temper on him, my Tom, but he wouldn't kill no one. I would swear to that on the Bible, I would."

"Leave it to me," Cecily said, following the jittery woman to the door. "I'll do my very best to find out exactly what happened last night. If I have any news, I'll send Samuel down to the shop to let you know."

Tears brimmed in Elsie's eyes as she looked up at Cecily. "Thank you, Mrs. Sinclair. Thank you ever so much."

"Don't thank me yet," Cecily said grimly. "P.C. Northcott is convinced he has the culprit, and he can be very stubborn at times."

"Cor, don't I know it," Elsie said with feeling. "But even

he's not as bad as that Inspector Cranshaw. Once he gets his teeth into something he won't let go."

Cecily couldn't agree more. She had the uneasy feeling that she was about to lock horns with the formidable inspector once again. Baxter would not be pleased.

CHAPTER

❊ 5 ❊

"Come now, ladies!" Phoebe clapped her hands in a vain effort to attract the attention of the group of young girls standing chattering in the corner of the spacious village hall. In spite of the fact that her voice echoed in the rafters of the drafty building, not one of the dancers appeared to notice.

Phoebe turned to the husky man standing next to her. She couldn't help noticing how the light from the gas lamps turned his thick white hair to silver. She couldn't be quite sure if the gleam in his dark brown eyes could also be attributed to the flickering light, or if perhaps a spark of interest in her appearance might have brightened his warm gaze.

Deciding that she would accept the gleam for approval, she fluttered her eyelashes and peeked coyly up at him. "I wonder if you could address the girls for me," she said, tilting the enormous brim of her hat in order to give him the full benefit of her face. "I don't seem able to raise my voice above their clatter."

Alec McPherson inclined his head with a smile. "My pleasure, ma'am. They do seem a wee bit inattentive this evening."

Basking in the effect of the smile, Phoebe watched as the Scotsman threw back his head. She jumped violently when a mighty roar erupted from his mouth, enough to make the walls tremble.

"Will ye be quiet, ye blithering numbskulls! Can ye no' hear a lady when she talks to ye?"

Phoebe clutched her hat with both hands as if afraid it would blow off. "Oh, my," she murmured.

The sudden silence was almost as shocking as the roar. All eight girls stood staring at the piper in openmouthed astonishment.

"That's better," Alec said, mercifully dropping his voice. Turning to Phoebe, he gave her a slight bow. "My apologies, ma'am, but sometimes a loud bellow works wonders."

"It does indeed," Phoebe gushed, fluttering a hand at her breast. "Most impressive, Mr. McPherson. Most impressive indeed."

"I thought we had agreed on Christian names," Alec said, nudging his head in the direction of the girls. "Two heads are better than one, if you remember?"

"Oh, I certainly do . . . Alec," Phoebe said, wishing she had more breath to spare. For some silly reason she found it hard to breathe when he looked at her in that roguish way.

"Now," Alec said, transferring his attention back to the avidly staring group in the corner, "I hope ye all remember the steps I showed ye yesterday."

"Oh, we certainly do . . . Alec," someone piped up from the back, in a fair imitation of Phoebe's breathless voice.

A chorus of giggles followed, and Phoebe's cheeks

flamed. Stepping forward, she fixed her stare on a dark-haired girl with barrel hips. "Marion, I will thank you to keep your place. You are the leader of this dance troupe and as such you should be setting an example. I must ask that you show a little more respect, if you please."

"It weren't me, Mrs. Carter-Holmes. I never said nuffing, honest."

"Very well. I sincerely hope that the rest of the girls follow your example. Now, if you will all please get into your positions, I will ask Mr. . . . Alec if he will kindly play the pipes for the Highland Fling."

A chorus of groans greeted this remark. "Why do we have to do flipping Scotch dances, just because the blinking Scotch are in town?" one strident voice demanded.

"Will we be wearing kilts?" someone else asked.

"I certainly hope not," Phoebe said in alarm. "It would be most disgraceful for young ladies to bare their knees in public."

"Be baring a lot more than that if the likes of us do the Highland Fling," Marion muttered.

A spindly girl with tangled blond hair elbowed Marion aside. "What's wrong with our knees?" she demanded. "If those bloody Scotchmen can do it, why can't we?"

"Shut up, Dora," Marion said rudely. "If you ask me, the sight of them bony knees flashing up and down makes me sick. Scotchmen should be wearing trousers, same as other men do. It ain't proper, that's what I say."

"*Scotchmen!*" Once more the awesome voice of Alec McPherson rattled the rafters. "We are not Scotchmen," he roared. "I've told ye all this before. Scotch is something you pour down your throat. We are Scotsmen. *Scotsmen!* Do I make myself clear?"

Several voices spoke dutifully in unison. "Yes, sir."

"Good. I'm very glad to hear that. Now, get in a circle while I prime my pipes."

Keeping a fixed smile on her face, Phoebe briefly closed her eyes as the dreadful wail drifted agonizingly to the ceiling. While she was quite fond of the stirring strains of the pipes once the melody became clear, she could not abide the awful whine as the bag filled with air from Alec's strong lungs.

The hall was quite large, and devoid of any furnishings, except for a few long tables and several chairs stacked against one wall. Remnants of streamers still hung from the rafters where some enterprising souls had risked their necks in order to decorate the hall for Christmas. Apparently they had not deemed the risk worthwhile enough to remove the decorations.

Barren as the premises were, the noise seemed to echo with quite appalling resonance throughout the building. Even so, Dora's raised voice could be heard quite clearly. "Strewth. Sounds like a hundred bleeding cats on the warpath."

"I'd rather have the cats," someone else said loudly.

"Not if they was peeing all over your house, you wouldn't," Marion chimed in.

Phoebe shot a nervous glance at Alec, who seemed too engrossed in getting enough air into the bag to listen to the disgraceful comments of the dancers.

"Get into a circle at once," she called out in a voice shrill enough to be heard above the racket.

There was a general shuffling and bumping among the girls, until finally they formed a ragged circle.

"Into positions everyone!" Phoebe pranced around the circle, doing her best to get fingers of the left hands resting on hips in the proper position, with right hands raised in a graceful pose above the head.

At least, they were supposed to be raised gracefully. Phoebe shook her head when she spied Dora's hand dangling limply over her head like a bunch of Tom Abbittson's sausages. "Do please try to look like dancers," Phoebe implored, as Marion wobbled precariously on one leg, the other bent at the knee.

"It's blinking hard to stand like this," Marion complained.

"Not if you balance your weight." Phoebe stood in the center of the uneven circle and inspected each dancer with a critical eye. "Isabelle, you are supposed to point your toes toward the ground."

"Can't." Isabelle uttered a loud moan. "I get cramps in me foot when I do that."

"That's what comes of creeping around in the damp grass with dopey David Hardcastle," Dora said with malicious glee. "Gives you rheumatiz, it does."

Outraged, Isabelle gave Dora a shove. "He's not dopey, so there."

Already off balance, Dora careened into the girl next to her. Phoebe closed her eyes as each girl crashed into the next, sending the lot of them toppling to the floor with shrieks that easily outclassed the wail of Alec's pipes.

In the midst of all the chaos, Alec bellowed, "I canna play music with all this commotion going on. Do you want me to play for ye or not?"

Phoebe opened her eyes. The girls sat on the floor, meekly staring up at him, though more than one struggled to keep a straight face.

Drawing herself to her full height, Phoebe took a deep breath. "Get up!" she yelled, forgetting for a moment that she was supposed to be a lady.

The girls scrambled to their feet.

Spinning around so that each dancer caught the full fury of her glare, Phoebe announced loudly and distinctly, "I will take no more of this ridiculous behavior. Either you act like young ladies, or I will tell Mr. . . . Alec to take his pipes out of here, and there will be no performance at the Tartan Ball."

"And for that we shall be eternally grateful," a low voice muttered.

Ignoring the comment, Phoebe turned to Alec. "I really must apologize, Alec. Please, do play the melody for us. I promise you the girls will do their best to master the Highland Fling."

"I thought we just did," Dora said, and someone snickered. Luckily Alec had already begun the opening notes, and only Phoebe heard the words. She sent up a silent prayer that somehow the girls would perform a miracle, and by the night of the ball at the very least manage to present the illusion that they knew what they were doing.

Watching them leap around, looking like wounded frogs, she had serious doubts about that. But then her gaze drifted to Alec, who stood in magnificent splendor in the center of the hall, looking so handsome and virile in his red and black kilt.

It was worth the effort, Phoebe told herself as she gazed admiringly at the impressive figure. Oh, yes, indeed, if nothing else, she will have enjoyed the pleasure of this fascinating man's company for a little while at least.

She would worry about the ball when the time came, she decided. Right now, it was enough to gaze upon the glorious sight of Alec McPherson and his pipes, and listen to the rousing melody that filled the hall.

Cecily waited until the evening meal had been served in the dining room before approaching Baxter. Her manager always ate his dinner in his quarters before the dinner gong summoned the guests. By the time she reached his office, he would be relaxing after his meal.

To her surprise, he was nowhere to be seen when she arrived at his office a few minutes later. Neither did he appear to be in his quarters. Wondering where he could be, she retraced her steps to the dining room and cornered Daisy, or perhaps it was Doris.

Daisy, as it turned out to be, informed her that Mr. Baxter was in the library. "He asked to have his coffee served in there," she said, shifting the heavy tray in her hands to get a better grip.

Cecily thanked the girl and watched her stomp off down the hallway. She couldn't help wondering if Daisy was happy working at the hotel. Doris seemed to have settled in very well, but Daisy still wore a perpetual look of bored indifference, and Cecily rarely saw her talk to anyone except her sister.

Her mind still dwelling on Daisy, Cecily made her way to the library. All of her staff were important to her, and she looked upon every one of them as family. It worried her a great deal that Daisy seemed despondent, even resentful at times. She made up her mind to have a word with the girl and perhaps find a way to make the child feel more at home.

Reaching the library, Cecily peeked into the room. Baxter sat in the armchair by the fire, a cup of coffee at his elbow, his expression somber as he gazed into the flickering flames.

He appeared not to have heard her open the door, and she watched him for a moment, feeling a pang of anxiety. Baxter was not a man of many words, but she knew most of his moods. He was rarely despondent, but looking at him now, she couldn't help wondering what it was that had put that look of melancholy on his face.

After a moment or two she had the odd feeling she was intruding on his privacy. She cleared her throat, and immediately he sprang to his feet. "Forgive me, madam, I didn't hear you come in."

She walked into the room, gazing intently at his face. He had the look of someone being caught in the act of committing a misdeed. Not quite sure how to respond, she said mildly, "I hope I'm not disturbing you?"

He looked shocked and drew a finger around the edge of his stiff white collar. "Not at all, madam. After all, you have every right to be in here."

She smiled. "So do you, Baxter."

"Thank you, madam. I meant that you had more right than I."

"I'm just surprised to find you here." She looked around

the vast room with its crowded shelves of unread books. "You usually prefer the comfort of your own suite."

"I was a little   restless tonight."

She looked back at him, peering up into his face. "You are not well? Can I get you something? Mrs. Chubb can no doubt find a remedy, providing it isn't something that needs a doctor's care."

"I'm afraid nothing can cure what ails me," Baxter said in a mournful voice that increased Cecily's concern.

Laying a hand on his arm, she said anxiously, "What is it, Bax? Please tell me. Perhaps I can help. If not, Dr. Prestwick—"

"Please, not Prestwick." Baxter moved away from her with an abrupt movement. "I hear he has more interest in curing the ladies than he does gentlemen."

Bristling a little, Cecily said stiffly, "It is not the doctor's fault if the ladies find him attractive. I'm quite sure he is just as attentive toward his male patients as his female ones."

"Your defense of him is admirable." Baxter moved even closer to the fireplace and once more gazed into the flames. "Even so, I can't help wishing that Dr. McDuff was still with us. He was a man I could trust implicitly."

Thoroughly alarmed now, Cecily moved swiftly to his side. "Baxter, please, what is it? You are frightening me with such talk. If you are ill, we must do something about it. Remember how James kept insisting he was feeling quite well, and just a few short days later he—"

She broke off and, to her consternation, heard Baxter curse softly, something he rarely did in her presence. And only then in dire circumstances. "Please, madam, do not upset yourself. I am perfectly well, just a little out of sorts, that is all."

She narrowed her eyes, again staring intently at his face. He still had good color, and his eyes looked clear enough. Except for the fact that he avoided her gaze, concentrating on a spot above her head, he seemed much the same as usual.

"You have a cold?" she demanded.

He shook his head. "No, madam. I assure you, this is not a physical illness. Just a slight case of the miseries. I have no idea why. Most likely this infernal weather. I never could tolerate the cold."

Unconvinced, Cecily continued to study him. "You are worried about something, perhaps? If it is a private matter—"

He unsettled her again by saying abruptly, "There is nothing in my life that is private as far as you are concerned, madam."

Wisely taking that as a subtle warning, she decided to postpone the questions. At least until he was in a better frame of mind. Under the circumstances, she was even more hesitant to say what she had come to tell him.

Deciding just to come right out with it, she sat down on the chair he'd just vacated and said quietly, "I had a visit from Elsie Abbittson this afternoon."

He was silent for a moment, then for the first time that evening he looked directly at her face, sighing heavily. "I am almost afraid to ask the reason why."

"I imagine you can guess. She believes her husband is innocent and has asked me to look into the case."

"Is the good lady aware that there are professional men who are paid to do that?"

"I mentioned hiring a lawyer. Mrs. Abbittson can neither trust nor afford one."

"So you have volunteered our services free of charge, as usual. Even though this murder does not implicate the hotel."

Warmed by his apparent cooperation in the venture, Cecily nevertheless felt obliged to justify her decision. "The victim was a guest here. That does give us some involvement, I would say."

Baxter turned back to the fireplace, his gaze shifting to the portrait of James Sinclair hanging above the mantelpiece. "Forgive me," he muttered to the dead man's image, "I tried my level best."

"I believe Tom is innocent," Cecily said, determined not to let him distract her. Before he could say anything else, she launched into an account of the conversation she'd had with Elsie earlier that afternoon.

Baxter, as usual, listened without comment. When she was finished, he stared thoughtfully into the flames for a long moment. Then he said quietly, "You are giving Tom Abbittson very much the benefit of the doubt."

"Perhaps," Cecily agreed. "But one thing sticks in my mind. As Samuel has already questioned, why would Tom send someone down to fetch a side of beef, knowing that the body would certainly be discovered?"

"Perhaps, for some unexplained reason, he wanted the body to be discovered."

She stared at him for a moment, wondering why he always seemed to have a logical answer to an illogical question. "Then why didn't he simply drag the body outside the shop, where at least his guilt would have been in some question? As it is, considering that there is only one key to the shop, his position is most compromising."

She paused, giving him a quizzical look. "Surely you are not suggesting that he wanted to be arrested for murder? I understand he complained quite loudly and bitterly about the injustice of being falsely accused."

She had thought that Baxter couldn't possibly surprise her more than he already had that evening. She was therefore astounded when, after another moment's thought, he pulled a pack of cigars from the breast pocket of his black morning coat.

"Something tells me that this situation calls for a cigar," he said in a tone of resignation. "May I offer you one for a change?"

"Why, Baxter, how terribly gallant of you." She laughed up at him as she reached out to take one. "I would love a cigar. I do believe this is the very first time you have given me one without my asking."

"There comes a time in every man's life, madam," Baxter said, striking a match, "when he must bow to the inevitable."

Cecily puffed on the cigar and wished she had more time to examine that cryptic remark.

CHAPTER

6

The place to start her investigation, Cecily decided the following morning, was at the George and Dragon Inn. Perhaps Michael could shed some light on the cause of the fight between Tom Abbittson and Peter Stewart.

Bowling along the Esplanade in the trap, she huddled into the corner for warmth. Even with the canopy closed, the bitter east wind found cracks to infiltrate, the salty air scouring out the comforting smell of soft leather.

Cecily's mind drifted from the immediate problem of murder to her son Michael, the present owner of the George and Dragon. When she had first heard that her eldest son had decided to retire from the army and settle down in Badgers End, she had been ecstatic, though hardly surprised.

Unlike Andrew, his younger brother, Michael had never really taken to the military life. Andrew's letters were few and far between, and always filled with glowing reports of his latest escapades, some of which made Cecily shudder.

Michael, on the other hand, had become bored once the real fighting had ceased in India. Cecily had long anticipated his resignation and had eagerly looked forward to spending some time with her son, who looked so much like his father.

Unfortunately things had not quite turned out the way she had hoped. Michael had brought home with him an unexpected companion—his African-born wife, Simani.

Not only had Cecily resented the fact that she had not been informed of the wedding, much less been invited to the primitive ceremony, which from Michael's comments appeared to have been presided over by a witch doctor, but much to her shame, she found it difficult to accept Simani as the much-longed-for daughter-in-law.

After raising two boys, a great deal of the time in the uncivilized tropics during James's military career, Cecily had looked forward to welcoming daughters-in-law into the family. Visions of grandchildren happily playing on the grounds of the Pennyfoot had helped keep her spirits afloat during the long cruel months after James's death.

Somehow the thought of a grandchild with mixed blood failed to arouse the same sense of delightful expectation. Thoroughly ashamed of her prejudice, Cecily tried to justify her sentiments with the fact that the scarcity of black people in the British Isles would cause problems for the children of a mixed marriage. Such a child would be considered a freak and would very likely be the target of ridicule and scorn.

Even the presence of Simani, a strikingly beautiful woman, had caused business to slack off at the pub, a fact that embittered Michael to no end.

Cecily found herself watching every word she said, fearful of uttering something that could be misconstrued in Michael's presence. She had done her best to make his wife feel welcome, but Simani, who possessed not only grace and beauty but also a high degree of intelligence, no doubt sensed a certain reluctance and remained somewhat distant.

Cecily took slight comfort in the belief that had Simani's skin been as white as the foam on Michael's ale, she still would have had trouble warming up to the aloof woman.

She was quite thankful to hear that Simani was shopping in the High Street when she entered the private saloon of the inn. Michael barely paused in his task of setting up the bar for the midday rush. He handled most of the work in the pub himself, except for the actual cleaning of the place. Business had not been brisk enough to afford help behind the bar.

This morning, however, Michael seemed rushed as he checked the pumps on the draught ales. "The only good thing about Scotsmen," he told his mother, "is that they have a fondness for beer. This pub has been the busiest I've ever seen it these past couple of days."

Cecily smiled and perched herself on one of the bar stools. Ignoring Michael's quick frown of disapproval, she said lightly, "I understand they also have a fondness for brawling. Although that can be said of a great many men when they have had more than enough to drink."

Michael nodded, looking gloomy. "You wouldn't want to be in here at night, Mother, I can assure you. Absolute shambles most of the time. Luckily nothing of any value appears to have been broken so far."

Cecily watched him hold a beer mug under a tap while he slowly pulled the long, slim handle down toward him. Dark brown liquid gushed from the tap, filling the glass with thick, yellowish foam. The potent smell of ale repulsed her. She never had been fond of the stuff, vastly preferring a cream sherry or the tangy taste of a good port.

Michael muttered something she couldn't catch and held the glass up in the light from the window.

"Is it all right?" Cecily asked, watching the foam settle until it left a measure of near-black beer in the lower half of the glass.

"Cloudy," Michael muttered. "Getting too close to the bottom of the barrel. I'll have to go down and change it. I suppose I should be jolly grateful it's selling, but it's a rotten job."

"Don't you have someone who can do it for you?" Cecily fidgeted on the high stool, bracing her foot on the thick brass rail that ran the length of the bar.

"Can't afford anyone. This spot of business will be gone as soon as the Robbie Burns bash is over. Jolly good job they had that contest, or I might have had to close down until the season. Business has been utterly frightful, I'm afraid."

Feeling a stirring of sympathy, Cecily decided to change the subject. She knew, only too well, how depressing business worries could be. "How is Simani?" she asked, forcing a brightness in her tone. "I hope she is keeping well in this dismal weather."

Michael shrugged. "That's another thing. Simani isn't well at all. She's had that hideous cough for weeks. Can't seem to shake it."

"Oh, I'm sorry to hear that," Cecily said with genuine concern. "Has she consulted Dr. Prestwick?"

"Two weeks ago. He gave her this ghastly-tasting stuff. She's sick every time she swallows it. Hasn't done any good, of course. It's this foul weather, you see. She's not used to it. Neither am I, for that matter." Michael began hanging the glass mugs on the hooks above the bar with a great deal of clattering and banging.

Cecily watched him for a moment or two in silence, then asked quietly, "What are you saying, Michael?"

"Damn." He gave her a guilty glance. "Never could keep anything from the old mater."

"So perhaps you should tell me what is troubling you," Cecily suggested, afraid that she already knew.

Michael shook his head. "I wasn't going to say anything until it was definite, but you might as well know. I'm thinking of selling the George. Simani feels she will do better in Africa, and I . . . sort of miss the tropics, you see. One gets used to all that sultry heat and wide-open spaces."

Not to mention the ready availability of cheap servants, Cecily added inwardly. Ashamed of her pettiness, she managed a smile. "You must do what is best for both of you, of course. I'm not going to say I'm happy about the news, but I know you haven't settled down here as well as you hoped."

"I really haven't, Mother. Sorry. I know it must be a frightful disappointment for you, but then you never did care much for Simani, so you won't exactly miss her all that much."

Cecily opened her mouth to protest, but Michael held up his hand. "Oh, it's all right, I quite understand. Simani hasn't been all that sociable, either. She feels out of sorts here. I'm afraid the villagers in Badgers End can't accept a woman like her."

"It's difficult to accept what you don't understand," Cecily said, wishing she didn't feel so guilty.

"I know. That's why it's best this way."

Michael gave her a tired grin, and for a moment Cecily saw James as he had been at that age. Determined not to disgrace herself with unnecessary tears, Cecily straightened her back. "I agree with you, Michael. I just want you to be happy, that's all. Both of you," she added quickly.

Michael nodded. "Thanks, Mother. I knew you would understand. Too bad Father isn't here to take care of you. I wouldn't feel so beastly guilty, then."

That actually made her laugh. "Don't worry about me, Michael. I am certainly capable of taking care of myself."

"I suppose so. And you still have old what's-his-name hanging around."

"Baxter, you mean." Aware of the faint animosity between her son and her manager, Cecily chose to ignore the slight. Michael had never trusted Baxter's motives, suspecting that her manager had designs on the family fortune.

Which was laughable, given the Pennyfoot's financial state of affairs.

"Baxter is a tremendous help, I must say," she added airily. "I really don't know what I'd do without him."

"I'd say it was more the other way around. Though, of course, it's none of my business. Though why Father asked him to take care of you instead of asking me, I'll never fathom."

"You weren't here," Cecily pointed out gently. "Under the circumstances, it was extremely generous of Baxter to give your father his word. I'm afraid he's had cause to regret that promise on more than one occasion."

"Well, I just hope the old boy knew what he was doing. I know he was on his deathbed and all that rot, but he should have given more thought to whom he assigned as his widow's protector."

Knowing that her son's resentment came out of concern for her well-being, Cecily merely smiled. "Darling, please don't worry about me. It sounds as if you have enough to worry about right now."

"I do. This rush of business is a mixed blessing, what with the fighting. And now with that young chap murdered after leaving here the other night, well, it gives the place a sort of bad name, doesn't it? Might not look too well when it comes time to sell it, you see."

"I'm sure all this will have blown over in no time," Cecily said, trying to sound convincing. "But now that you mention it, did you notice Peter Stewart fighting with Tom Abbittson that night?"

Michael's head disappeared behind the counter as he squatted down to close off the barrel. "I might have done, though I couldn't say for sure. The idiots were all fighting with each other, and as I told Northcott, I don't really remember who was fighting with whom."

He stood up again, dusting his hands on the smocked coat he wore. "I do know that not all of your ten pipers were in here. One of them was missing. Someone counted the rest of

them, saying something about the Christmas song. You
know, nine pipers piping . . ." He stared thoughtfully at
the dark beams that crossed the low ceiling. "Actually, now
I come to think of it, that's about when the uproar started."

"But you don't know who started it."

Michael shook his head. "Samuel was in here, I remember, and that daffy colonel. You could ask them, I suppose.
Though I wouldn't expect too much from Fortescue. That
man is an insufferable blighter. Ever since he found out I
was in Africa and India he's been bombarding me with his
asinine stories. I think he makes them up."

"I think Colonel Fortescue becomes muddled sometimes
and forgets what really happened."

"He's muddled, all right. Downright deranged, I would
say. You really should be more careful, Mother. Some of
your hotel guests are definitely barmy, you know."

"I'll be careful, dear," Cecily promised. "But now I must
get back to the hotel before the midday meal is served.
Samuel will be frozen stiff waiting outside for me. Please
give my regards to Simani, and tell her I sincerely hope she
will be feeling better soon. Perhaps we can have tea at
Dolly's some day soon."

It was an empty invitation, one offered almost as a matter
of habit. They both knew Simani would decline.

Leaving the warmth of the inn, Cecily shivered in the
crisp, cold air. The bare, twisted branches of the huge oak
tree stretched across the thatched roof, as if reaching for a
hold to support its centuries-old gnarled trunk.

A lonely crow sat high up on a broken branch, gazing
mournfully down on the field below. As Cecily approached
the trap, the huge black bird flapped its wings, then glided
into the air. Loudly cawing, it winged its way across the
field toward the dense woods behind the inn and disappeared.

Cecily watched it go, for some reason reminded of
Michael's intention to sell the inn. Maybe it was the thought

of him leaving, too, heading for some remote part of the world she would most likely never visit.

A deep sense of melancholy almost overwhelmed her, and she scrambled up into the trap, intent on reaching the warmth and security of the hotel . . . and Baxter.

She still felt concerned about her manager, wondering again what had caused his despondency the evening before. She would have to keep a closer eye on him, she decided, and if she detected some sign of illness she would summon Dr. Prestwick, no matter how loudly Baxter objected.

Thinking of the doctor, Cecily made a mental note to pay him a visit as soon as it was prudent. Kevin Prestwick would have been called in to examine the body of Peter Stewart, and might be able to give her some useful information.

Although he was bound by the irritating regulations that prevented him from discussing the finer details of the murder, Cecily usually managed to get some of her questions answered.

Upon reaching the hotel, she accepted Samuel's offered hand to alight from the trap. Thanking him, she added casually, "I understand you were in the George and Dragon the night of the murder, Samuel."

"Yes, mum. It was me night off, and I was feeling a bit down. When I heard some of the Scotch blokes talking about going down there, I thought it might cheer me up a bit, like, if I went down as well and had a drink or two."

Forgetting for a moment the purpose of her question, Cecily looked closer at Samuel's glum face. "Is something wrong, Samuel? You are not ill?"

"Oh, no, mum, nothing like that. It's just . . ." He twisted his cap around in his hands. "Well, it's sort of personal, mum, if you know what I mean."

Apparently the somber mood was contagious, Cecily thought, studying her stable manager's expression. "Is there something I can do to help?"

"No, mum, but thank you. It's something I have to sort out for myself."

After a moment, Cecily nodded. "Very well, but if you should need someone to talk to, I'm sure Baxter will be happy to oblige."

Samuel's mouth twisted. "Thank you, mum. I'll keep it in mind."

Deciding to let the matter rest, she remembered her initial question. "While I think of it, Samuel, did you happen to notice the fight between Peter Stewart and Tom Abbittson when you were at the inn?"

Samuel gave a decisive shake of his head. "No, mum, I didn't. I was in the other side, in the public bar, playing darts. I'm sorry that the man died, of course, especially like that. Must have been a horrible death. But I wouldn't be surprised if he didn't deserve it."

Shocked, Cecily stared at the young man. "Whatever gives you that impression?"

"Well, he's a bloody womanizer, isn't he, pardon my French." Samuel's face reddened, but he added bluntly, "It's Doris, you see. She's a bit impressionable, like, being as how she's so young and all. Peter Stewart was hanging around her a lot, turning her head with his fancy remarks, teasing her and everything."

"I see," Cecily said slowly.

"I told her as how he was just out for what he could get from her. Them Scotch blokes are all alike. They all think the ladies are falling over themselves to meet 'em. Just 'cause they wear those silly kilts and show off their hairy legs. Looks bloody ridiculous, if you ask me."

"Apparently Doris didn't think they look ridiculous," Cecily couldn't help pointing out.

"Ah, she's just trying to get some attention to her singing, that's all. At least, that's what she keeps telling me. Dead set on being on the stage she is. She's been talking to all them pipers, hoping someone can help her. That's all she thinks about, getting on the stage and meeting toffs."

He looked so miserable, Cecily's heart ached for him. A gust of wind tugged at her hat, which luckily was anchored under her chin with a silk scarf. Holding the flapping brim with one hand, she said soothingly, "Don't worry, Samuel. All young girls have fanciful dreams. They eventually grow out of them. Just give her a little time. She's very young, and it wouldn't be wise to push things right now."

Samuel nodded, looking unconvinced. "I know, mum. It's just that I get angry when I see her chatting and laughing with them blokes. Especially Peter Stewart. He was worse than any of them, though I shouldn't speak ill of the dead. I told him off myself, I did, that last night at the pub. Told him to keep his filthy hands off Doris."

"Oh, dear," Cecily murmured. "I don't imagine he took kindly to that."

"No, he didn't. He wanted to fight, but I wasn't having any of it. Not my cup of tea, all that scrapping. That's why I left the saloon and went and played darts. I could hear them all at it next door, but I don't know what it was all about."

"Well, try not to worry about Doris," Cecily said as another gust threatened to snatch her hat from her head. "I'll have a word with her myself, though perhaps Mrs. Chubb might do better than I."

"I don't want Doris to know I've been talking about her," Samuel said with some alarm. "She'd have my head, she would, if she knew."

"Don't worry, I won't say anything." Cecily started as a motorcar, belching smoke and fumes, stopped in front of them with an explosive bang. The chestnut whinnied, stepping sideways in alarm, and Samuel's attention switched immediately to the restless horse.

"I'd better get her into the stables," he said, glaring at the driver of the gleaming black monster, who had climbed out and was frantically cranking the starter handle in an attempt to get the motor running again.

Cecily watched the stocky young man lead the nervous horse around to the stable gate. His words still echoed in her mind. *I told him to keep his filthy hands off Doris.*

Not liking the way her thoughts were progressing, she made her way up the steps to the hotel. It seemed urgent now that she pay Dr. Prestwick a visit and determine exactly what time Peter Stewart had died.

She couldn't imagine for one moment that her stable manager was involved in murder. But Samuel had been extremely jealous of Peter Stewart. And Samuel had been the one to discover the body.

If Elsie was right about Tom, and her husband wasn't the killer, then someone else must have had good reason to cut the piper's throat. But then why choose the butcher's shop to do the ghastly deed? And how did the killer manage to get not only himself inside the shop, but his victim, too?

Nothing made sense—on the surface, that was. But Cecily had dealt with murder enough times to know that everything made sense once the truth was uncovered. It was unearthing that truth that could be so frustrating . . . not to mention dangerous.

CHAPTER

❈ 7 ❈

Gertie heaved the monstrous iron pot onto the stove, letting it crash down with a clatter that would have made Michel proud. Water slopped over the side of the pot, sizzling as it landed on the hot surface. Gertie barely noticed. She was too busy glaring at the two housemaids who stood in the corner of the vast kitchen.

The noise had at least interrupted their squabbling, which had been going on half the morning. Gertie, in charge of the kitchen during Mrs. Chubb's absence, had spoken sharply to the girls more than once. Now her nerves were as frizzled as fried bacon. Gertie had had enough.

"Now you listen here, you bleeding rattle mouths. I'm sick and blooming tired of listening to you two screeching at each other. It's a bleeding wonder my babies aren't screaming their bloody heads off, it is. What's the bloody matter with you?"

"Daisy called me a crybaby," Doris said, looking ready to prove her sister's words at any minute.

"Strewth, is that all? I thought she'd at least socked you one."

"It's all right for her, she hasn't lost someone she cared about." Doris stared mutinously at her twin. "She's cruel, that's what she is."

"You only knew him two days," Daisy muttered.

"He was my friend. He was going to help me get on the stage, he was."

Daisy snorted. "Anyone that believes that is stupid."

"'Ere, 'ere," Gertie said, sounding more like Mrs. Chubb than she cared to admit. "Put a sock in it, you two. I've got enough to bleeding worry about without having to bother with the likes of you. If you don't behave, I'll tell Mrs. Chubb. She'll lock you in your bleeding room without any grub, she will."

"Then you'll have to look after your babies yourself, won't you?"

Gertie scowled at Daisy. "None of your blinking sauce, now. I'm in bleeding charge here, I am, until Mrs. Chubb gets back. So you just watch your mouth, both of you. Now get on with your blooming work, before Michel comes in here chucking his weight around."

To her immense satisfaction, both girls sullenly headed toward the door, bumped into each other, snarled something at each other under their breath, and disappeared.

Gertie shook her head and gathered up the peeled potatoes from the sink. Dropping them a few at a time into the pot of water on the stove, she thought about her own twins. She could only hope they got along better than Doris and Daisy did.

It was Daisy who was the bloody troublemaker. Doris would be all right if her sister didn't keep on at her. It was as if Daisy was trying to be a mother instead of a sister, and Doris wasn't having any of it.

Gertie watched a large potato plop into the water and sink to the bottom of the pot. Maybe if Daisy smiled, she'd feel better, she thought. In the three months the sisters had been working at the hotel, she had never seen Daisy crack a bleeding smile. Of course, considering where they came from, and the cruel beatings they'd suffered at the hands of a tyrannical aunt, it was hardly surprising.

But then, Gertie mused as she let the smooth white potatoes slide from her hand, Doris had suffered just as much as her sister, and she was always bloody smiling.

Perhaps, Gertie thought, as she gathered up more potatoes, if she could make Daisy smile, the girl would stop being so blinking moody. Perhaps she would even start enjoying herself, instead of going around looking as if she had the troubles of the world on her bleeding shoulders.

The last of the potatoes plopped into the water and sank. Bending at the waist, Gertie grasped the poker and jammed it through the red-hot grating of the stove. Sparks flew as she prodded the lumps of coal, breaking them into small pieces.

The orange-red glow of the fire warmed her face and stomach, and she paused for a moment, staring into the intense heat of the coals. She was remembering the softly murmured words of Ross McBride. He had called her madam, and a bonny lass. And he'd had a twinkle in his bold eyes that had made her knees feel like blooming butter.

She was still holding the poker, smiling at the memory, when Mrs. Chubb's sharp voice behind her made her jump out of her skin. "Is this all you've got to do all day? Stand staring at the fire? What kind of example are you setting for those young girls, I ask you?"

Gertie hurriedly dropped the poker and slapped the lid on the potatoes, which were beginning to stir in the bubbling water. "They didn't see me standing here, did they? Besides,

I just told them off for squabbling. They've been at it half the bloody morning, they have."

"No wonder at it, the things that have been going on here. What with the murder of that poor chap and all. I still can't believe Tom Abbittson would do such a thing. Seemed such a nice man, he did."

"Just goes to show, you can't go by bleeding looks." Gertie glanced up at the clock on the mantelpiece. "You never know nowadays who you might be keeping company with. Could be blinking Jack the Ripper, and you'd never know it until it's too late."

"Go on with you, Gertie Brown. Talk like that isn't going to help those girls settle their nerves."

Gertie shrugged. "If you ask me, nothing will settle their blooming nerves. That Daisy's face is enough to upset anybody. Never smiles, she don't. I don't think she can. Her face must have been frozen that way when she was born."

"The poor child hasn't had much to smile about." Mrs. Chubb tutted as steam burst from beneath the lid of the potatoes, sending water hissing onto the stove. She reached for the bouncing lid of the pot and settled it with a gap for the steam to escape.

"Well, I'm going to make her smile," Gertie announced. "Somehow I'll find a way to cheer her up. And now I'd better go feed me babies, or I'll have a wet bodice."

She left Mrs. Chubb fussing over the stove and trudged down the hallway to her room, still trying to think up ways to produce a smile on Daisy's face.

"Dashed heathens, they are, that's all you can say for the blighters," Colonel Fortescue announced, standing with his back to the fire in the drawing room.

Cecily faced him across the otherwise empty room and tried to look sympathetic. "I'm afraid the pipers can be a little rowdy at times, but on the whole I think they mean well. Most of them have been extremely polite and well-mannered."

"Well-mannered? In my opinion, madam, they don't know the meaning of the word." The colonel flung a hand in the air, his face turning quite red with indignation. "Why, one of the bastards stole my drink the other night. Turned my back for an instant, and poof! It was gone. Just like that. Dashed ungentlemanly, to say the least."

"What night was that, Colonel?" Cecily murmured.

He coughed and cleared his throat. "What night? Dashed if I remember, old bean. One, two nights ago? They all seem pretty much alike, you know."

He clutched the lapels of his Norfolk jacket and rocked back and forth on his heels. "Not like in the old days, no, sir. Evenings in India were a great deal more exciting. Gin at sundown and all that rot, you know."

"Yes, I remember," Cecily said quietly.

"Oh, that's right, old bean. Keep forgetting you were one of the jolly old military crowd, what? Things are little tame around here nowadays, wouldn't you say?"

"Oh, I don't know, Colonel. There seems to have been a great deal of excitement at the George and Dragon lately. Not to mention the unfortunate murder of one of our guests."

Fortescue's bloodshot eyes seemed to bulge in his head. "Goodness gracious me, I'd quite forgotten about that. Dashed awful business that, what? Poor bugger left dangling with the meat like that?"

"It was indeed, Colonel. I wonder if you—"

"I say!" The colonel stopped rocking and stared at Cecily as best he could through his wildly blinking eyelids. "You don't suppose someone mistook him for a cow, do you? You know, found him stumbling around in the dark in a field, sozzled, so to speak. These chappies manage to down an unspeakable amount of beer, you know."

"No, I don't think—"

"Perhaps a farmer thought he was a cow and slit his damn throat. Good God, madam! The same thing could happen to me!"

Aware that the colonel was nearing a state of hysteria, Cecily reached for his arm and gave it a firm shake. "Calm yourself, Colonel, please. I can assure you that whoever killed Peter Stewart knew exactly what he was doing."

To her relief, Fortescue took a shuddering breath and let it out on a long sigh. She waited while he fumbled for the large white handkerchief in his breast pocket and mopped his brow, muttering something unintelligible.

"Now, Colonel, if you are feeling better, perhaps you can tell me if you remember seeing a fight at the inn the night you were there."

Breathing heavily, the colonel moved away from the fireplace as if he suddenly found it too hot on his back. "Fight? There were a good many scraps that night, if I remember. Everywhere I turned. Over the silliest things, too. Why, I remember one of those Scots bastards pummeling another because the poor bugger recognized him from somewhere. Seems a dashed stupid reason to fight, if you ask me."

"It does indeed, Colonel," Cecily said patiently. "But did you recognize any of the men who were fighting?"

"All of them, Madam. I've seen all of them about this hotel at one time or another." He suddenly leaned forward, his hand in front of his mouth. Out of the side of his luxuriant white mustache he muttered, "They're all bastards, you know. Any one of them would run you through with a saber as soon as look at you."

"Well, I'm sure you have nothing to worry about, Colonel." Cecily looked deliberately at the clock on the mantelpiece. "Oh, my, is that the time? I really have to run."

"Had them in Africa, you know. A whole blasted regiment of them. Caused more trouble than the damn natives, they did, by Jove. Why, I remember once—"

"If you'll excuse me, Colonel," Cecily murmured, edging toward the door.

"—when I was out in the jungle. Nighttime it was, black as the ace of spades. Couldn't see a damn thing in front of me. I was leading a group of natives on patrol, creeping along one behind the other, we were. Complete hush except for the occasional growl or scuffle in the bushes."

Cecily reached the door and nodded politely.

Fortescue appeared not to notice her. He stood staring into space, one hand clutching his lapel, the other hovering in the air ready to emphasize whatever crisis he was about to describe.

"Anyway, there we were, sneaking along like weasels, when all of a sudden the most ghastly noise you ever heard rattled the damn trees. It sounded like a herd of wounded elephants, all screaming at once. I shot up in the air, of course, but managed to keep my feet. Not like those blasted cowards behind me. Turned tail, madam. Every last one of them back down the trail."

"How upsetting for you, Colonel," Cecily murmured. "Now, if you'll excuse me—"

"I hollered at them, of course, but what with all that dashed crashing through the bushes and that blistering racket going on, they couldn't hear me. Had to get my rifle and send a couple of shots over their damn heads. Of course, that scared them even more. Ended up in the river, by Jove. Wonder they weren't all drowned."

"I do believe the bar is open," Cecily said desperately.

"What?" The colonel blinked at her several times. "Oh, jolly good show. I'll toddle off, then."

Smiling, Cecily nodded and stepped back to let him pass.

"Damn Scots pipers, of course," the colonel announced as he reached the doorway. "Must have heard us coming and thought we were guerrillas. Decided to scare the wits out of us with their blasted bagpipes. Never thought to check first, of course. Not exactly cricket, what?"

"Absolutely, Colonel." She held her breath until the portly gentleman stepped out into the hallway and headed for the bar. There were times, she thought as she sped off in the opposite direction, when she could use a drink herself. Or maybe a good cigar.

* * *

Gertie stood in the empty dining room and looked around at the messy tables. Them bleeding Scotch were an untidy lot, she thought gloomily. Left her a bloody mess to clean up, that was for sure. Crumpled serviettes lay in a sea of dirty plates, wine and brandy glasses, silverware, half-eaten bread rolls, and overflowing ashtrays.

Gertie sighed and balanced the immense tray more firmly on her hip. It would take her the best part of the afternoon to clear that lot up. Then it would be time to lay the bloody tables for afternoon tea. Get that lot cleaned up, and they'd be scrambling to get the tables laid for dinner. No bleeding ending.

She moved to the first table and rested the edge of the tray on the white linen tablecloth. The clattering of china as she stacked the plates together drowned the sound of footsteps on the polished parquet floor.

Therefore she nearly dropped the blinking lot when a voice spoke right in her ear. "Well, now, if it isn't the bonny lass wi' the feisty tongue."

Turning her head, she almost bumped noses with the wickedly grinning piper, Ross McBride. "You scared me half to death," she said crossly, jerking her head back away from him.

"I'm sorry, lass, I didna mean to frighten you. I just came back for my pipe. Left it right on the table over there."

"I'll get it for you," Gertie muttered, trying not to notice the trembling of her hands. She shoved several plates out of the way and edged the tray further onto the table.

"Whist, lass, I'm perfectly able to get it for myself." The piper strode over to the table, his pleated kilt swinging briskly just above his knees.

Gertie did her best not to stare at his calves, which were encased in black socks trimmed with a tartan ribbon. She concentrated instead on the soiled silverware, laying the pieces carefully between the plates so they wouldn't roll off on the

trip back to the kitchen. She had the tray loaded by the time
Ross McBride came back.

"Here," he said, seizing the tray, "let me carry that for
you."

"Not on your bleeding life," Gertie said resolutely. "I'll
catch it in the ear from Mrs. Chubb, I will."

"And I'm sure you'll give as good as ye get." The piper
dragged the tray from her hands and set off across the dining
room.

Speeding after him, Gertie managed to catch up with him.
Taking hold of his sleeve, she pulled him to a halt. "I'll get
into trouble, honest I will. It ain't heavy, in any case. I've
carried three times that load and not worried twice about it."

"I'm sure you have," McBride said, his eyes roving over
her shoulders. "You're a strong lassie, I can see that.
Wouldna surprise me if you could take on any one of these
strapping lads here at the hotel without any problem."

Gertie lifted her chin, wishing not for the first time that
she was small and dainty like Daisy instead of built like a
cow. "I could at that, so you'd better watch your step, Mr.
McBride . . . sir."

The piper's white teeth gleamed as he grinned at her.
"That's the spirit. Give me a lass who can hold her own,
that's what I like."

"And I like me job here, so you'd better step out of me
way before the housekeeper comes charging in here looking
for me."

"Do you get some time to yourself, then?" Ross McBride
asked, tilting his head on one side.

He looked so wickedly charming, Gertie found herself
stuttering. "And what if I do?"

Ross McBride winked. "What day do ye get off?"

"If you must know, I get one afternoon in the week, and
two evenings. Not that it's any of your business, of course."
Actually she had a lot more time off now that the babies
were born. Madam had been very good about giving her

extra time off, but there was no need to tell the cheeky bugger that.

"Of course," Ross McBride agreed with a broad wink. "So how would you like to meet me for a wee drink, then?"

Gertie took a firm hold of the tray, as well as her senses, and tossed her head. "I don't hold with hobnobbing with the guests. It ain't proper."

She marched to the door, her chin in the air, though her knees threatened to drop her to the floor any minute.

"Och, to hell with what's proper. There's nothing wrong with accompanying me to the pub now, is there? I'm not going to touch ye. I just want some company, that's all. It isn't every day I meet such a bonny lassie as yourself."

Gertie hesitated at the door. The invitation was very tempting. She hadn't been on a night out since Ian had left. It would be good to go out and have a few laughs with a good-looking chap like Ross McBride.

"Come on, Gertie, be a devil. You'll have fun, I promise you."

She had to be bloody crazy, Gertie told herself firmly. Her own common sense should tell her she'd be mad to go out with someone she'd only just met and knew nothing about. Why, Mrs. Chubb would have a pink fit if she knew.

Gertie pushed the door open wider with her foot. How did she know she could trust him? What with one of his mates being murdered and all. Bad as bleeding Doris, she was, letting one of them saucy blokes turn her head. She weren't going to fall for none of that blarney. Not on her life, thank you.

"I'll think about it," she said and rushed through the door before she said something she'd be sorry for later.

CHAPTER

❖ 8 ❖

"It is my considered opinion, madam, that you are smoking entirely too much these days."

Cecily shook her head at Baxter's look of disapproval. "You worry too much, Baxter. If I should develop a cough I will give up the cigars, but quite frankly there are times when I fear I should lose my mind if I didn't have a few quiet moments with a cigar."

She settled back on her favorite chair at the library table and drew on the thin brown cylinder. The smoke seemed to penetrate her mind, soothing and quietening the thoughts that tumbled around in there.

"I think Michael is going back to Africa," she said abruptly. "I believe he is considering rejoining the army."

Baxter's expression changed swiftly to one of concern.

"Oh, I'm so sorry, Cecily. I know how upsetting this news must be for you."

She glanced up at him, wondering if he'd realized what he'd said. His unsettling use of her Christian name had slipped out upon occasion lately, though she never knew if he meant to address her with such familiarity, or if he was even aware of it.

"Yes, it is upsetting," she murmured. "I had such high hopes when Michael came home from India. But it's not so much his leaving that I mind so much. After all, I have seen little of him since he arrived in Badgers End. I'm afraid that Simani and I do not have a close relationship. I know that Michael is upset by that, and I can't really blame him."

"We are not required to become attached to everyone we meet."

"I know. But one should be able to at least get along with one's in-laws. Michael says that Simani is finding it difficult to cope with the climate here, but I can't help wondering if I am perhaps part of the problem."

Cecily studied the glowing tip of her cigar. "Somehow I never imagined myself as the proverbial possessive, over-bearing mother-in-law, but I'm afraid that's how I must appear to Simani."

"If that young lady considers you as such, then she has not taken the time to become fully acquainted with you," Baxter said stoutly. "Rest assured, madam, that you are the kind of mother-in-law I would wish for myself."

Cecily raised her eyebrows. "I'm only two years older than you are, Baxter. That's hardly old enough to be your mother, in-law or not."

Baxter's face turned pink. He cleared his throat loudly and stretched his neck above his collar. "Forgive me, madam, I did not mean to suggest—"

"Please relax, Baxter. I was only teasing you."

"Yes, madam."

She glanced up at him, but he avoided her gaze, looking steadily above her head in the direction of the French windows. After a moment, she said quietly, "I'm afraid for him, Baxter. I'm afraid for them both."

At last his gray eyes rested on her face. She saw the compassion there and was warmed by it. "The boys, madam?"

She sighed. "They're not exactly boys anymore, are they? Both Michael and Andrew are fully grown adults, and well able to take care of themselves. With all this talk of war, however, I'm afraid . . ." She let her voice trail off, unwilling to put her fears into words.

"It may not come to that, madam. Politicians are noted for their doomsday prophecies. I'm convinced it is a prerequisite for the post."

She gave him a wan smile. "I hope you are right, Baxter. The world is changing so fast, and while I hate to admit it, not always for the better, despite the struggles of the oppressed."

"If I may say so, madam, it is my belief that the scaremonger rumors stem mainly from the working people. From what I hear, they are becoming quite militant in the industrial midlands. I believe they would welcome a war."

"I cannot imagine why anyone would welcome a war." Cecily tapped the end of her cigar, dropping ash into the silver ashtray. "Speaking of militants, our current guests seem to be causing quite an uproar at the George and Dragon, according to Michael."

"So I understand. I assume you were pursuing your investigation while calling on your son?"

She gave him a quick glance, but his expression remained impassive. It would seem that Baxter had indeed become resigned to her efforts at sleuthing. The discovery pleased her no end.

She had been quite flattered when Elsie had asked for her help. It was gratifying to know that her endeavors were appreciated by the villagers of Badgers End, even if the local constabulary did not share in their opinion. She also knew, without a doubt, that without the help and support of Baxter, she would not be nearly so proficient.

"I asked Michael a few questions, yes," she admitted. "I'm afraid I didn't learn much more than I already knew."

"If I may state my humble opinion, madam, I would suggest that the evidence points squarely to the butcher. Since there is only one key in existence, which is still in his possession, and it doesn't appear that anyone forced his way in, it would seem he is the only logical suspect."

"I agree," Cecily said unhappily. "Yet I can't help wondering why Tom would admit to there only being one key, since the presence of another one would put his guilt in doubt."

"On the other hand, since there is only one, how would another person be able to open the door, take a dead body inside to hang on the rack, then leave again, leaving a locked door behind him?"

"I admit, it is a puzzle. But somewhere, no doubt, is the answer."

They were both silent for a moment or two, then Baxter suggested tentatively, "Is it possible that someone could have borrowed the key from Tom Abbittson's pocket? Perhaps while he was lying unconscious in the street outside the shop? He could then have replaced the key in the butcher's pocket after ridding himself of the body."

"It is possible, I suppose. The killer could have murdered his victim before Tom arrived at the shop. Perhaps he saw Tom fall, and saw his advantage. It would be safe to assume that Tom would be blamed for the murder, especially since he would be unlikely to remember clearly what happened."

"Precisely," Baxter said, sounding pleased with himself.

"There is just one small flaw with that reasoning," Cecily said, regretting that she had to dampen his enthusiasm. "Elsie saw her husband arrive at the shop. Had the killer entered the shop after that, Elsie would no doubt have heard him, since she is quite positive she didn't fall asleep again until after her husband was safely in bed."

"She could be mistaken."

"So she could. Perhaps I should question her further."

Baxter's gaze sharpened. "You will be careful, madam? Perhaps I should accompany you."

"Thank you, Baxter, but that won't be necessary. Elsie is far more likely to talk freely if I am there alone."

"Very well, madam." His expression suggested that he was not at all happy about the situation.

He would be even less happy, Cecily thought guiltily, if he knew that she planned to call on Dr. Prestwick that afternoon. Wisely she decided to delay that information until after the event. Now that she finally had Baxter's cooperation, she hated to say anything that would be likely to upset the new understanding between them. It was much too fragile, and entirely too precious.

"Strewth," Gertie exclaimed, as she tried for the third time to fold the serviette into a tulip shape. She seemed to be all fingers and thumbs lately. Normally she could fold the serviettes without even thinking about it.

It were that Ross McBride's fault, asking her to go out with him, indeed. The bleeding sauce of the man. Yet she couldn't stop her face from burning or her knees from wobbling whenever she thought about it.

"Haven't you finished those serviettes yet, Gertie?" Mrs. Chubb exclaimed as she bustled into the kitchen. "Daisy has already finished laying the silver for dinner. She'll be looking for the serviettes any minute."

"I know, I know. I'll be finished in a bleeding minute." Gertie took a firm hold of the corner of the linen square and deftly flipped it over, catching it between her fingers while she tucked the opposite corner inside.

"Well, perhaps if you light the lamps you'll be able to see what you're doing," Mrs. Chubb said irritably. "What's the matter with you today, Gertie? You're not usually so absentminded."

Gertie shrugged. "Dunno. Got things on me mind, I have."

"It's not those babies, is it?" The housekeeper stared worriedly at her. "Nothing wrong with them, is there?"

Gertie shook her head. "They're both fast asleep. Soon as I get finished with this lot I'm going back to feed them. Hungry little buggers, they are. I'll be needing a cow to help me feed them soon."

Mrs. Chubb shook her head, her round face wreathed in smiles. "Just so precious, they are. I looked in on them a short while ago, just to make sure they were still sleeping. Though I daresay we should hear them if they start crying."

"The whole bleeding village can hear them. I sometimes wonder if madam wishes she hadn't asked me to live here with them. What if they disturb the guests?"

Mrs. Chubb hurried over to the stove and opened the oven. "Don't you worry yourself about that, ducks. No one is going to hear those babies abovestairs. The floors are much too thick."

The warm, rich smell of baked fruit puddings made Gertie feel hungry. She reminded herself she still had some fat to get off her hips if she was ever going to wear her nice clothes again. It would be a long time before she could eat the way she used to before the twins were born.

"Have you given any thought to who's going to be their godparents yet?" Mrs. Chubb asked as she carried the steaming puddings over to the windowsill.

"No, not yet," Gertie mumbled.

"Well, you'd better hurry up, my girl. The christening is on Sunday. There isn't much time left, you know."

Gertie folded the last of the serviettes, feeling the niggling twinges of worry in her stomach again. The truth was, she didn't know how to solve the problem without hurting someone's feelings.

She would have liked to ask Mrs. Chubb to be the babies' godmother. After all, she was always fussing about them, that was for sure. But the housekeeper was getting on and might not be around to take care of the twins if anything happened to their mother.

What Gertie really wanted was to ask madam and Mr. Baxter, who were really the only parental figures she knew. But that might upset Mrs. Chubb.

It was all a bleeding nuisance, Gertie thought crossly as she stacked the serviettes on a tray. She had enough on her mind without worrying about bloody godparents.

"If I were you," Mrs. Chubb said, fanning her face with her apron, "I'd ask madam and Mr. Baxter. I'm sure they'd make wonderful godparents for James and Lillian. After all, you did name James after Mr. Sinclair, didn't you?"

Amazed and immensely relieved at the sudden miraculous solution to her problem, Gertie nodded. "Well, he was the one what hired me to work here in the first place. I always liked the name, too. You know, madam looked like she was going to bleeding cry when I told her I was going to call one of the babies James."

"I'm sure she did," the housekeeper said softly. "Just like I did when you chose my middle name for Lillian."

Gertie grinned. "Well, I like that name, too."

"Well, I'm sure both madam and Mr. Baxter will be pleased as punch to be asked to be godparents. But I wouldn't wait too long to ask them if I were you."

"I won't." Gertie looked up as the door swung open.

One of the twins stood in the doorway. Gertie took one look at the scowl on her face and knew it was Daisy. "I'm waiting for the serviettes," she said, glaring at Gertie.

"All right, all right, I'm coming." Gertie shoved the tray at her. "Here, if you're in such a bleeding hurry, take them yourself."

Daisy grabbed the tray and spun around.

"Is that you, Doris?" Mrs. Chubb asked, peering at the young girl across the room.

"No, it ain't," Gertie said as Daisy turned back. "Can't you tell by that ugly frown on her face?" She looked across at the housemaid. "Don't you ever smile?"

"Ain't got nothing to smile about, have I?" Daisy said sullenly.

"Course you bloody do," Irritated by the girl's attitude, Gertie slumped down in a chair. "You've got a good job, you've got a bleeding warm bed and good food, and you've got your health and strength. What more could you blinking ask for?"

Daisy opened her mouth to answer, but at that moment the door flew open, nearly knocking the petite girl off her feet. Her twin rushed into the kitchen, hair flying and eyes as wide as tea trays.

Gertie saw the girl's chalk-white skin and felt a chill in her stomach. Even Mrs. Chubb seemed struck dumb for a second, standing there with one hand clutching her throat.

Doris seemed unable to speak, but just stood trembling in the middle of the kitchen, her throat working and her hands plucking at the folds of her apron.

Daisy was the first one to find her voice. "Whatever's the matter with you?" she demanded. "You look like you've seen a ghost."

Doris nodded her head up and down. "I . . . I have!"

"Mercy me, whatever next!" Mrs. Chubb exclaimed, still staring at Doris.

"Whatcha mean?" Gertie said, getting up from the chair. Her hands felt cold all of a sudden, and she could feel the hairs on her neck prickling her skin.

"I saw *Peter*," Doris whispered. She started trembling, so hard her teeth rattled.

Mrs. Chubb sprang into action, drawing the girl closer to the fire with an arm about her shoulders. "Now, now, my love, you've had a nasty fright, that's for sure. Why don't you tell us what happened? Here, sit down on the coal bin, next to the fire. It'll get you warm in no time."

Doris sank down on the leather lid of the bin, her knees shaking beneath her gray skirt. "I was coming out of room seven, when I saw him walking down the hallway. I went up to him, 'cause I forgot for a minute that he was . . ." She gulped, then finished in a high-pitched voice, " . . . dead!"

"Course he's dead," Gertie said loudly, more to convince herself than anyone. "The police took his body off the rack, didn't they? So you couldn't have seen him."

"But I did!" Doris's voice rose on a wail, and Mrs. Chubb patted the thin shoulders.

"Now, now." She sent Gertie a swift frown. "Be quiet, Gertie, and let the girl tell her story."

Gulping down a sob, Doris nodded her head. "It were him, Mrs. Chubb, honest it was. I saw him as plain as the nose on me face. I know what he looks like, I spoke to him long enough. It were him, I'd stake me life on it."

"What did he say when you went up to him?" Daisy asked, looking as if she were fascinated by the story.

"Nothing." Doris's frail body shook violently, and Mrs. Chubb tutted.

"I'd better get you a spoonful of Michel's cognac," she muttered. "Hold still a minute, love, I'll be back in a tick."

She rushed off to the pantry, leaving Daisy and Gertie staring at Doris, who sat huddled by the fire as if she would never get warm again.

"Come on," Gertie said, rubbing her cold hands together, "it had to be one of the other pipers. Playing a joke on you, he was, though I don't think much about his bleeding sense of humor."

"It weren't anyone else," Doris whispered. "I tell you, it were him. I know, I went right up to him. I touched him."

"Well, that proves it, doesn't it?" Gertie said with relief. "You can't touch a bleeding ghost. Your hand would go right through him."

Doris started shivering again. "I know," she whispered, her voice barely audible in the quiet kitchen. "That's exactly what happened. I put out my hand to touch his arm, and it went right through him. Then he just . . . disappeared."

Gertie hardly noticed Mrs. Chubb come back with the brandy. She was too busy trying to still the quivers in her stomach. It wasn't so much what Doris had said, as the way she had said it. Somehow Gertie knew the housemaid was telling the truth. And it scared the bleeding daylights out of her.

CHAPTER

❈ 9 ❈

Stepping out of the trap late that afternoon, Cecily was happy to see a thin stream of smoke rising from the chimney of Dr. Prestwick's cottage. It would appear that the good doctor was at home, unless some poor soul had called him out on an emergency.

She paused at the gate as Samuel called out, "Would you like me to wait, mum?"

"I shall be but a moment." She had no intention of going inside the cottage, and it was much too cold to stand for long outside of it. Already the first stars could be seen in the rapidly darkening sky. It would be cold and frosty that night, with perhaps a hint of snow in the wind.

Shivering at the thought, Cecily made her way up the path to the porch. Her shoes crunched in the gravel, apparently alerting the doctor to her presence, as the door opened before she reached it.

"Cecily, my dear! What a very great pleasure, as always." He took her proffered hand and pressed his lips to her gloved fingers. "Though I trust you are not ill? I hope this is a social visit?"

"I am quite well, Doctor," Cecily assured him. Withdrawing her hand from his hold, she added, "Though I must confess, this is not entirely a social call."

Dr. Prestwick shook his handsome head. "I feared as much. But do please come inside, out of this miserable weather. As much as I should be delighted for an excuse to see you again, I prefer it not to be in my surgery."

"Thank you, Doctor, but I shall not take up too much of your time. Just long enough for you to give me the answers to a question or two."

Kevin Prestwick's dark brown eyes regarded her solemnly. "In the first place, my dear, I thought we were well enough acquainted for you to call me by my Christian name. In the second place, you could never take up too much of my time. I find your charming presence both stimulating and thoroughly fascinating."

"Thank you, Doctor, but—"

"Kevin, if you remember. And in the third place, if the questions you refer to have anything to do with the recent murder of Peter Stewart, you know full well that I am unable to give you the answers."

Cecily pursed her lips. "I'm quite sure, Kevin, that you can tell me what I need to know without violating any of Inspector Cranshaw's illogical regulations."

Dr. Prestwick uttered an audible sigh. "Perhaps if you were to tell me the reason for your interest?"

She hesitated, then said quietly, "I believe that P.C. Northcott has arrested the wrong man."

For a moment longer the doctor continued to regard her with a serious expression, then his engaging smile brightened his face. "Ah, Cecily, as always I am powerless when you look at me with such charming appeal. Come inside and I will tell you what little information I am permitted to give you."

Cecily shook her head, sending a backward glance over her shoulder. "Samuel is waiting. In any case, I prefer not to risk your reputation, Kevin. You know how tongues wag in this village. Entertaining a widow alone in your cottage would no doubt be the subject of conversation in every drawing room by morning."

Dr. Prestwick sighed and rolled his eyes heavenward. "As always, you are quite right, my dear. As I have said before, were it only my reputation to worry about, I would not care one whit, but I will do nothing to besmirch your impeccable standing in Badgers End."

Cecily had to smile. "I'm not so sure it's all that impeccable. I have been known to kick over the traces now and again."

"So I have heard. I greatly admire a woman who can fly in the face of convention. I only wish it could be me with whom you defy the proprieties, instead of that granite-faced manager of yours."

Cecily raised her eyebrows. "Why, Kevin, I am surprised at you. Everyone knows that Baxter was appointed my protector by my late husband. He is simply doing his duty, at considerable risk at times."

"To his reputation or his health?" Dr. Prestwick asked dryly.

"Both, very likely," Cecily admitted. "I'm afraid that Baxter is far more concerned with decorum than I, and it is with a great deal of reluctance that he accompanies me in my misadventures."

"Then the man is a fool," the doctor said crisply. "I would dearly love the opportunity to cavort with you all over the countryside."

"I assure you there is a great deal less cavorting than there is simple investigation."

"Which might be better left to the local police officers, if I might be so bold."

Cecily lifted her chin. "There are times when our local constabulary are hampered in their efforts. I enjoy the privilege of the villagers' trust and can therefore learn a great deal more than the police, simply by asking questions. Most of the people in Badgers End refuse to talk to the officers, for fear of reprisal. I'm afraid our local police constable can be quite obtuse at times."

"Obtuse and quite stubborn." Prestwick shook his head. "Very well, if I can't persuade you to step inside, I will answer what I can as quickly as possible. It is decidedly chilly out here tonight."

Feeling the wind cutting through the cloth of her coat at her back, Cecily had to agree. "Do you know what time Peter Stewart was murdered?"

The doctor's face became grave. "I would say somewhere around midnight. Not too long after he apparently left the George and Dragon."

"And where would you say he was killed?"

He looked surprised at that. "There's no doubt the victim was killed inside the shop. There were no bloodstains outside on the street. Judging by the amount of blood on the floor at the victim's feet, he was most likely killed after he was hung on the rack. His throat was neatly slit with a butcher's knife. Much as a butcher would slaughter beef."

Cecily gave a violent shudder, and Kevin Prestwick looked at her with concern. "My dear, please forgive me. This is gruesome talk for a lady's ears."

"Not at all, Kevin. Merely the bite of the wind, I assure you." Which was not strictly true, but she was not about to admit that to him. "What about the knife found at his feet? Did it belong to Tom Abbittson?"

The doctor lifted his hands in a gesture of appeal. "Please, Cecily, I really am not at liberty to discuss the details with you. I am sorry."

She gave him a resigned nod. "I understand. I have taken

up enough of your time, in any case. I must be getting back to the hotel." He had been more than generous with the information, and she would not push him. Though she was very much afraid that what she had learned had done little to help Tom. Things looked very bleak for the butcher indeed.

"I will see you at the christening on Sunday?"

She looked at the doctor in surprise. "You will be at the church?"

"Miss Brown was kind enough to give me an invitation, since I delivered the babies. I sincerely hope that meets with your approval?"

She shivered and drew the collar of her thick wool coat closer about her ears. "Of course, Kevin. We shall be delighted to see you there."

"And I shall look forward to it. Until we meet again, Cecily."

He reached for her hand and once more pressed his lips to her fingers. He held them there just a little longer than was comfortable, and Cecily sharply pulled back her hand.

Although she liked the doctor quite well—in fact, there had been a time when he could easily fluster her with one of his warm looks—she had no wish to be included in the adoring group of women who flocked to his surgery on the merest of excuses. "Good night, Kevin. I appreciate your help in this matter."

"It has been a privilege and a pleasure, Cecily, as always. You will promise me not to take any undue risks in your investigation? I'm afraid I do not share your faith in your manager's abilities."

She smiled, lifting her hand in a wave of farewell as she moved down the path. "Please don't concern yourself, Kevin. There is no one in this world I would rather trust with my life than Baxter."

For some reason, those words warmed her far more than anything Kevin Prestwick might have said.

*   *   *

When Cecily returned to the hotel, she was greeted in the foyer by Gertie, who looked as if she had been wrestling with a bear. Her jet black hair flew in wild wisps from beneath her cap, which was tilted at a crazy angle on her head.

One strap of the housemaid's apron hung off her shoulder, and her blouse had been hastily tucked into the waistband of her skirt, leaving it bunched up in front instead of neatly smoothed out.

Cecily had long ago given up on Gertie's lack of attention to her appearance, preferring to leave any criticism for the sharp tongue of her housekeeper. Even Mrs. Chubb found it difficult to keep the girl looking neat and tidy, in spite of her constant harping on the subject. But this evening Gertie looked even more disheveled than usual.

Cecily was quite anxious to reach the warm comfort of her suite, the cold night air having seemingly penetrated her bones. She could hardly ignore the jittery state of Gertie, however, and paused to question her.

"You seem upset about something, Gertie. I do hope there is nothing wrong with the babies?"

"No, mum," Gertie said, bobbing a quick curtsey, "they are both very well, thank you, mum."

"I'm happy to hear that." Cecily peered closer at the young woman's strained face. "Then what is it that seems to have upset you so?"

Gertie looked over her shoulder into the dark corner of the lobby, where the light from the gas lamps could not reach. "I hardly like to say, mum. It don't seem bleeding possible, but—"

Becoming alarmed now, Cecily said sharply, "There was not another murder, I hope?"

"Oh, no, mum, nothing like that. At least, I bloody hope not."

"Then what is it?" Impatiently Cecily curbed her impulse to shake the housemaid's arm.

"It's the colonel, mum," Gertie said quickly. "He's in the drawing room. In a right bloody state, he is. I think you'd better have a word with him, begging your pardon, mum."

Cecily sighed. "Very well. Thank you, Gertie."

"Yes, mum."

Frowning, Cecily watched the housemaid scurry off. She had the distinct feeling that Gertie hadn't told her everything, but no doubt she'd find out when she confronted the colonel. Thinking wistfully of her comfortable settee and warm fireplace waiting for her in her suite, she set off down the hallway in search of the unpredictable gentleman.

She found him seated in the drawing room, a large glass of brandy clutched in his shaking hand. He was staring into the fireplace as she entered the room, apparently absorbed in the flames.

Two of the Scotsmen staying at the hotel sat in the opposite corner, poring over a chessboard. Cecily spared them no more than a glance as she headed across the room to the fireplace.

"Good evening, Colonel," she said quietly, hoping that perhaps whatever had troubled him had now passed. Her hopes were dashed when Fortescue jumped as if he'd been shot. Brandy spilled from his glass, staining his jacket, but he seemed not to notice.

"What? What? Oh, there you are, Mrs. Sinclair. Didn't see you standing there." He started out of his chair, muttering, "'Pon my word, madam, you gave me quite a fright."

"I do apologize, Colonel. Please remain seated. I'll take the other chair."

Cecily sat down and waited until the colonel had rather fussily settled himself again. His eyelids flapped up and down at quite an alarming rate, and his cheeks were almost as red as his nose.

When he seemed reasonably calm again, she said gently, "Gertie tells me you are upset. Is there something I can do to help?"

Fortescue looked at her as if he had trouble focusing. "What? Oh, that." He looked over his shoulder at the two men in the corner, who were seemingly engrossed in their game. Leaning forward, he whispered hoarsely, "Found one of them in my room a little while ago. Damn bastard was standing by my bed, just looking at me."

"One of whom, Colonel?" Cecily asked, wondering if he was being plagued by visions of his past enemies again. There were times when Fortescue's attempts to escape from imaginary warriors could be quite disruptive.

"One of those blasted pipers, of course."

Cecily shot a glance at the two Scotsmen, but neither appeared to have a heard the colonel's frantic whisper. Lowering her voice, she said soothingly, "I'm sure you are mistaken, Colonel. You have the only key to your room. No one would have access to it, unless it was one of my staff, and I'm quite sure the housemaids would not be in your room at this time of the day."

"No, no, madam. It was not one of your staff. Couldn't mistake the blighter, he was wearing a kilt. I've never seen any of your staff wearing a kilt, what?"

Again Cecily glanced at the pipers. One of them sat leaning forward, his chin propped up by his elbows. The other stared intently at the board, apparently just as absorbed in the next move.

Deciding to humor the agitated gentleman, she kept her voice low as she asked, "Did this man say anything to you?"

"Nothing, old bean. Not a word. Just stood there staring at me."

"Did you recognize him?"

"Well, yes, as a matter of fact, I did." The colonel shook his head, as if confused by his own thoughts. "Dashed if I can remember his name now, but it's definitely one of the blighters staying at this hotel. I've seen the chap more than once."

"Did you speak to him?"

The colonel took a large gulp of brandy, coughed and

spluttered, then dug in his breast pocket for his handkerchief.

Cecily waited impatiently while he blew his nose loud enough to disturb the concentration of the pipers in the corner. One of them lifted his head and glanced across the room, then returned his attention to the game.

"Of course I did, madam. I told the bastard to leave at once, or I'd run him through with my saber." The colonel's eyelids resumed their frantic blinking. "Used to be a dab hand with the saber when I was younger. Why, I remember once bagging a wild boar with a saber."

Relieved that the colonel seemed to have forgotten about the imaginary man in his room, Cecily welcomed the change of subject for once. "That must have been quite an experience."

"What?" The colonel blinked at her. "Oh, it was, old bean. But you haven't heard the best of it yet."

Having heard more than she cared to about Fortescue's adventures in the tropics, Cecily glanced at the clock.

Before she could speak, the colonel added, "He disappeared, you know." He tried to click his fingers, but after failing twice, gave up the effort. "Just like that."

"How interesting." She really didn't care to hear about a wounded boar running around with a saber stuck through him. "You must tell me more about it some other time. But right now I'm afraid I must return to my suite."

She was about to make her leave when the colonel muttered, "I expected him to walk out of the door, of course. I even opened it for him."

"I beg your pardon?" Confused, it was a moment or two before she realized the colonel was still talking about the mysterious intruder in his room.

"Yes, madam," the colonel said, raising his voice. "I opened the blasted door for him. I was going to give him a piece of my mind as he went out, but the bastard tricked me. He vanished right in front of my eyes. One minute he was standing at the foot of my bed, the next he was gone.

Nothing there. It was as if he'd simply gone up in smoke."

Aware that Fortescue was becoming agitated again, Cecily said quickly, "Do finish your brandy, Colonel, and I'll have another sent in to you."

"What? Oh, yes, very kind of you, old bean. Much obliged, I'm sure."

She nodded and was about to turn away, when he added, "I told that young woman about it, you know."

"Young woman?"

"Yes, you know . . ." He waved his hand about as if trying to grasp an elusive butterfly. "What's-her-name. Tall, strapping girl with the loud voice."

"Oh, you mean Gertie." Cecily nodded. "Yes, I met her in the foyer. She told me you were upset, remember?"

"Yes, yes, I was. But she told me I wasn't the only person to see this damn Scotsman in my room. I think you had better be on your guard, old bean. Can't have these chappies running around willy-nilly, trespassing in other people's private quarters, you know. Could be stealing us blind, madam."

Determined to have a word with Gertie, Cecily sent a quick glance over at the silent men in the corner. The colonel's comments could be enough to start a rumpus right there in her own drawing room. Happily, both men had their heads bowed above the chessboard.

"I hardly think anyone would be stealing from you, Colonel," Cecily said firmly. "But I'll look into it."

The colonel nodded, and with a quick gulp drained his glass. "I remember Gertie when she was just a chit. Your late husband had just hired her, if I remember rightly. Always had a bit of a mouth on her, but very willing. Grown into a nice-looking woman, she has. Surprised some young man hasn't snapped her up before now."

Obviously the colonel had forgotten that Gertie had been married briefly to Ian and was now the mother of twins. There would be no point in reminding him, of course.

Cecily was almost at the door when the colonel added,

"Might be a good idea to ask her about that Scots blighter in my room. She said she knew who it was."

Spinning around, Cecily was just in time to see one of the pipers in the corner drop his gaze back to the board. He had obviously been staring at the colonel with acute interest.

Deciding that perhaps it would be better to tackle Gertie instead of questioning the confused gentleman further, Cecily left the room. But somehow she couldn't quite forget her brief glimpse of the piper's sharp hazel eyes staring at the colonel with such intense concentration.

CHAPTER

❊ 10 ❊

There were days, Gertie thought as she finished stacking the glasses on their shelf in the dresser, when the hands on the bloody clock seemed to be stuck. The last hour had crawled by, but any minute now she'd hear the nine chimes that would end her long day. She was looking forward to getting to her room to enjoy the sheer luxury of taking her weight off her feet.

Not that she'd get much rest, if the babies kept her up half the night again. Gertie shook her head as she crossed the kitchen to the stove. It didn't seem possible that two tiny babies could be so much trouble. What with the feeding, changing, rocking, and singing, it seemed all her spare time was taken up with her son and daughter.

In spite of her weariness, Gertie smiled to herself. It was

still hard for her to think of herself as a mother. It didn't seem that long ago when she was just a blinking kid herself, starting work for the first time at the Pennyfoot. Like Doris and Daisy were now.

Thinking of Daisy, Gertie looked once more at the clock. The young housemaid had offered to stay with the babies again, giving up a precious evening off. She had nothing else to do, she'd insisted, when Gertie had halfheartedly said she could manage.

It was a load off her mind, Gertie thought, not having to run back and forth making sure the twins were still peacefully sleeping in the cradle. Although, as Mrs. Chubb had said, once they were awake they made enough noise to wake the dead.

Gertie lifted the heavy pot of hot water off the stove and carried it to the sink. She'd just have time to clean the bugger before finishing for the day. She reached for the scrub brush, and almost dropped it as a deep voice spoke behind her.

"I knew this would be my lucky night."

She didn't have to turn her head to know it was Ross McBride standing in the kitchen. She hadn't heard him open the door. Glancing at him over her shoulder, she said tartly, "If you're looking for Mrs. Chubb, she's not here."

"Ay, I can see that. As I said, it's my lucky night."

Gertie felt her stomach quivering, the way it always did when he spoke to her like that. She'd better watch it, she thought grimly, or she'd be getting herself into more trouble than she could handle.

Reminding herself that he was a hotel guest, and therefore had to be treated with respect, she turned to face him. "Is there something I can do for you, sir?"

"Ay, you can stop calling me sir and call me Ross instead." He stood just inside the doorway, looking at her with a funny expression in his eyes. She couldn't tell if he was cross with her or if he was teasing her.

"I'm not allowed to call the guests by their Christian names," she said primly.

To her surprise, Ross burst out laughing. "Come off it, Gertie. What's the harm between two friends?" He moved farther into the kitchen, making her nerves jump.

"You're not supposed to be in here. You'll get me into bleeding trouble," Gertie said a little desperately.

"You said yourself Mrs. Chubb isn't here." He pulled out a chair from the table and sat down. The kilt barely covered his knees.

Gertie hastily snatched her gaze back to his face. "She'll be back any minute. She's just gone to inspect the dining room."

"Then I'm sure she won't mind if I sit here and have a cup of tea, now will she?"

Gertie stared belligerently at his face, but he continued to look at her with that strange half-serious expression. "I'll get it for you," she said at last, knowing she'd be in for it if the housekeeper knew she'd refused a guest a late-night cup of tea.

Turning her back on him again, she reached for the kettle and stuck it under the tap. The cold water gushed into the pot, and she filled it almost to the top.

"Will ye no' join me with one?" Ross said as she carried the kettle to the stove.

It was time, Gertie told herself. He had to know sometime. Maybe it was just as well, then he'd leave her alone and she wouldn't be getting all these funny feelings in her stomach.

"I haven't got bleeding time," she said, dumping the kettle with a loud bang on the stove. "I have to get back to me babies."

She could feel the silence grow heavy behind her as she bent down to grasp the poker. Shoving it violently through the bars, she raked the coals until sparks flew in all directions.

"I dinna know you were married," Ross said at last.

"I'm not." Gertie straightened, her face flushed more from the conversation than the heat from the fire. "Not anymore, anyhow." She avoided looking at him as she crossed to the china cabinet. Opening the door, she took down a bone china cup and saucer.

"Widowed?" Ross asked softly.

She shook her head. "Nah. I never was married proper like. I found out he was already bloody married to someone else. Went back to her, he did. Course, it were too bleeding late for me, then. I already had a bun in the oven. Two of them, in fact."

"I'm so very sorry."

He sounded so sincere she couldn't help looking at him. He had a different look in his eyes now. Sort of soft, like he really cared. Dragging her gaze away from him, Gertie put the cup and saucer on the counter next to the sink. "I'll be back in a jiff. Got to get some milk for the tea."

She was glad of the brief respite. It gave her a chance to cool her face and gather her senses. Leaning up against the wall of the pantry, Gertie gave herself a good talking-to.

She couldn't bleeding ignore him or she'd get into trouble. But she didn't have to be bloody friendly to him either. Just treat him like she treated all the bleeding others. Except that none of the other guests had nice hazel eyes with a look in them that made her go all warm and soft inside.

Grabbing hold of the milk jug, Gertie did her best to pull herself together. He was just another blinking man, after all. And she was off men for good. None of them could be trusted, except for Mr. Baxter, and he was a bleeding stuffed shirt.

Men like Ross McBride were another kettle of fish altogether. Him and his blooming bedroom eyes. The further she kept out of his way, the better.

Ross McBride still sat where she'd left him, staring into space as if he were far away. Gertie headed for the sink and poured milk into the cup. "You take sugar?" she asked as she carried the jug back to the pantry.

"Ay, just a spoonful, if you please."

She could feel his gaze following her when she crossed the room once more. Taking down the heavy teapot, she poured some of the hot water from the kettle into it and swished it around for a moment. Then she carried the teapot to the sink and emptied the water.

"I had two children myself," Ross said, his voice sounding a little strained.

Surprised, she glanced at him as she set the warmed pot on the side of the stove. "You married, then?"

"Widowed."

A long pause followed while Gertie digested that. "I'm sorry," she said awkwardly at last. She didn't like to ask how his wife had died, or what had happened to the children. Carefully she measured a level spoonful of tea leaves into the pot.

The kettle started singing on the stove, and she stood watching it, waiting for the steam to pour in a steady stream from the spout.

"My wife and bairns were killed in a house fire," Ross McBride said, so quietly she barely heard him above the singing kettle. "I wasna there at the time."

For once Gertie didn't know what to say. She could feel a knot in her throat as big as a fist. All she could think about was how she would feel if something like that happened to her twins. "Oh, Gawd," she whispered.

Just then the steam burst through the spout, and she lifted the kettle to pour the boiling water on the tea leaves. Settling the kettle back on the stove, she wondered desperately what to say to him. To just say she was sorry seemed so bloody useless, yet there wasn't anything else she could think of.

Very carefully, she fitted the lid of the teapot in place. "I'm sorry," she said, without looking at him. "That must have been bloody awful."

"Bloody awful," Ross McBride agreed. "Your bairns must be of some comfort to you."

She looked at him then. "They're me whole bleeding life," she said simply.

"Ay, I imagine they are."

She couldn't seem to look away from him.

They might have gone on staring at each other half the bleeding night, she told Daisy later, if Mrs. Chubb hadn't chosen that moment to come bustling into the kitchen, full of concern in case one of madam's guests might not be taken care of properly.

Gertie had left the kitchen then, with Ross McBride's firm assurances to Mrs. Chubb that he'd been taken very good care of still ringing in her ears.

She sat now on the edge of the bed, recounting the entire episode to Daisy. She wasn't sure why she was confiding in the younger girl, except that she was bursting to tell someone, and somehow she didn't think Mrs. Chubb would take too kindly to her being so familiar with the guests.

Daisy sat in the rocking chair, a baby sleeping in each arm, and listened quietly as Gertie described the way Ross McBride had looked when he told her about losing his wife and children.

"It gave me quite a turn, it did," Gertie said, her heart aching at the thought of it. "It must have been a bloody terrible experience."

"It can't bother him too much anymore," Daisy said. "Not if he wants you to go out with him."

"I think he's just lonely, that's all." Like she was, she thought, though she didn't say it out loud.

"Well, lonely or not, I wouldn't go out with him. Like I keep telling Doris, you can't be too careful. Not with blokes, you can't."

Gertie smiled. "Wait until you get to my age, Daisy Hoggins, you'll change your tune. You'll be glad of a bit of attention by then." One of the babies stirred with a faint whimper, and she held out her arms. "Here, I'll take them now. You must be tired of holding them."

Daisy shook her head, but carefully handed the babies over all the same. Getting to her feet, she smoothed the wrinkles out of her skirt. "I like looking after them," she said as she moved to the door. "I like taking care of things what can't take care of themselves."

Holding her babies close to her breasts, Gertie stared at the closed door. Funny one, that Daisy, she mused. Sometimes she talked as if she was an old woman. It didn't seem possible that two girls who looked so alike could be so bloody different inside.

Doris was so easy to get along with, always willing to do anything you asked her, and always with a smile. Yet in spite of Daisy's sullen moods, Gertie felt more at ease with her than her twin. Maybe because she reminded her of herself when she was that age.

If only she could fetch a smile to the girl's face, Gertie thought as she gently rocked her babies, she'd feel like she'd achieved something worthwhile. She owed Daisy a lot, she did, her taking such good care of her James and Lilly.

Settling down in the chair, Gertie closed her eyes. It was very pleasant to sit there with the warm weight of two tiny bodies in her arms and let her thoughts drift back to a roguish, smiling face and a pair of warm hazel eyes.

The snow started falling during the night, leaving a light dusting on the sweeping lawns of the hotel grounds. There wasn't enough to coat the streets for long, however, and by mid-morning the clopping hooves and rolling wheels had dried out the road, much to Phoebe's relief.

Normally she didn't mind the walk along the Esplanade. It was excellent exercise, and helped to keep her waist from expanding, as it was wont to do during the winter months. There were times when she had quite a struggle to lace her corset tight enough to get into her favorite wasp-waisted frocks.

It was Algie's fault, of course, she told herself as she pranced briskly alongside the wrought-iron railing that divided the street from the sands. The vicar was entirely too fond of rabbit stew and dumplings, not to mention the roly-poly puddings smothered in treacle.

As it was, Phoebe had even more reason nowadays to watch her figure. A smile flitted across her face as she thought about Alec McPherson. Such a charming man. Quite well-educated, all things considered. The last few days had dawned considerably brighter, with the prospect of such gracious companionship.

She crossed the street to the hotel, looking carefully each way in case one of those dreadful motorcars should come charging at her. They traveled so fast one hardly saw them coming. Twelve miles an hour, so she'd heard. The thought of it made her feel quite dizzy.

Of course, most of the time they made so much noise one could hear them coming long before they were in sight. Nasty, noisy, dirty things with all that black smoke belching out everywhere. Enough to make one choke.

Phoebe waited for a horse and trap to pass before crossing over to the steps of the Pennyfoot. Nothing, she told herself with assurance, would ever take the place of the nice, clean, steady pace of a horse and carriage.

Inside the hotel, Cecily waited with Madeline in the library for Phoebe to arrive.

"I do think it would be fun to decorate the balconies for the Tartan Ball," Madeline said, drawing arcs in the air with her expressive hands. "Something dramatic, like masses of pure white chrysanthemums, with perhaps arches of thick green pine, absolutely covered with red and white roses."

"Very dramatic," Cecily said dryly. "And horribly expensive, I daresay."

Madeline sighed. "I'm afraid so. If only we poor mortals were not bound by the necessity of pounds, shillings, and pence—just think how much more creative we might be. It is the dire lack of wealth that holds many an artistic soul in bondage."

"Who is in bondage?" a light voice trilled from the doorway.

Cecily smiled at Phoebe, who held her graceful pose in the doorway just long enough for the other two women to admire her burgundy two-piece with its fox collar and her magnificent rose-trimmed hat.

"Women," Madeline muttered, in answer to Phoebe's question. "Unfortunately most of them are too stupid to realize it."

Luckily her comment went over Phoebe's head. She settled herself on the brocade seat of her chair and smiled at Cecily. "I'm so thankful the snowfall was light last night. I do hate trudging through snow. So inelegant."

"I only hope it stays dry until after the ball," Cecily said, sending a wary glance toward the end of the table. To her surprise, Madeline failed to utter one of her derisive remarks. In fact, she seemed preoccupied, staring at a spot beyond Cecily's head.

"Oh, I certainly hope so," Phoebe murmured. "I can't imagine how I would get my dancers to the village hall if we should have a snowstorm."

"How is the dancing coming along?" Cecily asked, deciding to leave Madeline to her woolgathering for the moment.

"Oh, my dear." Phoebe shook her head in a mournful way that did not promise good news. "I don't know how Alec keeps his patience, I really don't. Those girls can be absolute horrors. No matter how hard Alec works with them, showing them the steps over and over again, they absolutely refuse to dance the Sword Dance in their stock-inged feet."

Cecily, watching Madeline out of the corner of her eye, nodded absently. "Well, I don't suppose it will matter too much if they keep their shoes on, will it?"

Phoebe uttered a small gasp. "Keep their shoes on? My dear Cecily, that's the entire point of the dance. Alec explained it all very carefully. The idea is to perform the intricate dance between the razor-sharp blades of the crossed swords without cutting one's toes. The girls are absolutely terrified, of course."

"I don't blame them," Cecily said in some alarm. The thought of Phoebe's clumsy troupe attempting such a risky maneuver was too disturbing to contemplate.

"Oh, Alec assures me it's quite safe, as long as the dancers are nimble." The roses on Phoebe's hat trembled as she uttered a loud sigh. "Unfortunately I seriously doubt that my dancers will ever begin to approach nimble. Even their version of the Highland Fling, which is quite a simple dance really, has more fling than finesse."

"Oh, dear," Cecily murmured. "In that case, I fervently suggest that they keep their feet shod."

"I suppose so," Phoebe said gloomily. "Though it does rather take away the element of suspense. If that wasn't enough to deal with, Algie is being very difficult about this entire celebration. He despises the sound of the bagpipes, and considers it an outrage that this outlandish music, as he calls it, should be played in a place of worship."

Cecily frowned. "They're playing the bagpipes in the church?"

"Oh, no, my dear, that would never do. No, in the village hall. Unfortunately the sound does travel rather. One can hear it quite clearly from the vestry, I'm afraid."

"Well, it won't be for much longer." Cecily glanced once more at Madeline, who had been uncommonly quiet throughout Phoebe's chatter. The lack of barbs from Madeline's caustic tongue was quite mystifying.

Madeline's face wore an expression of deep concentration. Something about the way she held herself so still unsettled Cecily.

"Algie never did have much time for the Scots," Phoebe

was saying. "Although he did quite surprise me by mentioning that he was partial to their kilts. Mind you, I could never imagine my son in a kilt. Somehow I think a vicar might not command too much respect with his bare knees displayed."

"We have a presence in the room," Madeline said suddenly, in a voice that sent chills racing down Cecily's back.

Phoebe stopped talking and stared at Madeline as if she'd gone quite mad. "A presence? Whatever are you talking about?"

"I can feel it." Madeline narrowed her eyes, peering into the dark corners of the library. "I can't see it yet, but it's there. Watching . . . waiting . . ."

"Waiting for what?" Phoebe asked sharply.

"For us to notice it, of course." Madeline turned her dark eyes on Phoebe. "Perhaps it's waiting for you."

"Oh, good Lord, Cecily," Phoebe said crossly, "you might be perfectly willing to listen to such nonsense, but I'm quite sure I am not. I have better things to do with my time." She got up from her chair with a great deal of fussing, tugging at her gloves and smoothing down her skirt.

"It is an unhappy spirit," Madeline said in the same toneless voice. "An unhappy spirit is a dangerous spirit."

Phoebe straightened her hat with a firm tug. "I am quite sure my girls will be more than adequate with their performance at the ball, Cecily, so please do not worry. Alec will whip them into shape, I have no doubt."

Cecily nodded, her attention still on Madeline's trancelike expression. "Thank you, Phoebe. I have complete faith in you, as always."

Apparently gratified, Phoebe moved to the door. "Good day, Madeline. I do hope your return to our world is imminent. We should hate to lose you to your hallucinations." With a final toss of her head, Phoebe disappeared through the door.

Cecily hardly saw her go. Her gaze was on Madeline, but

in her mind she could hear Colonel Fortescue's rambling voice. *He vanished right in front of my eyes. One minute he was standing at the foot of my bed, the next he was gone. Nothing there. It was as if he'd simply gone up in smoke.*

CHAPTER

❀ 11 ❀

"I tell you, Gertie, it's far too cold to take those babies outside." Mrs. Chubb shook her finger in Gertie's face. "Why, it snowed last night, remember? Little mites like that don't have the lungs to breathe in that cold air. It could kill them both, it could."

Gertie wiped her hands dry on a kitchen towel and stared defiantly at the housekeeper. "Dr. Prestwick said that fresh air will do them good. As long as they've wrapped up warm enough. He says as how the babies are breathing all the bleeding dust and smoke from the fires, and they need fresh air to clean out their lungs."

"Well, how are you going to carry them, that's what I want to know."

"I don't have to bleeding carry them, do I. Madam is

lending me her pram that she had for her boys. It's a bloody big one, it is, so there's plenty of room for little Lilly and James."

Mrs. Chubb jerked her chin in the air. "Lilly? You're calling her Lilly?"

Gertie sighed. "Well, Lillian is such a bleeding mouthful for a tiny baby. Sometimes I have trouble getting me bloody tongue around it."

"And how will she feel if everyone calls her Lilly when she grows up?"

"Then I suppose she'll have to decide what she wants people to call her, won't she."

"It might be too late then." The housekeeper opened a cupboard door and peered inside. "I don't know what Michel does with the sugar, I really don't. It's nearly all gone again. I only ordered it last week."

Gertie pulled a face at Mrs. Chubb's back. It didn't seem as if she could do anything nowadays without the housekeeper jumping on her. Mrs. Chubb turned around at that moment and Gertie hastily straightened her face.

"Have you asked madam and Mr. Baxter about being godparents yet?" Mrs. Chubb asked.

"No, I haven't. I'm going to today, after I take the babies for their first walk."

The housekeeper shook her head. "I do wish you wouldn't take them out just yet, Gertie. Wait another month or two until the weather warms up a bit."

"They're nearly bleeding three months old and they don't know what the sky looks like yet. I won't have them out for long. Besides, they'll have to go out for the bloody christening, won't they?"

Burying her resentment, Gertie crossed the room to the door. Mrs. Chubb meant well, she knew, but sometimes her constant fussing over the babies drove Gertie crazy.

Give her Daisy's sensible attitude anytime, she thought as she opened the door. Leave it to Mrs. Chubb and she'd have both babies so mollycoddled they'd grow up horrible spoiled brats, like that fat Stanley Malton who had given her such blooming trouble last summer when he was here with his parents.

"Just make sure you wrap them up well," Mrs. Chubb called out as the door closed behind Gertie. "It's almost midday, and the sun will be going down again soon. Wrap a wooly scarf across their little mouths . . ."

Her voice faded away as Gertie hurried down the hallway to her room. It was time for the babies' feeding, then she had about half an hour before she had to be back for the midday meal. And Gertie wasn't about to miss a minute of precious time she was able to spend with her twins.

She was almost at the door of her room when she saw one of the housemaids coming toward her. She couldn't see too clearly in the dim light of the passageway, and she wasn't sure if it was Doris or Daisy who halted in front of her, with a scared look that made her eyes look huge in her white face.

For a second or two Gertie's heart stopped. "Daisy? Is something wrong? Not my babies, is it?" Her hand was on the door handle, already turning it when the young girl shook her head.

"No, Miss Brown, I'm Doris. I just come from the conservatory. I was watering the plants in there, and I saw him again."

"Saw who?" Gertie demanded, her relief making her voice sharp.

"Peter Stewart. He was standing by the windows, as large as life."

Gertie's stomach gave a little jump. "You're bleeding seeing things again, Doris 'Oggins. Not been at Michel's brandy, have you? He'll cut your bloody tongue out if you have."

"No, I haven't. And I'm not seeing things." Doris reached out a shaky hand and clutched Gertie's apron. "I don't know what to do, Miss Brown, honest I don't. It's like he's following me around, watching me all the time. Fair gives me the creeps, it does."

Gertie could feel the girl's hand trembling. She must have been really frightened. Curbing her impatience, Gertie said briskly, "It's just someone playing tricks on you, that's all. All them Scotch blokes look alike when they're wearing them kilts. You know it can't be Peter Stewart. He's bleeding dead, isn't he?"

"It's his ghost," Doris said in a soft moaning voice that gave Gertie chills. "I see him everywhere. He's following me, and I don't know what to do about it."

Determined not to be spooked by the jittery girl, Gertie squared her shoulders. She didn't believe in ghosts, not in any way, shape, or form. There had to be a simple explanation for everything that happened. It was just that sometimes things weren't always what they seemed.

"You sound as daffy as that bleeding Colonel Fortescue," she said, gently dislodging Doris's frantic grip on her apron. "He kept on about seeing a ghost, too. Scared me silly, he did, until I remembered all the other times he'd seen things. All in his mind, it were. Same as you."

She ignored the emphatic shake of Doris's head. "You're all upset 'cause you liked Peter Stewart, that's why you keep thinking you can see him." She took hold of Doris's frail hand and started down the hallway. "Come on, I'll go back with you. I'll show you there's no ghost in the conservatory."

"No, no, I'm not going back there. You can't make me." Doris snatched her hand away from Gertie's and flew off in the opposite direction.

Gertie watched her go, her face grim. Someone was bleeding playing jokes on the poor girl, and it weren't funny. Maybe the bugger was still there. If so, she'd give him a piece of her mind.

Hurrying up the stairs to the conservatory, she hoped and prayed the twins wouldn't wake up and start screaming for their blinking milk before she got back to them. Bugger those Scotchmen, they were more trouble than they were worth. Even Ross McBride spelled trouble. He seemed to be on her mind far too bloody much lately.

She'd be bleeding glad, she decided, when the Robbie Burns celebration was over and done with and they all went back to bleeding Scotland, where they belonged. Then maybe she could stop thinking about Ross McBride and his blooming come-hither eyes.

Gertie smiled as she reached the conservatory door. Come-hither eyes. She'd been fascinated by that phrase ever since she'd first heard it. She'd never really known what it meant until now.

Still smiling, she pushed the doors open and went inside the cool conservatory. In the summer the glass walls on the outside kept the narrow room hot and moist, but in the winter it was always cold in there. In fact, Gertie thought as she stood shivering in her thin white linen blouse, it was bloody freezing in there now.

Unwilling to spend a second longer in there than she needed to, she cast a quick look around then turned to go. As she did so, a slight movement near the glass doors that led to the outside caught her eyes.

For a moment she thought she was seeing things. Outlined against the glass she could see what looked like the shadow of a piper. Blinking, Gertie stared harder. She could actually see the bushes and trees outside right through him.

For a moment she froze in shock, then her common sense took hold. It had to be a reflection of someone standing outside, probably bloody hiding around the corner where she couldn't see him.

Even so, she couldn't make herself go closer to look. As she watched, the shadow grew fainter, until it disappeared altogether. Gertie wasn't totally surprised to feel her teeth chattering. Whoever it was, he was doing a good job of frightening everyone, she thought grimly. Maybe she should have a word with Mrs. Chubb about it. Or even madam.

Making up her mind that she would speak to madam

about the shadow when she went to see her that afternoon, Gertie hurried back to her room and the solid comfort of her babies.

Cecily paused in the act of tapping on the door of Baxter's office. He would not be happy to know that she had been to see Dr. Prestwick, yet she needed to discuss the information she had learned from the doctor. Wishing things didn't have to be quite so complicated, she gave the door a sharp rap, waiting a moment before opening it.

Baxter looked up from the desk and immediately rose to his feet. "I suppose there is no point in reminding you that we have staff who will bring me a message that you wish to see me," he said, struggling into his morning coat. "Thus eliminating the necessity for you to visit me in my office."

She had heard the slight rebuke so often she hardly listened to it. "I sometimes think, Baxter," she said mildly as she seated herself on a deep leather armchair, "that you have things to hide from me in this office."

He looked down his nose at her, his mouth drawn in a tight line of resentment. "That, if I may say so, madam, is pure poppycock."

She peered up at him. He did not appear to be in too good a humor. Hazarding a guess as to the cause of his tension, she asked softly, "Problems with bills again?"

"There are always problems with bills, madam."

"But more so in the winter, I would say."

"Yes, madam."

She tried a smile. "Never mind, Baxter, spring is just around the corner."

"Unfortunately, madam, I'm afraid there will be even more bills waiting around that corner. Samuel informed me that a portion of the ceiling has collapsed in room two, the roof is leaking again, and the chimney in suite four is smoking quite badly. I imagine it needs refacing."

"Oh, dear. We have that suite booked for this weekend."

"Yes, madam. I doubt if the work can be done before

then, so I have suggested that the Halliwells take room five. It's not as spacious as the suite, but it is the largest of the rooms."

"Lady Halliwell will not care for that. She has always insisted on a suite."

"Yes, madam. I shall attempt to be diplomatic when they arrive."

"Thank you, Baxter. I'm quite sure you will handle things beautifully."

"I will do my best, madam."

"Tell me something. Do you believe in ghosts?"

He looked startled at the swift change of subject. "Ghosts? I'm not sure what you mean."

"Ghosts, Baxter. Those transparent ethereal beings who haunt old castles and scare everyone to death."

"I haven't given it much thought, madam."

"Well, give it some thought. And please, do sit down. I have a crick in the neck from peering up at you."

He stretched his neck above his collar. "You know very well my views on that subject."

"I also know that you have been attempting to relax your strict ethics of late." She smiled sweetly at him. "I was hoping that might include being seated in my presence. After all, I have left the door ajar to satisfy your unnecessary concerns. Our discussions would be so much more comfortable if I could look at you eye to eye."

"Yes, madam. But . . ."

"But what?"

"I'm not sure if I would be comfortable, madam."

Cecily sighed. "Try it, Baxter. You can't live in the Victorian age forever. However are we women going to be accepted as equals if we are constantly dealing with outdated modes of behavior?"

"I do not want to give the staff the wrong impression."

She studied his flushed face for a moment before asking, "Which wrong impression?"

He cleared his throat, shifting his weight from one foot to

the other. "I do not want to give the impression that I am becoming too familiar with my superiors."

"Piffle." She leaned forward. "I don't care what the staff think. Let them think what they want."

"Yes, madam."

He looked so uncomfortable, she gave up. "Very well. So tell me if you believe in ghosts."

His expression relaxed slightly, though his gray eyes remained wary. "I have heard stories about people who have encountered apparitions, yes. While I haven't exactly studied the subject, I understand that the theory of spirits being able to communicate with people has never been authenticated. On the other hand, neither has their presence been refuted. Therefore, since I prefer to base my judgment on matters that have a logical explanation, I prefer not to pass an opinion."

Cecily stared at him, then shook her head in disbelief. "For a man of few words, Baxter, you have a remarkable propensity for taking the longest way around of saying no."

"I did not say no, madam. Merely that I had no opinion either way."

She could tell by the sparkle in his eyes that he was beginning to enjoy himself. Now, perhaps, was the time to mention Dr. Prestwick.

"I paid a call this afternoon," she said, rearranging the folds in her skirt. "I went to see Dr. Prestwick about the murder. He was quite helpful, actually, though of course there's so much he's not able to tell me. I really don't know why everything has to be such a secret. The truth comes out eventually, doesn't it?"

Aware of the growing silence, she peeked up at his face. To her dismay, his expression had hardened considerably.

"I cannot imagine why you insist on exposing yourself to gossip in this manner," he said stiffly. "It is well known that Prestwick's reputation with the ladies is questionable—"

"Through no fault of his own," Cecily felt compelled to point out.

"—and I find it deplorable that you should feel perfectly at ease when visiting such a man alone in his home."

Stung by his tone, she said fiercely, "I did not go inside, Baxter. Even if I had, it is not up to you to question my morals. Just because James asked you to watch over me, that does not give you the right to dictate my every movement."

"Damn it, Cecily, let us please leave your late husband out of this. My promise to James Sinclair has nothing to do with my concern over your inappropriate activities."

Stunned, Cecily stared at him, aware of the sound of his harsh breathing in the quiet room. After a tight pause, she said very quietly, "May I ask what your concern does have to do with?"

She saw him swallow, as if trying to rid himself of something stuck in his throat. "My concern stems from my deep respect for your welfare and your standing in this community."

She was about to speak, when he added as an after-thought, "Madam."

She didn't know whether to feel grateful for his consideration or insulted by his lack of trust in her ethics. "Might I suggest, Baxter," she said at last, "as I have mentioned just a short while ago, that you are living in an age that no longer exists. Women are working in offices with men, working alongside men in factories, waiting on men in shops and restaurants, and even, in too few instances, performing surgery on men."

He refrained from answering, his expression unyielding.

Irritated by his rigid beliefs, she added crossly, "I wish now that I had gone inside the doctor's cottage, if only to prove that it was perfectly safe and proper for me to do so. There are times, Baxter, when I find your attitude quite tedious. When are you ever going to relax that moral code that is so hopelessly outdated?"

She was startled when fire suddenly blazed in his eyes. "You tend to forget, madam, that I also have feelings, I can assure you, were you anything but my employer, I would be more than willing to modernize my behavior."

Try as she might, she could find no answer to that volatile statement.

After a short pause, Baxter muttered rather bitterly, "Please forgive me, madam. I am afraid I overstepped the boundaries of protocol."

Still flustered, Cecily wished she had a fan to cool her warm face. His apology had been offered halfheartedly, to say the least. She had the distinct impression he was not in the least sorry for what he had said.

"That's all right, Baxter," she said when she finally recovered her voice. "I owe you an apology, too. I have no right to criticize you for your beliefs, no matter how unpopular they might be."

His raised eyebrow told her that he was not happy with her apology either, but she adroitly changed the subject. "Anyway, as I said, Dr. Prestwick did give me one piece of useful information about the murder. It would seem our theory of the key having been taken from Tom's pocket while he lay unconscious will not hold water. Dr. Prestwick assures me that Peter Stewart was killed inside the shop."

Baxter's chin relaxed just a little. "The key could still have been taken and returned. Maybe the victim was merely unconscious when Abbittson arrived on the scene. The killer could then have taken the key, dragged Stewart inside the shop, finished him off there, and left the shop again, returning the key to Abbittson's pocket."

"Why would anyone go to all that trouble? Unless he was deliberately trying to make it look as if Tom was the killer." Cecily tapped her fingernails on his desk. "If so, he's certainly succeeding. It would seem that Peter Stewart died just about the time Tom arrived home from the George."

She shook her head in a gesture of despair. "Moreover, as I've mentioned before, I don't understand how someone could have done all that without disturbing Elsie. I'm afraid that the more I learn about this matter, the more Tom appears to be guilty."

"In which case, his wife is most likely inventing lies in order to protect him."

Cecily gazed up at him. "Indeed," she murmured. "I had arrived at the same conclusion. I think the time has come for me to call on Elsie Abbittson. I shall do so this afternoon. Perhaps if she is not too busy, I shall have an opportunity to talk to her."

Baxter looked down at her with an odd expression on his face. She waited for a moment or two, and when he didn't speak she said with a frown, "What is it?"

He cleared his throat and clasped his hands behind his back, but still said nothing.

Watching him with faint suspicion, Cecily said quietly, "If you have something to say to me, Baxter, please get it out before you drive me crazy with your inane pantomime."

He raised his chin. "I was merely going to caution you, madam. Since you tend to get somewhat peevish if I do so, however, I thought it prudent to keep my council to myself."

"Peevish?" She pursed her lips. "If I get peevish, Baxter, it is because you fail to trust my common sense. When have I ever given you good cause to fear for my safety?"

Baxter looked as if someone had just handed him a tasty cream bun. He opened his mouth, but Cecily hastily forestalled him.

"Don't answer that. I admit there might have been a time or two when you might have had cause to worry, but you have to agree, it was through no lack of prudence on my part. One cannot always foresee the pitfalls, particularly when conducting an investigation into murder."

"Precisely, madam."

She made a sound of impatience deep in her throat. "What would you have me do? Trust Stan Northcott to ferret out the truth?"

Knowing how he felt about the local constable, she was fairly certain of his reaction. To her immense satisfaction, his expression altered at once. "Had we left matters to that dolt in the past, we might very well have lost a great deal of business."

"Possibly the hotel as well." She smiled sweetly at him. "I'm so happy you agree with me, Bax."

His face was inscrutable as he gave her a stiff little bow. "How can I venture to do anything else, madam?"

How indeed, she thought smugly. Chalk up one more victory to her.

CHAPTER 12

Gertie lifted her nose in the damp chilly air as she pushed the pram along the Esplanade. It was bleeding cold, she thought. At least Mrs. Chubb had been right about that. She could smell bloody snow in the wind.

Glancing down at the two small bundles in the pram, she hoped they were warm enough. They bleeding should be, the way she'd wrapped them up in woollies. It was a wonder they could breathe with all that lot on them.

The hoarse cry of a sea gull disturbed her thoughts, and she lifted her face toward the sky. The bird wheeled in slow circles beneath the dark gray clouds, watching her. He was waiting for a few crumbs, she reckoned. He'd have a bloody long wait.

There was a time when she might have shoved a slice of

stale cake or a dry crust in her pocket for the hungry birds. But feed one and the bloody lot descended on her, and she didn't want blinking bird shit all over her clean covers, thank you.

The sea looked angry, spitting white froth as it pummeled the beach. Higher up the sand the waves had strewn limp seaweed in a straggly line beneath the tall cliffs. She could smell the salty tang of the stuff in the cold wind.

She was the only one on the Esplanade. All the little shops, usually crowded with eager visitors in the summer, were closed now, their windows shuttered against the winter storms. A few shriveled dried-up leaves leapt and swirled as the stiff breeze drove them along the pavement.

A strip of paper, torn by the wind from one of the summer posters advertising the pier, had wrapped itself around one of the railings. It looked so forlorn, like the ragged remnants of better days.

The seaside could be a lonely place in winter, Gertie thought, feeling a sudden rush of melancholy. She didn't know why she should feel so bloody lonely. She had her friends at the Pennyfoot, and her two precious little ones. Though they'd be a lot better company once they'd bleeding grown up a bit. All they seemed to do now was eat, cry, and sleep.

It could be a lot worse, Gertie told herself as she watched the sea gull swoop low over the water then soar with graceful ease up and over the cliffs of Putney Downs.

She could be on the street, she reminded herself. Out in the cold with nowhere to go and two hungry mouths to feed. There were too many people like that, without a home and a fireplace to keep them warm. She had the best home in the world—the best bleeding hotel in England.

Marching along with grim determination, Gertie tried to outpace her gloomy mood. No matter how much she counted her blessings, however, the fact remained: She was bloody lonely.

It wasn't easy being responsible for two little ones. The

older they got, the harder it was going to be. There were times when the enormity of her situation almost overwhelmed her.

Deeply engrossed in her troubled thoughts, she paid no attention to the swift footsteps approaching her, until the man reached her side, then spun around and fell in step alongside her.

Looking up into the face of Ross McBride, Gertie could feel her spirits rising. There was just something about those bedroom eyes that made a girl feel all warm and cozy inside.

"I can hardly believe my luck," Ross McBride said cheerfully. "Here I was, walking back from band practice, and suddenly there you are in front of me, looking just like a page out of my favorite picture book."

Determined not to let her foolish fancies sway her common sense, Gertie kept her gaze on the cliffs ahead. All she could seem to think about was how bloody cold his knees must be in that blinking kilt. She just hoped he was wearing warm drawers underneath it.

Thin columns of smoke rose from the fishermen's cottages dotted along the harbor. She wished she was inside one of them, warm and snug, instead of out there in the blinking freezing wind trying to ignore a man she just knew was up to no good.

In spite of her good intentions, the question slipped out. "What picture book?"

"*Alice's Adventures in Wonderland.*" Ross laughed, a warm rich sound that helped chase some of the chill out of her bones. "That's who you remind me of, you know."

"I do?" Caught by surprise, she looked up at him. It was sort of nice, looking up at a man. Ian had been the same size as her. Shorter if she wore her fancy shoes with the heels.

"Ay, lass, you certainly do. I can just imagine you chasing rabbits down a hole or arguing with the Queen of Hearts. I'd put odds on you winning and all, right enough."

"I wouldn't let no bleeding bugger chop my bloody head off, that's for certain." Thinking about chopping heads off made her think about Peter Stewart and the shadow she'd seen on the windows. Perhaps it were Ross McBride who was playing tricks, she thought. He seemed the type what would enjoy a bloody good joke.

Hoping to catch him off guard, she said abruptly, "Dreadful thing, that murder of Peter Stewart, wasn't it? Poor sod, it must have been awful for him. Shouldn't wonder if he doesn't come back and haunt whoever killed him."

She didn't really think he would take that much notice of what she said. But he surprised her by saying sharply, "Whatever makes you say that?"

Unsettled by his tone, she shrugged. "Oh, I dunno. Sometimes people do come back as ghosts, don't they?"

"That's rubbish. I've certainly been in enough Scottish castles to meet one, I can tell you, and I've never seen one."

Well, that settled one bloody question, she thought. If he'd been the one playing tricks, he would have told her the ghost was real. Still, it was bloody funny the way he got upset about it.

She was about to change the subject when Ross said quietly, "I dinna like to speak ill of the dead, but I never liked the bloke. He was too familiar with the ladies, always leading them on, until he got bored with them and went looking for someone new."

"You knew him, then?" Gertie said in surprise. "Before you came here, I mean."

"Ay, I knew him. But I dinna want to talk about him. He's dead, and he can't hurt anyone else now." He looked down at her, the twinkle back in his eyes. "I'd much rather talk about you."

Gertie tossed her head. "Seems as if Peter Stewart wasn't the only bloody flirt around." She gave the pram a firm push, sending it bowling along ahead of her.

Before she could grab the handle again, Ross had taken hold of it. Pushing it easily with one hand, he gazed down at the two little mounds beneath the blankets.

"These are very young bairns," he said, his voice sort of hushed.

"Almost three months." Gertie felt a fierce rush of pride. All of a sudden she wanted to show off the babies to him.

"I had no idea." He looked at her then, his eyes full of warm sympathy that made her stomach go squishy. "It must be very difficult for you, having to take care of two wee bairns all by yourself."

She managed a casual shrug. "Nah, it's not so bad. Mrs. Chubb and the twins, Doris and Daisy, help me take care of them. It's handy having the babies near me when I'm working. I can hear them when they're crying, and when it's time to feed them I can just—"

She broke off, her face growing hot.

Ross paused, bringing the pram to a halt. "I bet you don't get out much at all, do you?" he said gently.

Gertie shook her head. For some strange reason, she felt like crying. "I don't mind. I have the babies now, you see, and they take up all me time. Don't know what I'd bleeding do with meself if I did go out, anyhow. Not much to do down here, 'specially in the winter. In the summer we're too bleeding busy to go anywhere."

"I'm going to be playing the pipes at the Tartan Ball tomorrow night."

"Yes," Gertie said awkwardly. "I know."

"I'd like it fine if you could be there to hear me play."

She shook her head, furious with herself for wishing so bad that she could be there. "I'm not allowed to go. Not unless madam invites me, and she's not bloody likely to do that. The only time I went to a ball was after my blinking wedding, when everyone went back to the hotel after the service."

"I see."

She daren't look up at him. She was afraid that one look into those wicked eyes and she'd agree to anything.

"Well, how about joining me for a drink afterward? We could go down to the George, or perhaps there's somewhere in the hotel we could go? Somewhere where we could have a spot of privacy?"

She made the mistake of looking at him then. "I have to go back," she said abruptly, and whisked the pram around before he had a chance to protest.

"Please, Gertie." Once more he fell in step beside her, keeping pace with her furiously marching feet. "I get awful lonely here. I don't know a soul, except for one or two of the pipers, and none of us really get along. I really would like some company."

"I can't bloody get away just like that," Gertie said desperately.

"I miss my wife and bairns, Gertie. Just like you must miss your husband. What's the harm with a wee drink or two? Just between two lonely friends, that is."

Gertie gritted her teeth.

"I promise that's all it is, Gertie. I swear, on God's honor, I willna lay a hand on you."

She had reached the steps of the hotel. All she had to do was wheel the pram down the path along the wall to the kitchen yard. He could hardly follow her into the bleeding kitchen.

"Can I at least push the pram for you across the yard?"

She shook her head, refusing to look at him again.

"Very well, I can see I'm wasting my time. I'm sorry I bothered you, Gertie. Never fear, I willna bother you again. God bless you, lass."

She watched his back as he slowly climbed the steps. He had almost reached the door when she called out. "I could meet you in a card room."

She didn't think he'd heard her, but after a slight pause he turned around and came back down the steps. She almost cried at the look of hope on his face.

"A card room?"

She nodded, eager now that she'd made up her mind. "We've got six of them, down in the cellar. No one's supposed to know about them except for the ones what pay to play down there, so don't tell no one, all right?"

Ross grinned, showing his even white teeth. With a swift movement of his hand he made a sign of the cross across his chest. "Swear to God. Where do I find this card room?"

"I'll have to take you down there. Meet me in the conservatory after the entertainment tomorrow night."

"Ay, I will that."

She nodded, her heart pounding so hard she felt sure it was going to come right through her chest. "All right, then. I'll see you tomorrow night."

Ross lifted his hand and touched his forehead. "Until tomorrow night, Gertie." He seemed to spring up the steps this time. Reaching the top, he turned and blew her a kiss. Before she had fully recovered, he'd disappeared inside the doors.

Cheeky bugger, she told herself, but she smiled at the thought. It was bleeding funny, but now she didn't feel cold at all.

"I think," Cecily said as she rose from her chair in Baxter's office, "that I shall have lunch in the dining room for a change. I have been taking my meals in my suite of late, but that can be a little lonely at times."

"Yes, madam. I am quite familiar with that feeling."

She gave him a quick glance, but he seemed to be preoccupied with the open ledger on his desk. "Would you care to join me, Baxter? I should enjoy your company for lunch."

She expected him to appear shocked, and perhaps utter a faint rebuke. Instead, he surprised her by saying mildly, "Thank you, madam. I would enjoy your company, also. Unfortunately I have a pressing engagement with an expense ledger. I regret I shall be unable to join you in the dining room."

She was still wondering how to answer that when a light tap was followed immediately by Gertie's voice saying,

"Excuse me, mum, could I have a word with you, if you please?"

Cecily smiled at the housemaid, who stood in the doorway looking unsure of herself for once. "Of course, Gertie. I was on my way to the dining room. We can talk on the way."

"As a matter of fact, mum," Gertie said, casting a quick glance at Baxter, "I wanted to talk to Mr. Baxter as well. To you both, I mean."

Cecily frowned. "This sounds serious, Gertie. You had better come in and close the door." She watched the housemaid edge inside the door and close it behind her. Noticing the dark shadows under the girl's eyes, she felt a twinge of anxiety.

Gertie stood with her back to the door and pushed the strap of her apron higher over her shoulder. She'd tied her black hair back in a knot, and her prominent cheekbones seemed to stand out above the hollows in her cheeks. "Mrs. Sinclair, Mr. Baxter, I wanted to ask you a favor, like."

"You are not well, Gertie?" Cecily laid a hand on the housemaid's shoulder. "If you need more rest—"

"No, no, mum. It's nothing like that. I'm all right, honest I am. Bit tired, that's all."

"Well, then, girl, what is it?" Baxter demanded, sounding impatient.

Really worried now, Cecily continued to study the nervous girl. This wasn't like Gertie at all. Usually she had no trouble saying what she wanted to say, often to the point where it was difficult to shut her up.

"Well, it's two things, actually, mum." Gertie visibly straightened her back when Cecily dropped her hand. "First, I wanted to report that someone is bleeding playing tricks on the housemaids. One of the bloody pipers, I think, mum. And the other thing is that I wanted to ask you and Mr. Baxter if you would like to be godparents to my twins."

The words had come out in such a rush it took Cecily a

moment or two to absorb them. "Oh, my," she said as she met Gertie's beseeching look. "This is a surprise."

Behind her, Baxter cleared his throat.

Cecily dared not look at him. Instead, she said warmly, "Thank you, Gertie. I am very flattered that you wish to entrust the care of your babies to me. Of course, I would love to be their godmother."

A smile of relief lit up Gertie's face. "Oh, thank you, mum, I don't know what I would have bleeding done if you'd said no. There ain't no one else to ask, and I—"

Again Baxter cleared his throat. Louder this time.

Gertie snapped her mouth shut and sent him a nervous look.

Steeling herself, Cecily turned to face him. She'd intended to signal with her eyes that he should accept, no matter how he felt about it. She was determined to spare Gertie any hurt feelings.

To her surprise, Baxter's face was pink, and she could tell he was pleased, even though his mouth barely moved in a tight smile.

"Thank you, Gertie," he said, inclining his head in a small bow. "It is indeed an honor. I accept with the greatest of pleasure."

"Oh, Gawd." Gertie breathed a sigh. "Thank you, sir. Thank you ever so much. Oh, wait till I tell Mrs. Chubb. She'll be tickled pink, she will."

"Yes, well, don't spend your day tattling about it to one and all," Baxter said, reverting to his pompous tone again.

"Yes, sir . . . mum . . . oh, thank you." She bobbed a curtsey. "Me babies will be in bloody good hands if anything happens to me, that they will." She started to open the door, but Cecily stopped her with a hand on the housemaid's arm.

"One moment, Gertie. You mentioned something about someone playing tricks?"

"Oh, yes, mum. In all the bleeding excitement I forgot about it. It's Doris, mostly, mum. Bloody hysterical, she is sometimes. Keeps thinking she's seeing ghosts. She says as how it's that Peter Stewart who got murdered what's following her around. Course, I told her she was blinking daft, and that it was just someone playing tricks, but you know how Doris is, mum. Silly little bugger sometimes, she is."

Cecily jumped in while Gertie paused for breath. "Yes, but what exactly did Doris see?"

Gertie shrugged, losing her strap over her shoulder again in the process. "Dunno exactly. Doris said he kept disappearing like. Anyway, I went into the conservatory to have a look."

She paused, as if not quite sure what she had seen.

Cecily felt a small flutter under her ribs. "What did you see?" she prompted gently.

"Well, it was queer, mum, but it was like a shadow, on the French windows. I think it was someone standing outside, but I couldn't see no one. Then it sort of . . . disappeared. I didn't wait around to look anymore. I just left."

Cecily nodded gravely. "Thank you, Gertie. We'll look into it."

"Yes, mum." Again Gertie dropped a curtsey, then hurried off down the passageway.

"Well," Cecily said, turning back to Baxter, "what do you think of that?"

"I think that the young lady has excellent taste." Baxter puffed out his chest and stuck his thumbs inside the armholes of his waistcoat. "She has chosen the best possible godparents for her offspring, if I might say so."

Cecily laughed. "I happen to agree, Baxter. But I wasn't referring to her request. I was talking about Doris and her ghost."

Baxter uttered a scornful sound in his throat. "If we were to take notice of the hysterical imagination of the younger members of our staff, we would be wasting our time constantly investigating such nonsense."

"I hardly think it nonsense that someone is deliberately

frightening the girls," Cecily said in mild reproof. "Upsetting someone to that degree goes beyond the bounds of innocent mischief."

Baxter sighed. "Very well, madam. I will look into it. Where would you suggest I start?"

"Never mind, Baxter. You have enough to do at the moment wrestling with that ledger. I'll have a word with Doris when I get back from Abbittson's."

"Yes, madam."

Cecily paused at the door and looked back at him. "I think you will make a wonderful godfather," she said softly, then quickly left the room before he had time to answer her.

CHAPTER

❖ 13 ❖

Cecily was quite disturbed to find Abbittson's butcher shop closed when she arrived there later that day. She hoped the butcher's wife was at home, and not at the police station visiting her husband. Taking hold of the brass door knocker on the front door, she rapped the lion's head sharply against its base several times.

Waiting for Elsie to answer, she watched Samuel guide the chestnut and trap around the corner, no doubt heading for the George and Dragon before returning in an hour as Cecily had ordered.

Several women were shopping in the High Street, carrying loaded baskets on their arms as they hurried in and out of Wilson's the greengrocer's or Shuttleworth's the grocer's.

A motorcar pulled up with a great deal of noise and

smoke in front of Botham's Chemist Shop on the corner.
Cecily watched the driver hurry into the chemist's, his head
heavily swathed in cap and scarf and his face hidden behind
a pair of large goggles.

Farther down the street she could hear the bell jingling on
the door of Dolly's Tea Shop as the primarily female
customers jostled for a space in the crowded dining room,
all eager for their afternoon tea.

The door of the butcher's shop opened with a loud jangle,
taking Cecily by surprise. She turned to see the worried face
of Elsie Abbittson peering at her through the crack in the
doorway.

Upon seeing her visitor, Elsie opened the door wider.
"Why, Mrs. Sinclair! This is a surprise."

"I'm sorry to disturb you, Elsie," Cecily said, thankful to
find the woman at home. "I wonder if I might have a word
with you?"

Elsie's face turned white, then pink. "Have you found out
who done it?"

Regretfully Cecily shook her head. "I'm sorry. I wish I
had better news."

Elsie clutched her throat. "It's not Tom, is it? I mean, they
haven't . . . he's not . . . ?"

"Oh, no, this has nothing to do with Tom," Cecily
hastened to reassure the woman. "Well, it has, I suppose—"
She broke off as Elsie made a little moaning noise. "Perhaps
if I could come inside? I promise I won't keep you long."

"Oh, forgive me, Mrs. Sinclair. Don't know what I was
thinking of, really." Elsie stepped back and allowed Cecily
to step through the doorway.

The odor inside the shop was unpleasant, and Cecily
gladly followed Elsie as she hurriedly led the way up a
narrow staircase to the flat above.

The drawing room into which Elsie ushered her was quite
spacious, with two very large windows that looked down
upon the busy High Street. The steady clop of hoofbeats

outside could be heard quite clearly in the quiet room as
Cecily took a sat on a worn padded armchair.

Resting her elbows on the wooden arms, Cecily smiled at
Elsie, who hurriedly snatched her fingers away from her
mouth.

"Can I get you some tea?" Elsie offered, looking as if
she'd faint away if Cecily accepted.

"Thank you, no. I have not long finished my lunch."
Cecily looked around the shabby room. One wall was
dominated by the fireplace, a rather glamorous affair in
black marble edged in gold.

The High Street had once consisted of quite elegant
Victorian homes. With the advent of the tourist trade in
Badgers End, most of the houses had been converted into
shops on the lower level, leaving what would have been the
bedrooms at one time to serve as the living quarters of the
shop owners.

Glancing up at the high ceiling, Cecily admired the
ornamental rose in the center. The heavily decorated centerpiece must have been quite spectacular at one time, with
perhaps a gleaming chandelier to softly light the room.

Now the ceiling was bare of any fixtures, the room
apparently lit by the small gas lamps on the pedestal tables
in each corner. The rose-patterned carpet, once quite luxurious, had worn through almost to the backing in some
spots.

"What did you come to tell me?" Elsie said, her voice
pitched high with nervous strain.

"Oh, I'm sorry," Cecily said hastily. "I was admiring this
room."

"Thank you," Elsie murmured, looking taken aback.

"Have you seen your husband since he was taken away?"

Obviously unnerved by this unexpected question, Elsie
sat down a little too abruptly in a heavy oak rocking chair.
The chair rocked back sharply, and Elsie clutched the arms
with a little gasp.

Righting herself, she said breathlessly, "They won't let

me see him. Not until he's properly charged, that is. P.C. Northcott is waiting for Inspector Cranshaw to come from Wellercombe. He said that could take days."

Cecily sighed. "I'm afraid that it usually does take the inspector some time to get here. He always seems to have something more important to take care of in Wellercombe."

"Well, he'd better hurry up and get here soon. I can just imagine my Tom, shut up in that awful dark room in the police station. Though I daresay prison's worse."

"Infinitely worse," Cecily said quietly. "I'm sorry, Elsie, but I'm afraid that things do not look too encouraging for Tom. It seems the evidence is piling up against him."

She paused, watching the other woman's face closely. "It's the fact that he had the only key to the door in his possession, you see. The police are quite convinced that there was no forced entry into the shop. It just doesn't seem possible that anyone else could have entered the shop, committed the murder, then left again, locking the door behind him."

"I suppose it doesn't," Elsie said miserably.

Cecily waited a moment or two, while a horse pulled a loudly creaking carriage down the street. The sound faded, and she folded her gloved hands in her lap. "I'm very much afraid, Elsie, that Tom is almost certain to be convicted of murder."

Elsie uttered a sharp cry. "No, he can't be. I can't let them take him away." She started to cry, causing Cecily to regret the necessity of her harsh words.

She swiftly rose and patted the weeping woman's shoulder. "There, there, my dear. Can I get you something?"

Elsie shook her head. She poked her fingers into her sleeves and came out with a large white handkerchief. Cecily waited while the butcher's wife blew her nose, then tucked the handkerchief back in her sleeve.

For a long moment she stared into her lap. Then she looked up again, with a look of defiance on her flushed face. "There is another key."

"I see." Feeling somewhat more justified for her ruthlessness, Cecily returned to her seat. "Perhaps you had better tell me about it."

Elsie nodded and started nibbling on her thumb. After a moment, she looked at Cecily, tears still glimmering in her eyes. "I couldn't say anything before, Mrs. Sinclair. I wanted to, but I was afraid Tom would kill me. He's got such a temper and . . ." She gulped as a sob took her breath away.

Cecily nodded, her face creased in sympathy. She said nothing, waiting for the woman to regain her composure.

Finally Elsie went on. "I knew Peter Stewart, you see. I met him when he came into the town." Fishing in her sleeve again, she pulled out the handkerchief and once more loudly blew her nose.

"He was in Dolly's Tea Shop," Elsie continued, her voice quavering. "He was in such a state, Mrs. Sinclair. He'd overslept, you see, and he'd missed the first day of the band practice at the church hall. He was feeling sorry for himself, and he wasn't looking what he was doing. He knocked his hot cup of tea all over me."

She pulled back her sleeve and showed Cecily a red stain on her arm. "Scalded my arm, he did. Of course, he was full of apologies. Such a gentleman he was."

Tears filled her eyes again, and she blinked them back. "He never meant any real harm, Mrs. Sinclair. We got to talking, and one thing led to another, like it does sometimes."

Cecily pursed her lips. "Is that the reason Tom was fighting with Peter Stewart in the George and Dragon?"

Elsie lifted her shoulders in a gesture of despair. "I don't know. I haven't been able to talk to either of them since . . . since . . ."

She gulped, and Cecily said quietly, "Take your time, Elsie. Take a few deep breaths, and go on when you feel ready."

Elsie nodded and blew her nose again. "Anyway, it was

partly Tom's fault really. He was always down the pub, leaving me alone every night. I mean, there was nothing to do except sit and wait all by myself for him to come home."

She sniffed loudly. "It wouldn't have been so bad, you see, if we'd had babies. But the good Lord hasn't blessed us with any, and I was so lonely. When I met Peter, he was so nice to me. He was such a handsome man, younger than me, he was, and he made me feel like a beautiful woman when he looked at me with those big admiring eyes of his."

She paused for a moment, half smiling at the memory, and Cecily felt a stirring of pity for the neglected woman.

"Anyway," Elsie said after a moment of silence, "when I told Peter how Tom was always off, leaving me alone all the time, he suggested he come over and see me. While Tom was down the pub, like."

"So Peter was coming to see you the night he was killed," Cecily said, beginning to understand at last.

Elsie nodded her head. "I suppose he must have been, otherwise why would he have been in the shop? I don't really know for sure, of course. But he did come the night before he was killed. I know I shouldn't have done it, but I sort of lost my head. It's been a very long time since anyone made me feel like a real woman."

Once more she seemed on the verge of tears. Cecily leaned forward and said quietly, "I do believe I will take that cup of tea, Elsie. I think it might do us both good."

Elsie nodded and jumped to her feet. "I'll get it right away, Mrs. Sinclair."

She disappeared into a small room off the living room, while Cecily mulled over in her mind what she had heard. Apparently Tom had a violent temper, judging by Elsie's fear of him. If he had learned about Peter Stewart's visit to his wife, it would give him a very strong motive for murder.

Perhaps, Cecily thought uneasily, for once she was mistaken in her judgment. Perhaps this time P.C. Northcott had been right for a change.

Within a few minutes, Elsie was back with the tea. Taking

the cup and saucer from her shaking hand, Cecily thanked her. The room was quiet for a minute or two, while both women sipped at their tea. Then Elsie put her cup down in her saucer with a clatter.

"I gave Peter my key, you see," she said, as Cecily put down her own cup and saucer. "I thought it best. Peter wasn't sure if he could come, and I didn't want to have to wait all evening for him in the shop. I couldn't have him knocking on the door, or the neighbors would have heard him. Nosy lot, our neighbors. More likely than not they would have asked Tom who it was who was visiting his wife while he was away down the pub."

"So Peter took your key?" Cecily prompted, after another long moment of silence.

Elsie nodded. "He let himself into the shop and came up to the flat. We spent a lovely evening together. He made me laugh a lot, that's something I haven't done in a while. We danced a bit, and he kissed me a few times, but that was all. I wouldn't let him do anything else." She looked up as if remembering to whom she was speaking. "Oh, forgive me, Mrs. Sinclair. I didn't mean to sound vulgar."

"That's all right, Elsie. Go on." Cecily reached for her cup and saucer again.

"Well, anyway, when he left, Peter asked if he could take the key with him again. He wanted to come back the next night, you see. We'd both had such a lovely time, and he said the pub wasn't much fun, what with all the fighting and everything."

"So he did plan on coming to see you the night he was murdered?"

"Yes. He said he had to go down there first, so it wouldn't look strange him not being there, but he'd slip away as soon as he could." Elsie's voice was so soft, Cecily had to strain to hear it. "I waited all evening for him," she said. "When he didn't come, I thought maybe he couldn't get away from the pub. Instead of that, someone had cut his throat and . . . left him hanging on a hook . . . in our cellar. Poor Peter."

Dissolving into a flood of tears, Elsie sat rocking herself back and forth, while Cecily did her best to comfort the distraught woman. Finally Elsie seemed to get herself under control again.

"I need to know something," Cecily said, when the tears had finally dried on Elsie's drawn face. "And I must insist that you tell me the truth this time."

Elsie nodded. "I've told you everything now. Honest I have."

"I need to know," Cecily said firmly, "if you were speaking the truth when you said that you saw your husband walking up the street from the George and Dragon, and that you saw him fall down in front of the store, apparently unconscious."

"I swear it, Mrs. Sinclair. On the Bible, I swear it. I saw him fall down. I was upset, you see, about not seeing Peter, and that's why I didn't go down at first. Let him sleep it off, I thought. It was his own bloody fault if he caught cold. Always coming home drunk. But then after a while I felt sorry for him. I went down there just as he was waking up. Just like I told you."

"And you heard nothing in between the time you saw Tom fall down and when you went down to bring him back up to the flat?"

"Nothing. I tell you, Mrs. Sinclair, if Tom, or anyone else for that matter, had come into that shop after I woke up and saw my husband coming up the road, I certainly would have heard him. I didn't go back to sleep until after Tom came back to bed with me."

Cecily finished her tea and put down the cup and saucer. "If there had been a fight while you were asleep, would you have heard it, then, do you think?"

Elsie took her time thinking about that. Finally she said slowly, "It's possible, I suppose. I sleep pretty soundly at times. The cellar is two floors below this one. There could have been a fight down there without me hearing it, but I would have to be sound asleep."

Cecily smiled as she rose to her feet. "Thank you for being honest with me, Elsie."

"You won't have to tell Tom about Peter Stewart, will you?" Elsie sprang up from the chair, leaving it rocking furiously behind her. "I don't want Tom to go to prison for something he didn't do, but he has such a temper on him . . ."

"I can't promise anything," Cecily said gently. "I'm sorry. I can only say that if it's at all possible to keep your relationship with Peter Stewart a secret, I will do so."

Elsie seemed satisfied with that. "I'll come down to the door with you," she said, and led the way back down the dark narrow stairs to the shop below.

Standing at the door to the street, Cecily shivered in the cool wind. "One last question," she said. "You said that something woke you up in time for you to see your husband walking up the road. What do you think it was that disturbed you out of a sound sleep?"

Elsie thought about that for a moment or two. Finally she said slowly, "I think it might have been this door closing. I remember thinking at the time that it was Tom coming back from the pub, until I looked outside and saw him walking up the road."

Cecily nodded. "Thank you, Elsie." She turned to leave, but paused as Elsie spoke again.

"Strange thing, now that I come to think about it. I thought I saw Peter walking away from the shop at that time. I thought perhaps he'd come to see me and had seen my Tom coming. Then, of course, he'd have to leave."

Elsie gave a little laugh that held no humor. "But it couldn't have been Peter, could it. Unless it was his ghost. I mean, he was dead by then, wasn't he?"

"Yes," Cecily said quietly, "I do believe he was." She stepped out into the street, trying not to think about all the stories she'd heard lately about Peter Stewart's ghost.

"Try not to worry," she said, smiling at Elsie. "Now that I know there is another key, there's a chance we may discover who else might have been in this shop the night of the murder."

"The thing is," Elsie said with a worried little frown, "where is the key now? I don't think the constable could have found it on Peter Stewart's body, or he would have known there was more than one key."

"That's a very good question," Cecily said, "and one that I have already asked myself. Which brings up yet another question. Why do you think Tom lied about the existence of your key?"

Elsie shrugged. "I can't imagine, Mrs. Sinclair."

"Well, it's something to think about," Cecily said. Looking down the street, she saw Samuel driving the trap toward her. Steam poured from the chestnut's nose as it halted in front of the shop, pawing the ground impatiently at this undesirable delay in getting back to the warm stables.

"Thank you, Elsie," Cecily said, giving the other woman an encouraging smile. "You've been very helpful."

"You will do your best to find out who done it, Mrs. Sinclair?" Elsie asked anxiously.

Cecily patted the woman's arm. "Don't worry, I shan't rest until I find out the truth. You can be assured of that."

Bidding Elsie goodbye, Cecily stepped across the pavement to the trap.

Samuel sprang down and offered her his hand. She took it and stepped up into the draughty compartment. Settling down in the corner of the seat, she ordered Samuel back to the hotel as quickly as possible. The wind seemed to have grown considerably colder since her visit to the butcher's shop.

As the trap drew away, Cecily looked out through the narrow slit in the back of the canopy. Elsie Abbittson was still standing in the doorway, staring after the trap as if she was waiting to make sure it moved out of sight.

Settling back in her seat, Cecily thought about her

interesting conversation with the butcher's wife. She couldn't help but wonder if Elsie had been completely honest with her. After all, she had lied before.

Somewhere in the back of her mind, the words of Dr. Prestwick echoed persistently. *His throat was neatly slit with a butcher's knife. Much as a butcher would slaughter beef.* After all, who would know as much as a butcher about slitting throats and hanging carcasses if not his wife?

The carriage jogged at a smart pace along the Esplanade, past the lonely, windswept beach and the deserted gift shops. Deep in thought, Cecily hardly noticed the tiny flakes of snow drifting from a leaden sky.

If Tom didn't have the missing key, she silently reasoned, and neither did Elsie; if that lady was telling the truth, and it wasn't found on Peter Stewart's body, then, as Elsie so succinctly put it, where was it now?

Looking up, she saw the solid white walls of the hotel waiting for her at the end of the Esplanade. As always, the sight comforted her. There the security of her home and her friends waited for her.

As for Peter Stewart, if the rumors that abounded were to be believed, that poor man could not find rest even in death. It was a very sobering thought.

CHAPTER

❈ 14 ❈

A short time later Cecily sat in an armchair in the library, allowing the heat from the glowing coals in the fireplace to thaw out her bones. Mrs. Chubb had brought her a pot of tea and some warm scones, together with her homemade lemon curd, while Gertie had been in to stoke up the fire so that the flames roared up the chimney.

Setting her feet on the fender, Cecily hoped she wouldn't get chilblains. The itchy sores on one's hands and feet seemed to be a constant nuisance for some people during the cold winter months. Fortunately Cecily had remained immune to the condition. She had always maintained that plenty of exercise kept the circulation moving.

A light tap on the door made her lift her head expectantly.

The door opened, and she smiled as Baxter poked his head around it.

"Ah, there you are, madam. I thought I might find you in here. May I come in, or would you prefer some privacy?"

"Do come in, Baxter, and please, close the door behind you. I am absolutely frozen, and I don't want the heat escaping from the room."

"Yes, madam." He stepped inside and gently closed the door, but remained standing with his back to it, watching her with a slight look of concern on his face. "You must take better care of yourself during the winter, madam. It is so easy to catch a chill in this weather."

She gave him another smile. "Don't worry, Baxter. I shall soon warm up now. These scones are excellent. Would you care for one?"

He gave a negative shake of his head. "Thank you, madam. I have not long eaten two of them. Mrs. Chubb was kind enough to give them to me hot from the oven."

Cecily shook her head at him in mock disapproval. "Very bad for the digestion."

"Yes, madam."

"But delicious, I grant you." She took a bite out of the scone, relishing the tangy flavor of lemon curd and clotted cream.

Baxter waited for her to finish the tasty morsel before asking, "I trust all went well at the butcher's shop this afternoon?"

"Yes. Very well, as a matter of fact." She drained the last of her tea and replaced the cup in its saucer. "Baxter, do move closer to the fire, for heaven's sake. This room is so large you can't feel the warmth of the fire unless you are standing on top of it."

Baxter hesitated for a moment, then slowly edged over a few steps.

"There," Cecily said happily, "that's better, isn't it? Much more cozy, don't you think?"

He gave her an inscrutable look and said quietly, "Indubitably, madam."

Sighing, Cecily leaned back in her chair. "I must admit, I find the cold weather rather tiring. It's so much easier to get around in the summer, without having to wrap oneself in a ridiculous amount of clothing to keep warm."

"Yes, madam."

He'd sounded uncomfortable with the course of the conversation, and she took pity on him. "I talked to Elsie Abbittson," she said, changing the subject. "I do believe she was telling the truth when she said she saw her husband walk up the street then fall down in a drunken stupor outside the shop."

"Then that leaves the question of how someone else managed to take possession of the key."

"Well, that's the point. As a matter of fact, there are two keys after all." Quickly she recounted the gist of the conversation that had taken place between her and Elsie. After she had finished, Baxter was silent for a long moment, apparently digesting everything she had told him.

"According to Samuel," Cecily went on, "Peter Stewart fought with Tom Abbittson in the George and Dragon the night he was murdered. Peter then left the pub, apparently to meet with Elsie."

"Someone followed him, do you think?"

"If Elsie is telling the truth, yes, I think someone might have followed Peter Stewart to the shop. He waited until his victim was inside the shop, then followed him inside and killed him there. He then took the key from the piper, let himself out of the shop, and locked the door behind him. No doubt he intended that Tom Abbittson should be suspected of the murder."

Baxter clasped his hands behind his back, lifting his chin in contemplation. Finally he said, "It is a valid theory, I agree. Isn't it possible, however, that Tom Abbittson followed Stewart back to the shop? Then, realizing that the piper intended calling on Elsie, he could have killed him in a jealous rage."

"He could have," Cecily agreed, "but he didn't. I'm quite sure that Peter Stewart was already dead when Tom arrived back at the shop."

Baxter raised an eyebrow. "You are certain that Elsie was not lying in order to protect her husband?"

"I am certain she was telling the truth about Tom's innocence. You see, if there were two keys, why would Tom lie and insist that there was only one? It's the most damaging piece of evidence against him. He had nothing to gain by insisting he had the only key."

"It does seem a strange thing to do."

"Unless, that is, he suspected the murderer to be the only other person who could have been inside the shop at the time." She leaned forward to make her point. "His wife, Baxter. He lied to protect her."

"Good Lord," Baxter said, looking impressed. "In which case, if he suspected his wife, he could hardly have done the murder himself."

"Baxter, it is so comforting to join forces with a man of intelligence."

"Thank you, madam."

Cecily wiggled her slowly warming toes inside her house shoes, enjoying the smug look on Baxter's face. "Now that we have eliminated Tom as the suspect, either someone else did indeed follow Peter Stewart and take the key from him, or we are left with Elsie. She could have had an argument with Peter, I suppose. Perhaps he threatened to tell her husband about their little tryst."

She paused, staring thoughtfully up at him. "In any case, it would seem that whoever has the key is mostly likely to be the murderer. In other words, Baxter, find the key, and we find the killer."

"There is one small problem that might arise," Baxter said, rubbing his hands together as if to warm them.

"Knowing that the key could incriminate him, the killer could well have thrown it away by now."

"That is entirely possible." She stared into the flames for a moment or two, then said quietly, "In which case, we shall have to give him a reason to use the key again, won't we?"

"Cor blimey, Doris, there you bloody go again." Gertie stared at the broken pieces of china sitting in a puddle of milk, which spread rapidly across the pantry floor.

"I'm sorry, Miss Brown, really I am." Doris wrung her hands together as she stared at the mess. "It were those blessed cats again. One of them was hiding under the shelf. I sneezed, and it jumped right across my feet. It startled me so, I dropped the jug."

Gertie tutted and lifted the hem of her skirt out of the way of the white rivulets. "Well, don't stand there bleeding dithering, get something to clean this mess up."

"Yes, Miss Brown."

Doris scuttled out of the pantry, and Gertie leaned over to pick up the jagged pieces of china. Mrs. Chubb would be good and bleeding mad about this one, she thought. The third jug this week, smashed to bloody smithereens. Doris won't half bleeding cop it this time.

The timid housemaid rushed in carrying a mop and bucket of water. "Don't cut yourself, Miss Brown," she said, squatting down in the puddle. "I'll pick this up."

"You're getting your blinking skirt all wet." Gertie reached for another piece of broken china, lifted the corners of her apron, and dropped the piece inside the fold. "You're more bloody likely to cut yourself than I am. I never seen no one as nervous as you. You're getting bleeding worse, you are."

"It's the ghost, Miss Brown. He keeps following me around, he does."

"There ain't no such thing as bloody ghosts," Gertie said, wishing she could feel as convincing as she sounded. "I keep telling you, it's someone playing tricks on you.

Anyhow, I told madam about it, so whoever it is better bloody watch out."

"Ooh, 'eck, I hope he doesn't get mad at me for telling on him," Doris muttered.

"Telling on who?" Gertie picked up the last of the broken pieces and dropped it in her apron.

"Peter. He might get mad at me and do something terrible."

Gertie sighed. "I don't know how many times I have to tell you—"

She broke off as Mrs. Chubb's voice rang out from the kitchen. "Doris? Where is that girl?"

"In here, Mrs. Chubb." Doris jumped guiltily to her feet. "I'm going to catch it now," she said miserably. "This being the third one and all."

Gertie felt a stab of sympathy for the girl. It wasn't so long ago when she was terrified of the housekeeper herself. "Tell you what," she said quietly, "I'll tell Mrs. Chubb it were my fault this time. She won't yell at me as loud as what she'd yell at you."

Doris's mouth dropped open. "Go on! You really mean it? Why would you do that?"

Gertie shrugged. "Let's just say I'm feeling in a good mood today. But you'd better bloody get out of here quick like, before I change me bleeding mind."

"Thank you, Miss Brown," Doris whispered, looking as if she was about to cry. "I won't forget this, on me honor I won't."

"Go on with you," Gertie muttered, her face growing hot. She hated anyone making a fuss of her. But after Doris had gone to find out what Mrs. Chubb wanted, Gertie had to admit to feeling all nice and warm inside. Sometimes it felt really good to do something nice for somebody.

Smiling to herself, she finished mopping up the floor. Tomorrow night she would be alone in a card room with Ross McBride. Her stomach went all squishy again when she thought about it. Tomorrow night. She would never bloody sleep tonight thinking about it. Not that she slept much with the babies, anyway.

But somehow that didn't seem to matter anymore. Nothing mattered, except that she had twenty-four hours to get through before she could slip away to meet the most fascinating man she'd ever known.

Hearing the light tap, Cecily opened the door of her suite to find one of the twins waiting outside. The housemaid bobbed a curtsey and said in a nervous, high-pitched voice, "Mrs. Chubb said as how you wanted to speak to me, mum."

"Yes, Doris." Cecily peered closer. "It is Doris, isn't it?"

The young girl nodded. "Yes, mum. Daisy's in Miss Brown's room with the babies."

Cecily stood aside to allow the girl to enter the room. "Daisy seems to like taking care of the babies, so Gertie tells me."

Doris, who was standing in the middle of the Axminster carpet gazing around at the walls, dragged her gaze back to Cecily. "Yes, mum. Daisy likes taking care of helpless things. She was always getting in trouble for bringing strays home when we lived with our aunt."

Cecily's smile faded, reminded of the cruel treatment the girls had suffered at the hands of their spinster aunt. "Well, I'm happy that your sister has found an outlet for her need. I'm sure Gertie appreciates the help."

"Yes, mum." Doris's eyes grew wide as she spied the huge elephant tusk hanging over the fireplace.

"Doris," Cecily said patiently, "Gertie tells me someone has been playing tricks on you. She seems to think you are quite frightened by them."

Doris jerked her face around, a look of terror in her eyes. "It's no one playing tricks, mum. It's Peter Stewart, come back to haunt me."

"Now why would he want to do that?" Cecily asked gently.

Doris's thin shoulders jerked up and down. "P'raps he's

cross with me, 'cause I wouldn't go for a walk with him."

Cecily sighed. "Doris, Peter Stewart is dead. He can't hurt anyone now."

"He might be dead, mum, begging your pardon, but he's not gorn. I've seen him. Lots of times. I always know when he's around 'cause it gets really, really cold. Freezing cold. Even if there's a fire in the room. That's when I see him."

Cecily could feel a chill right then. Now that she thought about it, the hotel had seemed uncommonly cold of late. Shaking off her absurd thoughts, she said a trifle sharply, "You really must stop this nonsense, Doris. If you insist on talking about ghosts, the word could spread to our guests. I really don't want my guests upset any more than they are already by this dreadful murder."

Doris chewed her bottom lip and nodded. "Yes, mum. I won't say nothing more, mum. Only—"

She broke off, and Cecily frowned. "Only what, Doris?"

"I just hope he stops following me around, that's all. He's driving me bonkers, he is."

"Perhaps you'd better tell me exactly what it is you see." Cecily moved closer to the fire, seeking more comfort from its warmth.

"It's him, all right. I know what he looks like—I talked to him often enough. He stands there just looking at me. I touched him once, and me hand went right through his arm. I swear to God it did."

"It could be a trick of the light, a reflection of someone standing out of sight. In the shadows we can often mistake what we see."

"I touched him, mum. I went right up to him. He weren't there, and yet he was."

Seeing that the child was thoroughly convinced, Cecily gave up. "Very well, Doris. I don't quite know what I can do about this, but I'll try to find out what is happening. In the meantime, I would appreciate it if you didn't talk about it to anyone else."

"Yes, mum. I mean no, mum, I won't." Doris bobbed an awkward curtsey and headed for the door.

Long after she had gone, Cecily was still trying to convince herself that Doris's fears were nothing more than an active imagination.

Belowstairs, Gertie reached her room just in time to hear a lusty howl from the babies. She'd timed it just about right, she thought grimly as she opened the door. Daisy was walking up and down holding one of the twins in her arms, while the other one yelled in outrage at being neglected.

Scooping up the baby in her arms, Gertie muttered a few soothing words. Immediately the baby turned its small face toward her, seeking a breast.

"Bloody always hungry, these two," Gertie mumbled as she sank onto the side of the bed. She peered into the red face of the baby as it drew strongly on her milk. "Can tell you're a boy, all right. Never bleeding satisfied."

She looked up at the housemaid, who sat quietly murmuring to the squalling baby in her arms. "You doing anything special tomorrow night?"

Daisy looked up in surprise. "I'm off after I've helped get the ballroom ready for the ball. I have to clear the tables away so they can dance."

"Yeah, I know. I mean after that."

"I'll probably want to go to bed after that. I have to be up at four in the morning."

Gertie nodded, feeling guilty. She knew how miserable it was, getting up in the dark on a cold winter's morning to light the fires. She'd done it often enough herself.

"Did you want me to look after the twins, then?" Daisy asked, raising her voice to be heard above Lilly's yelling.

"Well, I was going to ask you, if you wouldn't mind. I'll pay you thruppence to do it."

Daisy shook her head. "Nah. I don't want no money for it."

"All right, then I'll get up the next morning and light the bloody fires for you. That's only fair."

Daisy regarded her with her usual solemn expression. "Will you be gone all night, then?"

Gertie shook her head. "Course not. No more than half an hour, I shouldn't think."

Daisy looked back at the baby writhing in her arms. "You don't have to do my job, Miss Brown. I like taking care of the babies. Besides, they wake you up in the night, and you need your sleep. I'd only have to get up the next morning to look after them if you were doing the fires, wouldn't I?"

Gertie grinned at her. "S'pose you're right. Thank you, Daisy. I won't bleeding forget it. I swear I won't."

"It's nothing. Like I said, I like taking care of them."

Pulling James from her breast, Gertie handed the baby over to Daisy and took Lilly from her.

"Where will you be going, then?" Daisy asked, pushing her finger into James's tiny fist. "That's if you don't mind me asking?"

Gertie hesitated. She was dying to tell someone about it, but she wasn't sure Daisy was the person to confide in. But then, who else could she tell? Daisy was the closest thing she had to a sister, and somehow she knew she could trust her. Even if the poor sod did go around with a gloomy face all the time.

"Well," she said with an air of imparting a confidence, "if you want to know, I'm meeting someone. Only don't tell no one. This is our little secret."

Daisy looked up, with the first spark of interest Gertie had ever seen in her eyes. "You meeting a man?"

Gertie felt the squishy feeling again in her stomach. "Yeah, a real nice man. We're just going to have a chat, that's all. But we want to have some privacy like, where no nosy bugger is going to listen in on us."

"Where you meeting him, then?"

Gertie put a finger to her lips. "Don't tell no one," she

whispered. "I'm going to meet him in one of the card rooms."

Daisy looked shocked. "In the hotel?"

"He's staying here in the hotel, ain't he? It'll be bloody easy enough."

Gertie felt uneasy as Daisy stared at her in growing horror. "You're not going to meet that piper, are you?"

"Yeah, I bloody am. Why not?"

"After what happened to Doris? She got friendly with one of them, and he got murdered."

Gertie managed a strained laugh. "Well, don't you worry. No one is going to murder this one." Glancing down at Lilly's face, she said softly, "Well, look at that. Fast asleep."

Thankful for the opportunity to change the subject, she laid Lilly down in the cot and held out her arms for James. "I'll see you tomorrow night, then," she said, trying not to let her uneasiness show in her voice. "After you're finished with the ballroom."

Daisy nodded, looking worried. "I'll be here, Miss Brown. But if I were you I'd think twice about what you're doing."

Gertie managed a fairly decent laugh. "You worry too much, Daisy. I'll be fine, I will. I'm old enough in the tooth to know what I'm doing, I reckon." She jerked her head at the babies. "It's not as if I haven't been around, now is it? It'll be all right, you'll see."

She watched the door close behind Daisy, her own words still ringing in her ears. "It will be all right," she whispered. But the squishy feeling in her stomach had turned into something else. Something that didn't feel half as good. In fact, it didn't feel good at all.

CHAPTER

❄15❄

Saturday morning, the day of the Tartan Ball, dawned clear and cold. Phoebe, up with the lark as usual, had dressed with special care for the final dress rehearsal at the village hall.

Her favorite pearl-gray two-piece, which had been carefully re-tailored to meet the current fashion, fitted her to perfection, and the new peach organza collar she had sewn on to her blouse revitalized the entire outfit.

As always, her pièce de résistance was her purple hat, upon which she had labored for hours sewing into place the pink velvet rosebuds, several yards of pale green tulle, and, at great expense, three white doves.

Well satisfied with her appearance that morning, Phoebe pulled on her elbow-length gray kid gloves, placed her slightly moth-eaten fur wrap around her shoulders, and set off for the village hall.

Arriving somewhat out of breath several minutes later, she was irritated to find her young ladies, who were supposed to set an example of grace and elegance, engaged in a riotous version of a vulgar dance known as "Hands, Knees, and Bumps-a-Daisy."

The movements, as far as Phoebe could see, consisted of partners slapping each other's palms, then their own knees, and finally an utterly disgraceful "bumping" against each other's hips. All this accompanied by a shrill, tuneless rendition of the song, punctuated by annoyingly hysterical shrieks of laughter.

It did not improve Phoebe's frame of mind to discover Alec McPherson watching this shameful display with a certain amount of attention.

"Really!" she said to him, after having restored a somewhat tenuous order to the proceedings. "I would have thought that someone of your standing would have discouraged such uncouth shenanigans."

"Och, dinna fash yourself, Phoebe. The young ladies were only letting off a bit o' steam."

"Steam!" Phoebe emphasized this with a vigorous and quite magnificent toss of her head, which set the large brim of her hat wobbling up and down. "These young ladies, as you call them, were acting like hooligans."

She couldn't imagine why he had not supported her. Thoroughly disappointed with her companion's sudden and inexplicable lack of sympathy, Phoebe turned on the girls, who were standing in a group whispering and giggling together. "Ladies!" She clapped her hands to add emphasis to her command. "Give me your attention, *please*!"

The girls nudged each other and shuffled obediently around to face her. "Gawd," one of them whispered, loud enough for Phoebe to hear, "cast your peepers on them blooming sparrers."

Phoebe stiffened her back and flung out her bosom.

"They are not sparrows, Marion. They are doves. Not that you would know the difference, of course."

"Ooh, do-o-o-oves," Dora chanted in a singsong voice. "The birds of true lo-o-o-ove—"

"Shut up, Dora," Marion said, giving her a hefty shove that sent her into the next girl. "You sound like a blinking lost goat."

"You look like a blinking lost goat," Dora retorted, shoving back.

"Ow," someone complained. "Get your bony elbow out of my face."

"You need something there to improve it."

"Is that so? Well, Miss Big Mouth—"

"*Girls!*" Phoebe clapped her hands again sharply. "I will tolerate no more of this outrageous behavior. Either we have complete cooperation from each and every one of you, or I shall—" She broke off, staring in horror at one of the dancers who until now had been largely hidden behind others.

Phoebe had spent some time discussing potential costumes with Alec, who served as chief advisor, as well as Madeline, who had volunteered to work on the outfits.

They had finally decided on ankle-length black skirts and white blouses, provided by the girls themselves. Madeline had hemmed several yards of tartan cloth with a white wool fringe to be draped across the back and over one shoulder. The stole was then dramatically secured in the front with a very large safety pin.

The young lady standing at the back of the group, however, was not wearing the long black skirt as decreed by Phoebe. She was, it was true, wearing the white blouse. The tartan strip, that had been designed to drape becomingly over one shoulder, was somehow draped over her hips instead, leaving a quite appalling expanse of lily-white leg.

Phoebe shot a horrified glance at Alec, who appeared to be enjoying the spectacle. Now she knew why he had been so engrossed in the girls' crude capers earlier. No wonder he had turned traitor on her.

"Isabelle," Phoebe demanded, in a voice that would have made Goliath tremble, "where, pray, is your skirt?"

Speaking above the suppressed giggling of her companions, Isabelle said with a look of hurt innocence, "I thought this was supposed to be my skirt." She tugged at the tartan cloth, while Phoebe briefly closed her eyes.

"Why," she demanded, "would you form that assumption when all the other girls are correctly dressed?"

"'Cause she's stupid?" someone suggested.

"You mean blinking barmy," Dora said helpfully.

Isabelle held up her hands in a gesture of bewilderment. "I thought we was supposed to wear kilts."

"No, she didn't," someone piped up from the back. "Dora dared her to come dressed like that."

Dora spun round on the unfortunate girl who had spoken so recklessly. "Shut up, you tattling twit, or I'll sock you one in the eye."

"And I'll box your ears, young lady, if I have one more word out of you!" Phoebe's shrill voice echoed all the way to the rafters. Mortified by her outburst in front of Alec, she turned a beseeching eye on him.

Shaking his head, he held up one of his large hands. "All right, ladies, settle down. We have a lot of work to do before tonight. You are nowhere near ready to perform the Sword Dance yet."

"What about the Highland Fling?" Marion demanded. "We're getting good at that."

Alec picked up his bagpipes and stuck them under his arm. "What you term as good would never be tolerated in Scotland," he said bluntly. "Just thank your lucky stars you're performing in this puny little village, instead of a Scottish town. You'd all be stoned, right enough."

Phoebe, somewhat affronted at Alec for referring to Badgers End in such a derogatory manner, clapped her hands once more for attention. She had no idea what had got into the burly Scotsman that morning, but it was apparent that he was vexed about something.

In fact, Alec's unpleasant mood became even more apparent as the long morning wore on. The girls, suffering from the usual performance-day nerves, leapt when they should have stepped and flung when they should have twirled.

By the time Alec despairingly pronounced them as ready as they were going to be, Phoebe was quite exhausted. Left alone with the Scotsman after the girls had left the hall, she breathed a sigh of relief in the merciful silence.

"I do wonder sometimes why I take on such thankless tasks," she murmured as Alec helped her replace the chairs in their original position. "Thank heavens the whole thing will be over after tonight."

"Ay, I heartily agree. I'll be glad myself when the concert is over, then I can concentrate on the contest." Alec carefully placed his pipes in their case and closed it.

"I must admit, though," Phoebe said, brushing a speck of dust from her impeccable skirt, "I am rather looking forward to hearing your little group play for us this evening. I only hope the death of that poor man doesn't put a damper on the festivities."

"I wouldna worry yourself about it," Alec said as he led the way to the door. "No one will miss the sorry bugger. He was tone-deaf, that man. Couldn't play a note worth listening to for the life of him. I think he only came down here for the fun of the thing. He certainly wouldna have stood a chance in the contest."

"Well, we'll never know now, will we," Phoebe said soberly. Shivering, she stepped out into a chill gray mist that had rolled in from the sea. Even her fur wrap seemed inadequate protection against the damp cold. Hurrying to keep up with Alec's long stride, she hoped that the girls would put on a good display, after all the help the Scotsman had given them.

Even as the thought formed, she knew it was a forlorn

hope. Perhaps, for once, they could at least get through the performance without disgracing themselves. With that small consolation in mind, she gave up worrying about it for the moment, and concentrated on enjoying what could very well be her last moments alone with Alec McPherson.

After settling the twins down for their evening nap, Gertie hurried down to the kitchen, trying desperately to ignore the sensation of squirming worms in her tummy.

She could hear the crashing and banging of Michel's pots and pans long before she reached the door. It sounded as if the chef was in one of his right royal moods that evening. Taking a deep breath, Gertie pushed open the door.

She was just in time to see a large saucepan crash to the floor. Michel stood by the stove, his arms flailing the air, his tall chef's hat bobbing furiously as he yelled, "*Sacre bleu!* One hour to go before dinner is served and I am still waiting for ze herrings. Where is that girl?"

One of the twins flew out of the pantry with a large square pan in her hands. "Here they are, Michel. I had trouble finding them. Sorry."

"Everyone will be sorry, Daisy, if the roes fricassee are not on ze table before the pheasant gets there. Then it will be Michel who gets the bad name, *oui*?"

"Yes, I mean no, and I'm not Daisy. She's in the dining room setting up the tables."

Michel slapped the pan on the stove, causing the fish to jump in the air. "Doris . . . Daisy, what does it matter? As long as you answer to one of them."

Catching sight of Gertie, the chef waved a spatula at her. "Ah, there you are, Gertie. At least I know who you are. Where is that Mrs. Chubb? She is not in her room taking ze nap, I hope?"

"She's in the bleeding dining room with Daisy." Gertie winced as Doris picked up a loaded tray of silverware and tipped half of it back onto the table with a deafening clatter.

"Mon Dieu!" Michel muttered. "That girl has fingers of butter."

"Here, give it to me," Gertie said, pushing the girl to one side. "You get the bloody serviettes out for me to fold. I'll take this lot to the dining room."

"Yes, Miss Brown. Thank you, Miss Brown." Doris scampered over to the dresser and pulled open the drawer.

Ignoring Michel's expression of amazement, Gertie loaded the silverware back onto the tray and carried it from the kitchen. It was none of the chef's business if she wanted to be nice to Doris for a change, she thought as she hurried up the stairs. Though she was bloody surprised at herself lately. Must be getting bleeding soft. Smiling at the thought, she strode swiftly down the hallway to the dining room.

Daisy was placing the silver salt and pepper shakers on the tables when she arrived there. Mrs. Chubb loitered in the corner of the ballroom speaking to Madeline, who was arranging the last of the bouquets for the centerpieces.

Dumping the tray on the table next to Daisy, Gertie said cheerfully, "Here's the silverware, Daisy. Let me know if you need any more."

Daisy nodded, her usual scowl plastered across her grim face.

Gertie watched her for a moment or two, then edging nearer, whispered, "You won't forget about tonight, will you? Right after the entertainment's finished. All right?"

"Course I won't forget," Daisy muttered. "I said I'd come, didn't I?"

"All right, keep your bleeding hair on. I just wanted to make sure, that's all." Gertie picked up a fork and pretended to polish it with the corner of her apron. "After all, I don't want to take off unless I know my littl'uns are going to be looked after, now do I?"

"I'll be there." Daisy picked up a handful of knives from the tray. "I keep my word, I does. Just you be careful, that's all. I don't want nothing bad happening to you."

Gertie grinned. "Aw, go on, I didn't know you bleeding cared."

She had hoped to get a glimmer of a smile out of Daisy, but the housemaid merely sent her a dark look and muttered, "I just don't want to be lumbered with the babies all night, that's all."

Sighing, Gertie gave up. "Don't you worry about me, Daisy 'Oggins. I'm bleeding old enough and ugly enough to bloody take care of meself. I'll be back in half an hour, and that's a promise."

Daisy nodded without even bothering to look up.

Gertie took one last look at the housemaid's dismal expression and left the dining room. One day, she told herself, if it bleeding killed her, she'd see a smile on Daisy Hoggins's flipping face.

Right now she had better things to bloody worry about. Like her rapidly approaching rendezvous with Ross McBride. Although she didn't really believe that he would try anything, she couldn't help thinking about Daisy's warning.

After all, she didn't really know too much about the bloke. Then again, he just didn't seem the type who would want to do her any harm. Besides, she had promised Daisy she'd only be gone half an hour, so she'd have a good excuse to leave if he got too fresh.

All the way back to the kitchen she battled with indecision. She was half-tempted to ask Mrs. Chubb's advice, except she knew what the housekeeper would say. She'd tell her she was bleeding crazy and practically forbid her to go down there alone.

No, Gertie thought as she deftly folded the serviettes, the decision was entirely hers. And she bleeding knew what she was going to do. A chance like this might never come her way again. Anyhow, not much could come of it in half an hour.

Not that she wanted anything to come of it, she assured herself. After all, he lived in Scotland, and she lived in the south of England. Almost four hundred miles between them. It was like bleeding living on the other side of the world.

Still, it would be nice, just for a little while, to be treated like a proper lady. That's what she liked best about Ross McBride. He treated her like a bleeding lady. And that was the reason she was going to keep her appointment with him this evening. No matter what Daisy Hoggins thought about it.

Cecily stood on the balcony overlooking the ballroom and cast a critical eye over the floral decorations. Madeline had achieved her usual spectacular display, and Cecily couldn't have been more pleased with the results. The striking bouquets of red and bronze chrysanthemums made a dramatic centerpiece for each table, and the tartan ribbons added a festive touch.

Already the guests were drifting into the ballroom, most of them newly arrived from London for the weekend. Cecily was happy that her contribution toward the Robbie Burns celebration had turned out so well. The hotel rooms were full, and the Tartan Ball promised to be a spectacular and unusual event for the Pennyfoot.

That's if Phoebe's dance troupe managed to avoid one of the catastrophes. One never knew what to expect from them. At times their mishaps caused quite a sensation, but somehow Phoebe usually seemed to perform a miracle and avert total disaster.

Cecily watched the throng below for a moment or two, admiring the elegant women in magnificent ball gowns sweeping across the floor on the arms of their equally distinguished escorts.

Everything seemed to be going smoothly, and, satisfied with her inspection, Cecily turned to leave. As she did so, she saw something move in the shadows at the end of the balcony.

Peering at the still figure, she realized it was one of the

pipers. He stood by the rear door that led down to the backstage area at the back of the ballroom.

In fact, Cecily thought worriedly, that's where he should have been, down in the Blue Room with the rest of the pipers. They would be gathered there by now, waiting to make their dramatic entrance just as soon as the guests were all seated.

Phoebe, Cecily knew, would have a fit if she saw that there was a piper missing. She had her hands full as it was, no doubt, attempting to control her wayward dance troupe.

Deciding to ask him to go below immediately, Cecily hurried along the balcony toward the piper. She called out as she approached him. "Excuse me, but aren't you supposed to be in the Blue Room by now? It's almost time for the entertainment to begin. Mrs. Carter-Holmes will be concerned—"

She broke off, her words dying in her throat. She could see right through the man standing by the door. She blinked, certain that it was an illusion created by the poor lighting. If so, it was a remarkable illusion. For as she stared, the piper slowly turned, then walked through the closed door and disappeared.

CHAPTER

❖ 16 ❖

"Where is Isabelle?" Phoebe demanded, doing her very best to keep her voice calm and quiet. "She should have been here half an hour ago."

"She went back to her house to get her dance shoes, Mrs. Carter-Holmes," Dora said, sounding polite for once. "She should be here at any minute."

Phoebe sighed and tried not to give in to the quiver of panic fluttering under her tightly laced corset. "Speaking of shoes, how many of you have decided to perform the Sword Dance in stockinged feet?"

The girls stood huddled together in the small dressing room. Not one of them moved a muscle. They simply stood there staring at her in silence like a bunch of lovesick cows.

"Come, ladies," Phoebe said briskly. "In the interest of

drama, surely you can be courageous enough to risk a tiny nick on the toe?"

"Tiny nick?" Marion echoed indignantly. "You get your foot caught in the blade of one of those blooming swords and you won't be cutting your toenails again I can tell you."

The girls shuddered in unison.

Ignoring the hollow moans, Phoebe waved an elegant gloved hand at them. "Nonsense. If you are careful you won't get any more than a scratch. After all, a woman must suffer for her art, you know, if she is to be a proper artiste."

"Artists don't paint with their blinking toes," someone grumbled.

"Some of them do," Dora announced. "I saw a man at the fair once, he was painting with his toes. Put them in his mouth, too, he did."

This statement was immediately greeted with loud cries of disgust from the group.

"Hush!" Phoebe cried. "They will hear you in the ballroom. Please, I beg you, ladies, try to behave with at least a modicum of grace. Remember that some of the most respected members of the aristocracy will be watching you tonight. I trust you will not let yourselves down, nor me for that matter."

"Yes, Mrs. Carter-Holmes," the girls chanted.

Phoebe eyed them with suspicion. She never quite knew when they were being disrespectful. "Very well, then. I am going to look in next door, just to make sure the pipers are ready for their entrance. I will be gone no more than a minute, so please, do try not to get into mischief while I am gone."

"Yes, Mrs. Carter-Holmes."

Hoping she wasn't making a mistake in leaving the troupe alone, Phoebe hurried into the next room. In truth, she had hoped to have a quick word with Alec, but the burly Scot was deep in conversation with another of the pipers, and Phoebe had to be content with a brief nod and a smile from him. At least until after the entertainment, when she planned to engineer another meeting.

To cover her unannounced visit in a room full of men, Phoebe made it appear that she was taking a head count. To her intense dismay, she counted only eight pipers. Ross McBride, it seemed, had not as yet arrived.

"Where is he?" she demanded of the ginger-haired piper nearest the door. "Has anyone seen him?"

The piper shook his head. "Dinna fash yourself, Mrs. Carter-Holmes. I'm sure he'll be here. He might be a bit of a dark horse, but he's reliable."

"Well, I certainly hope so." Phoebe tugged on her hat brim to straighten it. "Please inform me when, and if, he arrives. I have to get back to my dancers right now."

The piper touched his cap with his fingers. "Yes, ma'am. I will do that."

"Thank you." Phoebe, upon hearing smothered giggles from next door, backed hurriedly out of the room and sped back to the dressing room.

Isabelle, it appeared, had finally arrived. She stood in the middle of the group, relating some hair-raising tale that had the rest of the dancers agog with excitement.

"I tell you, I could see right through him," Isabelle said, her voice rising above the awed murmurs. "It were a ghost, I swear it on my mother's grave."

"Your mother ain't dead yet," Dora said scornfully. "I think you're making it all up. You always did like all the attention."

"You shut your mouth, Dora Davis. I know what I saw, and I saw a ghost, so there."

"There ain't no such thing as ghosts, so you must be seeing things."

Cecily, who had just arrived at the door, was inclined to disagree. She was still trembling from her experience on the balcony, yet she could not bring herself to believe she had actually seen an apparition. It had to be a trick of the light, or more likely, someone playing tricks, as Gertie had suggested.

Cecily very badly wanted to find Baxter to tell him what she had seen. There were a few things that had to be taken care of first, however. Assuring herself that Phoebe had control of the situation in the dressing room was definitely a priority.

Fortunately her presence appeared to have a calming effect on the dance troupe. They chattered quietly amongst themselves while Cecily did her best to concentrate on her conversation with Phoebe, who seemed to be in her usual state of high anxiety.

She stood near the door, waiting for the first notes of the bagpipes that would signal curtain time for her troupe. Wringing her hands, she glanced continuously from the hallway to the dancers.

"I do hope the girls remember everything that Alec has taught them," she said anxiously. "He has worked so hard and given up so much of his time."

"I'm sure the girls will give us an admirable performance," Cecily murmured, convinced of no such thing.

"I really don't know. This is such a difficult dance, something they have never attempted before." Phoebe's hand fluttered at her throat. "Perhaps it is just as well they will be performing with their shoes on. I would hate to have someone cut her foot on those swords. Somehow I don't think the audience would take kindly to blood gushing all over the stage."

"Especially while they're eating dinner," Cecily agreed.

"The problem is, of course, they are used to Alec playing for them. I wanted to rehearse them with the entire ensemble, but the rest of the pipers wanted to attend the last band practice before the contest. I only hope they don't play too fast. You know how the girls are . . ."

Cecily, still thinking about the mysterious piper on the balcony, lost track of the conversation for a moment. Realizing that Phoebe had stopped talking and was waiting for some kind of comment, she said hurriedly, "Please try not to worry, Phoebe. I'm quite sure the pipers know what they are doing."

"Oh, I'm sure. But several of them are upset over the death of Peter Stewart. I'm just afraid it might have an effect on their performance."

"Effect?" With an effort Cecily put the vision of the ghostly piper out of her mind. "I wouldn't think the absence of one piper would make a difference to the music."

Phoebe shook her head impatiently. "Of course not the music, Cecily. In any case, Alec told me that Peter Stewart won't be missed at all. Apparently he couldn't play very well. Alec said he was tone-deaf, judging by his performance on the pipes."

She peered down the hallway with a worried frown. "Now, Ross McBride is another matter. He is one of their best musicians, according to Alec. In fact, Alec told me that Ross McBride might have had a chance at the Grand Prize, if it weren't for the fact that Alec is easily the best musician."

According to Alec, of course, Cecily thought wryly.

Phoebe uttered a little cry. "Oh, there he is. I was beginning to think we would have to go on without him."

Cecily smiled at the pleasant face of Ross McBride, who paused at the doorway of the dressing room. He gave her a polite bow, then turned to Phoebe.

"My apologies for being late, Mrs. Carter-Holmes. I had a wee bit of trouble with my pipes, but they are just fine now."

"Oh, thank goodness," Phoebe gushed. "It would not have been the same without you, Mr. McBride."

The piper backed away with a polite nod, while Phoebe smiled and waved after him. "Such a nice man," she said, casting a quick glance at the girls to make sure they weren't listening. "Such a tragedy. Apparently, so Alec told me, the poor man lost his wife and children when his house caught fire. It was a thatched roof, you see. There was nothing anyone could do."

Cecily felt a cold shock of sympathy. "How awful for him."

Phoebe nodded, her anxious eyes still on the girls. "Alec said that Mr. McBride is a very lonely man. He keeps himself to himself, and won't let anyone get close to him. Apparently he refused to join the other pipers at the George and Dragon every night."

"Drinking in the pubs is not for everyone, Phoebe."

"Oh, I agree entirely. Alec regards Mr. McBride as unsociable, but one can understand it. I don't suppose the poor man feels much like socializing after such a tragic loss."

Her heart going out to Ross McBride, Cecily had to agree.

Just then a small argument broke out among the girls, and Phoebe leapt into the fray. "You will be going onstage at any minute, ladies. Please try to tolerate each other until then."

As if on cue, a shrill whine sent ripples of goose bumps up Cecily's arms. The pipers, it seemed, were ready to descend on the guests. Praying that Phoebe would be up to the task, Cecily left her to marshal her skittish brood onto the stage, and hurried off to find Baxter.

She finally tracked him down in the drawing room, where he stood by the windows, examining the windowsill with a critical eye.

"Draught," he explained, when Cecily sent him a questioning look. "Apparently Mrs. Chubb has had several complaints. It appears that there is a gap between the windowsill and the wall. I shall have Samuel take care of it in the morning."

Cecily nodded. "It's the constant wind, I'm afraid. It does tend to batter the walls rather badly in winter."

Something in her voice must have given her away, as Baxter peered closely at her. "Is something the matter, madam?"

She dropped her gaze, moving closer to the warmth of the fireplace. Now that she had the opportunity to tell him about her experience, she wasn't too sure how to go about it. After all, she didn't quite believe it herself. It would be difficult to convince Baxter, of all people, that what she saw was not some easily explained phenomena.

After a short pause, during which Baxter waited patiently, she said quietly, "Do you remember me asking you if you believed in ghosts?"

"Yes, madam. I do recall the conversation. I believe it was after Gertie had complained about someone playing tricks on her."

"Yes, it was." She stood staring into the flames for a moment longer, then turned to face him. "I think I saw him."

Baxter's expression was inscrutable. "You saw whom, madam?"

"The ghost."

"The ghost?"

"Peter Stewart, if that is whose ghost is walking our hallways."

Baxter continued to look at her with a blank face. "You saw a ghost, madam?"

"Yes, Baxter, I did."

"In our hallways?"

"On the balcony, to be precise. It is Doris who sees him in the hallways."

"Ah." Baxter nodded, as if she were making perfect sense.

"And the conservatory," Cecily added lamely.

"Of course."

"So did Gertie. See him in the conservatory, I mean."

"Naturally."

She puffed out her breath in frustration. "You don't believe me, of course."

He dropped the fold of the curtain he'd been holding and advanced toward her. "I am quite sure you believe it, madam, which disturbs me."

"He was standing at the end of the balcony, next to the backstage door," Cecily said, beginning to feel a little foolish.

"Of course he was, madam."

"When I spoke to him, he disappeared."

"Disappeared."

"Yes." She glared at him. "Please don't humor me, Baxter. You are beginning to make me feel like Colonel Fortescue."

"I'm sorry, madam. Please forgive me."

Turning away from him, she stared into the fire again. "I don't know if I shall, Baxter." She felt perilously close to tears. Which was ridiculous. She had no idea why she felt like crying.

"Cecily."

As always, the sound of his voice speaking her name jolted her. She glanced back at him and saw the warmth of compassion in his gray eyes.

"I think," he said gently, "that you have too much on your mind of late. Apart from the unfortunate death of one of our guests, you have the constant worry of unpaid bills, and you are also troubled by the possibility of your son's return to Africa."

She managed a tremulous smile. "You know me well, Bax."

"I do indeed. I worry about you. I think you need a diversion."

"A diversion?" She looked at him suspiciously. "What kind of diversion?"

He continued to look at her for so long she became nervous. Finally, he cleared his throat. "I know how much you enjoyed dancing when your husband was alive."

"Yes, I did."

"And I am aware of how very much you miss the experience at times.

Frowning, she said slowly, "I do miss it. Very much. Though I sincerely hope you are not suggesting that I go into that ballroom and wait for one of the pipers to ask me to dance?"

She had meant it as a joke. Baxter, however, looked aghast. "Good Lord, I hope not."

"Well, then, perhaps you could tell me where all this is leading?"

Now he seemed nervous, fidgeting with his collar and looking everywhere but at her. "As a matter of fact, I was wondering if perhaps you would do me the honor of joining me in a waltz after the entertainment is over."

Aware that her mouth had dropped open, Cecily hastily closed it again. "You want me to dance with you?"

"That was the general concept, yes." Once more he cleared his throat. "On the other hand, I realize that it is somewhat unconventional. Please forget I mentioned it, madam."

Watching his cheeks grow warm, the cold feeling that had persisted around her heart for days suddenly melted. She smiled up at him, hoping he could see in her eyes how touched she was by his gesture.

"I had no idea you could dance, Baxter. I am immensely flattered that you should ask me."

"Then you accept?"

She hated to destroy that light in his eyes. "I would enjoy the experience very much. I am hardly dressed for the occasion, however. I would feel most uncomfortable joining all those fashionable ladies on the dance floor."

His expression didn't falter, but she could almost feel his disappointment. "I understand, of course, madam. Forgive me for the indiscretion." He started to turn away. "Now, if you will excuse me . . ."

"Wait." Unable to bear the thought of losing such a wonderful opportunity, she added quickly before she could change her mind, "It would not take me long to change my attire, if you would care to wait for me? By the time the entertainment is over and the dancing ready to begin, I could be, at the very least, presentable."

His rare smile spread across his face, and the look in his eyes made her feel quite breathless. "I will be happy to wait for as long as necessary, madam. Please, take your time."

"Very well. Give me an hour. I may be able to perform a miracle by then." She crossed the room with a spring in her step that made her feel like a young girl again.

"I will wait for you at the foot of the stairs," Baxter said as she reached the door, "and escort you to the ballroom."

She turned to look at him. "That would be very nice. Thank you, Baxter."

"The pleasure is entirely mine, madam."

She grinned at him in sheer delight, then hurried off to change her clothes, her mind already tussling with the problem of what she should wear. This was a very special invitation, and she was going to do her very best to rise to the occasion.

It had been years since she had dressed for a man, and she had forgotten the nervous anticipation of such an event. She could only hope she still knew how to dance. Just the mere thought of dancing in Baxter's arms could make her miss a step.

With a renewed energy she thought had gone forever, she hurried up the stairs to her suite.

CHAPTER

❊ 17 ❊

The grand entrance into the ballroom had been carefully planned by Phoebe. The dancers were to be in position behind the drawn curtains of the stage. The pipers would enter the ballroom from the opposite end, through the main doors.

They would march between the tables, playing their soul-stirring music, and continue up the side steps to the stage, where they would line up behind the dancers.

Having come to the end of their opening presentation, they would then launch into the musical accompaniment for the Highland Fling, followed by the Sword Dance. The dancers would then leave the stage for the pipers to perform their closing presentation, which would be played as they left the ballroom through the main doors again.

With that scenario firmly fixed in mind, Phoebe ushered her dancers onto the platform. They seemed unnaturally quiet after the high spirits in the dressing room, and she fervently hoped they hadn't been attacked by stage fright.

She remembered, only too well, the time a missing snake had suddenly materialized onstage, sending not only the dancers into an hysterical frenzy, but most of the female members of the audience as well.

Deciding that the best policy was a positive attitude, Phoebe gave one last round of commands to her fidgety performers, then retreated to her position in front of the stage. From there she hoped to control the proceedings with meaningful frowns or smiles, depending on the circumstances.

By now the high-pitched whine had developed into a recognizable tune, rapidly approaching the ballroom. Phoebe reached the floor just in time to see the pipers burst through the main doors, their colorful kilts swinging about their knees as they marched purposefully forward in time with the toe-tapping music.

A burst of applause greeted their dramatic entrance, and Phoebe felt a swelling of pride. She was responsible for this heart-stopping sight of nine pipers in glorious costume, striding out in unison to a rousing chorus of "Ye Banks and Braes of Bonny Doon."

Tears actually misted her eyes as she watched the proud tilt of their heads. This had to be her best effort yet. She would never forget the sight of these brave, talented men, marching purposefully down the room between the crowded tables as if into battle.

The music, deafening now, made her feel like marching with them. She could only hope that the sound of it would inspire her girls to give at least a passable performance.

The pipers reached the stage and began to march up the steps as the curtains drew back to more enthusiastic applause. Phoebe let out her breath when she saw the girls poised in position, one knee tastefully bent with the toe pointing down. Each dancer rested one hand on the hip, while the other was raised gracefully above the head.

Actually Dora's fingers still looked like a bunch of sausages, and Marion was visibly wobbling, but all in all, the troupe looked quite presentable.

Phoebe began to relax.

The pipers halted in their positions at the rear of the stage, and the music died away. A hush descended over the audience for a moment or two, then the whine began again. Phoebe felt her toe start to tap as the opening chords of the Highland Fling soared into the room.

Everything seemed to be going very well. The girls actually missed each other as they exchanged places, and although Isabelle seemed to have forgotten her steps and was attempting to follow the others without much success, the dancers managed to look as if they were executing a reasonable pattern.

The music died once more, and the dancers took their bows, faces flushed with success as polite applause greeted them. Marion and Isabelle rather spoilt the illusion when they dashed inelegantly offstage to collect the swords, but they returned promptly enough to lay out the gleaming blades in the cross formation on the floor.

Phoebe, still wishing that the girls had been brave enough to attempt the dance in stockinged feet, nevertheless prepared to enjoy herself. At last it would seem as if all her patience and hard work was about to pay off in a near-perfect performance. At least as perfect as the girls could manage.

Once more the wail of the pipes signaled the opening of the dance. Even the audience seemed to be enjoying the proceedings, for once. The dancers assumed their pose and began the hop-and-skip step around the sword blades.

It happened so fast that Phoebe could not recall the actual course of events afterward. Just when it seemed that the girls would get through the entire dance without mishap, Marion stumbled.

Even then, it might not have been quite so disastrous, had she not bumped into Dora, who blundered into the swords. Her toe slammed into the one closest to the edge of the stage.

While Phoebe watched in cold dread, the long blade spun on its handle. With astonishing alacrity, it sped off the stage, heading straight for the center table.

Every one of the dancers froze in various positions, their glazed eyes on the glittering weapon. Phoebe's heart threatened to stop as she watched the light flash off the deadly blade.

The horrified dowager seated in the direct path of the sword appeared too shocked to move, while the rest of her companions sat helplessly by. For one terrible moment it seemed as if the sword would bury itself in the heart of the terrified woman. Phoebe closed her eyes and prayed. She heard a scream, several screams in fact, which appeared for the most part to be coming from the stage. When she opened her eyes again, a portly gentleman in evening dress stood over the unfortunate lady.

At first Phoebe thought the woman had expired. Then she heard the dowager moan, while her worried escort cooled her white face with a large pink fan, delicately edged in black lace, Phoebe noticed.

The sword, its blade still trembling with the impact, protruded from the chair back, where it must have narrowly missed the dowager's ear.

The pipers, experienced artistes as they were, continued to play with grim determination. Seemingly oblivious to the drama taking place in front of them, to a man they kept their eyes fixed grimly on a spot above everyone's head.

The dancers, on the other hand, had totally fallen apart. They clung to each other, whispering and nudging, heedless of the efforts of the pipers to keep everything going.

Phoebe caught the shocked eyes of Marion, who stood with her hand pressed over her mouth. With a sharp gesture of her hand, Phoebe indicated that the dancers should continue. Marion simply gazed back with a blank look on her face.

The dowager was now moaning loudly, enough to distract the entire audience. Even so, the noise did not quite cover Dora's strident voice declaring, "Never mind the bleeding duchess. I could have cut off me blinking toes."

Muttering under her breath, Phoebe advanced on the stage. Standing as close to the edge as she could get, she glared up at Marion. "Get moving," she ordered loudly. "Finish the dance, for heaven's sake."

As if in a trance, Marion shuffled into position. One by one, with a great deal of reluctance, the rest of the dancers followed suit.

Just as they began to hop about like aging rabbits, the pipers played a final rousing chorus and, with a tremendous flourish, brought the music to an end. The girls halted and stood looking at each other as if not sure what was expected of them.

"Take a bow," Phoebe howled.

Dora obediently dropped a deep curtsey. No one else seemed to pay attention, until she tugged on the skirt of the girl next to her. Sporadic and watery applause rewarded the dazed dancers as they executed their ragged bows. With flushed faces they rushed offstage.

As the pipers left the ballroom, Phoebe couldn't help overhearing several comments from the guests seated at the tables, all of them expressing relief that the entertainment was mercifully over.

One day, she vowed as she made her way backstage, she would stage such a triumph that people all over England would talk about it for decades.

Right now, however, she had a few tart words to impart to some particularly inept young ladies. Bracing her shoulders, she headed for the dressing room.

Gertie had looked at the clock so many times that evening, she was beginning to see double. The entertainment part of the evening usually took about an hour. It was past that now, and time she was making her way to the conservatory, where she hoped Ross McBride would keep his promise to meet her.

It was too bad, Gertie thought as she vigorously polished a crystal water goblet, that she couldn't have dolled herself up for him. Her everyday black dress made her look like a witch. Mrs. Chubb would bleeding pounce on her the moment she saw her toffed up in her best Sunday frock. She could just hear the questions now.

Gertie put the last of the glasses away in the cupboard and took one final glance at the clock. If she didn't go soon, he wouldn't wait for her. She couldn't put it off any longer.

She waited until she was in the hallway before pulling off her cap and tucking it into her apron pocket. Her hand shook so badly she almost dropped the cap. She was beginning to wish she hadn't agreed to meet Ross McBride. Right then she would have given anything to be back in her blinking room, rocking her babies to sleep.

Actually they'd been asleep already when she left them with Daisy, who seemed happy to be settling down with the twins for a little while.

Gertie glanced at the grandfather clock in the lobby as she passed. She'd promised Daisy to be back within half an hour, so she hoped that Ross didn't keep her waiting too long. It would take them a few minutes to get to the card rooms.

The upstairs hallway was deserted. Everyone would be in the ballroom, enjoying the dance music. She could hear the violins all the way down the hallway.

A lot different to the sound of the pipes, she thought, as she hurried into the conservatory. She could bleeding hear them as far away as the kitchen. No wonder they sent their soldiers into battle playing the blinking things. It would be enough to scare the bloody wigs off the enemy, that it would.

She reached the conservatory, still without seeing anyone.

The sound of hushed giggles told her that someone was dallying behind the aspidistras. It was a favorite hiding place for courting couples who needed some privacy.

Where she was going was a bleeding lot more private than that, Gertie thought as she peeked into the long, narrow room, her heart thumping.

Ross McBride stood with his back to her, staring out at the darkness beyond the French windows. Her heart did a flip-flop as she stared at his broad shoulders. Gawd, he was a big man. Make bleeding twice of Ian, he would.

Gertie felt shivers chase each other up and down her back. She was a big girl, she assured herself. She knew what she was doing. Putting her hand up to her mouth, she uttered a loud hiss.

He turned around at once and gave her a smile that started her heart racing even more. She held up her hand in warning as he opened his mouth to speak.

Give him his due, she thought, he caught on bleeding fast. He gave a slight nod of his head, then sauntered across the room as if he'd just decided to leave.

Gertie waited out in the hallway until he joined her. "Come on," she whispered, "we'll have to be bleeding quick before someone sees us."

"Where are we going?" Ross whispered back.

"To the card room. I told you."

Gertie paused outside the drawing room, her head cocked to one side to listen for possible voices. Hearing none, she crept past the door and headed for the foyer, with Ross McBride on her heels.

The grandfather clock struck the hour, frightening her half out of her wits as she crossed the foyer. Looking over her shoulder, she saw the piper still following her, a slightly puzzled expression on his face.

Giving him an encouraging smile, she opened the door and stepped outside into the frosty night air. She wasn't sure if it was the bleeding cold or her frazzled nerves that made her shiver as she waited for Ross McBride to close the door behind them. Pulling her shawl closer around her shoulders, she headed down the steps.

"Will ye wait up!" Ross said, catching up with her. "I thought you told me the card rooms were in the hotel."

"They are, but we have to get to them from the kitchen yard." She looked up at him, her stomach going squishy again when she saw him smiling at her in the dim shadows of the hotel walls. "I couldn't take you through the bloody kitchen to get there, now could I? We have to go the long way around."

She reached the bottom of the steps and led the way around the side of the hotel to the kitchen yard. Light streamed across the courtyard from the windows, and for a moment Gertie felt as if she was shut out from the security the kitchen offered.

What was she bleeding doing, she wondered, creeping around in the bloody dark with a strange man? What with her being a bleeding mother and all.

Having a bit of fun, a devilish voice in her head answered. That's what she was doing. There was no blooming harm in that.

That was the voice she liked to hear. The voice that got her into trouble more often than not, her common sense warned her. It was too late now, anyhow. She could hardly back out without looking like a right proper idiot.

"Come on," she said quietly to Ross McBride. "Follow me."

Mincing slowly across the yard, she kept her eyes glued to the kitchen door. She could hear Ross's soft footsteps following her. It gave her a shivery feeling to know he was that close behind her.

She heaved a sigh of relief when she reached the door to the cellar. So far, so bleeding good. Ross paused beside her and put his mouth close to her ear. Her entire body got the quivers when he whispered, "I hope you won't get into trouble for this."

The excitement of it all made her feel reckless. She shook

her head at him, deciding that it would be worth a scolding from Mrs. Chubb. She'd never felt like this before, and she liked it.

The door uttered a loud creak when she opened it, and she froze. Nothing moved in the yard except the wind rustling the dry branches of the trees. The kitchen door remained firmly closed.

Opening the door further, Gertie beckoned to Ross with her finger and stepped through the doorway into the pitch-black darkness. Carefully closing the door first, she felt along the wall until her fingers touched the oil lamp that hung by a nail on the wall.

She'd brought matches with her, and it took a moment or two of fumbling before she finally got the wick alight. Holding up the lamp, she spilled light down the steps that lay directly in front of her.

"Where in God's name are you taking me?" Ross whispered behind her.

"I told you, the card rooms. They're in the cellar, remember?"

"People actually come down here to play cards?" Ross's voice echoed eerily as he followed her down the stairs.

"You can't get to them no other way." She looked back at him. "I hope you don't say nothing, or I'll really be in hot water. This is all supposed to be a big secret. The toffs don't want no one to know they're gambling."

"Don't worry, lass, I'm the last person to say anything. No one will know where we have been tonight. I can promise you that."

Something in the way he said it gave her goose bumps. She reached the floor of the cellar and held the lamp up above her head. Shadows danced up and down the shelves, glinting off the dark bottles of wine nesting there.

"The rooms are through there," Gertie said, nudging her head in that direction. "I brought the keys with me. There's no one down here tonight, thank goodness. So we have the place to ourselves."

She couldn't seem to stop shivering. It was freezing in the cellar, and the card rooms wouldn't be much better. That was the reason few people wanted to go down there in the winter. It was too bleeding cold.

Not for the first time that evening, Gertie was beginning to wish she had never agreed to this rendezvous. It had seemed so romantic and daring, but now that she was actually down here, her recklessness seemed bloody stupid. After all, what did she know about the piper?

She almost fainted as a vision popped into her mind of Peter Stewart, swinging from a rack in the butcher's shop with his throat cut. Daisy's warning rang loud and clear in her head now. She had to be crazy, she thought. She stopped and spun around to face Ross McBride. She couldn't go through with it. She'd have to tell him.

The light swung across his face. His eyes looked dark and mysterious in the shadows, and his mouth curved in a smile as he said softly, "What's the matter, lass? Not getting cold feet, are ye?"

Just looking at him gave her a warm feeling inside. "Course not," she said, turning back again. "Come on, let's get inside one of these bloody rooms before I freeze to death."

Cecily stood in front of her dresser and gave her reflection a critical examination. It had been a very long time since she had worn a ball gown. Such a long time, in fact, that the gown was obviously dated. Women wore their skirts straighter now, fitted snugly to the hips before falling in smooth folds.

The pale lilac gown she wore had been made when full, billowy skirts were still in fashion, and the train was a little long for the current mode.

She was pleased, however, that the gown still fitted her. Although she had never been blessed with a waist as small as Phoebe's, neither had she tortured her body with the tight lacing so popular when she was young.

In fact, she thought with a wry smile, she was only too happy to be rid of her corset the minute she was in the privacy of her own suite. She looked forward to the day when it would no longer be considered improper to go without such a restrictive garment, as she had heard some women were doing in France.

Leaning forward, she tucked a stray hair back into the chignon she wore. She had forgotten how it felt to be so concerned about her appearance. After all, she reminded herself, it was only Baxter. He had seen her many times at her worst, so anything she achieved this evening would be an improvement.

Even so, she couldn't stop the slight trembling of her hand as she applied a dab of perfume along the line of her low-cut bodice. In fact, she almost spilled the precious liquid when she heard the light tap on her door.

Frowning, she crossed the room, hoping that it would not be bad news. She wanted nothing to interrupt this rare opportunity to share a few special moments with her manager. Whatever the messenger brought, it would have to wait until after her dance with Baxter.

CHAPTER

18

"I'm sorry to disturb you, mum," the housemaid muttered when Cecily opened the door, "but it's Miss Brown. I'm worried about her."

Cecily peered closer. She still couldn't believe how closely the sisters resembled each other. When seen together, one could detect slight differences; but when they were apart, it was almost impossible to tell who was which.

Unless one knew their temperament, that was. The somewhat disagreeable tone suggested that this might be Daisy. Given that the girl usually sat with Gertie's babies, Cecily decided she had it right. "You had better come in, Daisy, and tell me about it."

"Yes, mum." The young girl edged into the room and stood by the door, looking uncomfortable. "I don't know what to do, mum. Miss Brown didn't want me to tell no one, but she said half an hour, and it's a while past that, and I can't help thinking . . ."

Her voice trailed off as she stared down at her foot, which was carefully tracing the pattern on the carpet.

Worried herself now, Cecily said quietly, "If Gertie is in trouble, you had better tell me about it. No matter what she told you."

"Yes, mum." Daisy hesitated for another moment, while Cecily grew more uneasy by the second.

Finally the housemaid blurted out, "Miss Brown is meeting with one of the pipers down in the card rooms. I told her it was stupid to go by herself like that, but she wanted to go, and I couldn't tell her what to do now, could I?"

Relief made Cecily's voice weak. "Is that all? I thought—" She broke off, unwilling to put into words what she had thought.

"She said half an hour, mum. I know she really likes this bloke, but it's over an hour since she's been gone. I have to get back to the babies, I left them alone—"

"Please try not to worry." Feeling somewhat surprised that Gertie had taken an interest in someone, Cecily silently rebuked the young mother for her thoughtlessness.

She couldn't blame Gertie for seeking consolation for her loneliness. It was, however, most inconsiderate to leave her two babies in the charge of a young girl for longer than promised.

"I'm sure she'll be back soon," Cecily said in an effort to reassure the child. "Perhaps she'll be there when you get back. She's just forgotten the time, that's all."

"And her babies," Daisy muttered darkly.

"Yes, well, I must say I'm a little surprised at her." Cecily smiled. "But I remember well how time flies when you are with someone special. Half an hour isn't very long under those circumstances."

Daisy's head came up. "She's only just met him, begging your pardon, mum."

"I know. But sometimes it doesn't take very long to know that someone is special." Cecily patted the girl's shoulder. "You'll understand when it happens to you."

"Yes, mum." Daisy turned back to the door. "I just hope that something hasn't happened to her."

"I'm sure she'll be just fine," Cecily said firmly. "If she isn't back within the next half hour, however, you must tell Mrs. Chubb. We can't have Gertie behaving irresponsibly when she has two young babies to take care of."

Daisy looked over her shoulder. "Miss Brown will kill me if I tell Mrs. Chubb. That's why I came to you." She let out a sigh. "Course, she'll probably kill me anyway when she finds out I told you."

"Don't worry, Daisy. I won't mention it to her. As long as she's back within the half hour. If she's not, then she'll only have herself to blame for being in trouble."

Daisy nodded. "Yes, mum. Thank you, mum. I wouldn't want her to be cross with me. I was worried about her, that's all."

She slipped through the door, and Cecily was about to close it when she added, a little diffidently, "If I might say so, mum, you look very nice."

Her face turned pink when Cecily gave her a warm smile. "Why, thank you, Daisy. That was very nice of you to tell me."

Daisy bobbed a hasty curtsey and fled down the hallway. Cecily watched her go, aware of a faint twinge of uneasiness. Then she shook her head and closed the door. Gertie knew how to take care of herself. She had proved that on more than one occasion.

Even so, Cecily couldn't help worrying just a little bit as she pulled on her long evening gloves. She made a mental note to look in on Daisy in half an hour, just in case.

Taking one more look in the mirror, she did her best to reassure herself that she looked presentable, then let herself out of the room. She had taken more than the allotted hour. She hoped she hadn't kept Baxter waiting too long at the foot of the stairs.

Now that the moment was at hand, she felt uncommonly nervous. Which was ridiculous, of course. It wasn't as if she didn't know Baxter. He was so much more than just her manager. He was a loyal and trusted friend, one she depended on a great deal.

Yet, somehow, something had happened that evening. For the first time since she had known him, Baxter was defying convention. In asking her to dance with him in public, he was offering far more than a simple whirl around the ballroom floor. He was taking a step beyond the business relationship they had enjoyed since James's death.

It was a small step, it was true, but nevertheless, it was against his rigid principles. Perhaps it was a sign that he might be starting to care for her in a more personal way.

Cecily sighed as she reached the head of the stairs. She valued Baxter's friendship and his loyal support above everything. But for months now she had longed for more. Knowing her manager, it could be many months, perhaps years, before he overcame his strict sense of propriety and offered her the kind of relationship she longed for.

But this event was a precious step in the right direction, and she would grasp it with both hands and enjoy it. For he had given her hope, and with hope she could wait. After all, she had nothing better to do.

She rounded the curve of the staircase and saw him waiting at the bottom, looking very distinguished in his black morning coat and striped gray trousers. He had tucked a white handkerchief in his breast pocket, and the light from the gas lamps played across his hair, glinting on the silver streaks that she found so becoming.

When would he realize how she felt about him? she wondered. For she could never tell him. It would embarrass him greatly, and perhaps ruin the fragile thread that so tenuously bound them together.

She could only hide her feelings behind the friendly banter that he seemed to enjoy so much, even if he did usually receive the worst of it. Dear Baxter. How would she ever manage without him?

He looked up as she descended the last flight of stairs, her silk skirt billowing out in front of her with each step. Her matching lilac shoes had a higher heel than she'd been used to for some time, and she had to concentrate to tread gracefully down the stairs. Even so, she almost lost her step when she saw the warm admiration in his eyes.

In that moment she forgot she was middle-aged with two grown sons. She forgot that the gray hairs were multiplying at a depressing rate and that every time she looked into a mirror she discovered a new wrinkle. She forgot that her ball gown was outdated and just a tiny bit too tight in the waistline.

Looking into Baxter's appreciative gray eyes, the years fell away, and once again she was young and more beautiful than she ever remembered.

As she reached the floor, he held out his hand, and, laughing, she gladly put hers into his warm grasp.

"You look . . . enchanting, madam."

"Baxter?"

"Yes, madam?"

She smiled up at him. "Do you think you could call me Cecily? Just for tonight?"

"I'll try, madam."

She raised her eyebrows, and to her utter delight, he laughed.

"Forgive me, Cecily. I'll do my best to honor your request." He inclined his head in the direction of the ballroom, from whence he could hear the beautiful strains of a popular melody. "Shall we?"

"Let's."

With her hand still clasped in his, he led her to the ballroom.

Several couples waltzed gracefully around the room

when they entered. No one seemed to care, or indeed even notice the owner of the hotel taking the floor with her manager.

Pausing at the fringe of the dancers, Baxter turned to her and executed a slight bow. "May I have the pleasure, madam?"

Cecily pursed her lips, and he added hastily, "I beg your pardon. May I have the pleasure, Cecily?"

"I should be delighted, Baxter."

She fitted into his arm as if she belonged there. The music seemed to swell, inside her head as well as her heart. Her feet floated across the floor with no effort, her hand resting on his strong shoulder, the other clasped in his fingers.

Round and round they twirled, until she felt dizzy with the exhilaration of it all. She felt like thistledown, spinning in a late summer wind, and immediately felt foolish for her fanciful notions.

Looking up at him, she said lightly, "Why, Baxter, you surprise me. I had no idea you could dance so well."

"I would not be nearly as proficient had I not such a graceful and skillful partner."

"You are also a flatterer."

"No, Cecily, I speak the truth. I always admired the way you and Major Sinclair seemed to float across the floor when you danced."

She looked at him in surprise. "You watched us?"

"Often." He looked sheepish. "Do you mind?"

"Not at all." She sighed. "James loved to dance."

"He did indeed. Almost as much as you do."

"And I'm enjoying it now, Bax. Very much."

"And so am I."

She tried to give herself up to the sheer enjoyment of the dance. He was a good dancer, almost as good as James had been. There was a difference, however. She had been completely relaxed when dancing with her late husband.

With nothing to distract her from the touch of Baxter's hand in the small of her back, and his fingers firmly clasping hers, she found it difficult to keep her steps as smooth and effortless as they once had been.

She knew that Baxter felt the same tension. His shoulders were braced as if he were facing a deadly foe, and he held his chin so high she found it difficult to look into his eyes.

After a while, when the silence between them threatened to become awkward, she made an attempt at conversation. "I wonder how the entertainment went tonight. I should find Phoebe and ask her."

"I don't think she is particularly happy. From what I hear, the dancers caused a bit of a stir."

"Oh, dear." Cecily smiled at one of the guests as they glided by. "Do you know what happened?"

"According to Doris, one of Mrs. Carter-Holmes's dancers did her best to stab Lady Dappleby through the heart with one of the swords used in the Sword Dance."

"What?" Cecily stared up at him, only partly reassured by the bland expression on his face. "Whatever did she do?"

"From what I understand, the girl's foot caught the sword, which spun off the stage and buried itself in the chair upon which Lady Dappleby was seated. It gave the poor lady a nasty fright, I'm afraid, but she is otherwise unharmed."

"Oh, good heavens." Cecily raised her eyes to the ceiling. "Whatever will those girls do next? Poor Phoebe, she simply will not give up. I'm quite sure that one day those girls will be the death of her."

"They were almost the death of Lady Dappleby," Baxter said dryly. "I'm afraid those young ladies are becoming quite a menace."

"It certainly sounds like it. I had better have a word with Phoebe later. Though it's not entirely her fault, of course."

"Might I suggest that if Mrs. Carter-Holmes were to hire professional dancers, instead of those inept, bumbling fools, the entertainment at these events would be more successful."

"I know, Baxter. You are right, of course. I'm afraid it's mostly my fault. Phoebe is so proud of her dance troupe, I really hate to turn her down when she offers their services."

"If we accept much more of their services, we might very well lose some of our guests."

She paused to get her breath as Baxter spun her around. "Most of the time," she said when she could breathe again, "the girls manage to get through a performance without causing any damage. To tell you the truth, I think the guests rather enjoy their antics. It must be quite refreshing after the precise performances they are used to seeing onstage."

Baxter gave her a sardonic look. "I hardly think refreshing is the word. From what I understand, even the pipers had trouble keeping in tune while watching the antics of Mrs. Carter-Holmes's protégées."

"Poor Phoebe." Cecily shook her head. "She really has had a dreadful night. When I saw her earlier, she was quite flustered, though I'm not sure if her concern was more for the girls or the pipers."

Baxter said something, but she barely heard him. She was hearing Phoebe's breathless voice as she talked about the pipers. Suddenly she jerked to a stop, almost tripping up Baxter, who stared at her in surprise.

"Is something wrong? I didn't step on your foot, did I?"

"No, no, I'm perfectly all right." She shook her head. "I don't know why I didn't see it before."

"I beg your pardon?" With a concerned frown, Baxter led her off the floor. He paused at the door, looking down at her with worried eyes. "For heaven's sake, Cecily, what is the matter?"

"I'm sorry, Baxter. I have just realized who murdered Peter Stewart." She looked up at him in dismay. "Oh, my goodness. I should have asked Daisy which one."

He looked at her, his face a mask of confusion. "Which one?"

"Yes." She pulled her hand from his grasp. "Quickly, Baxter. Gertie is with one of the pipers right now. I must know which one. She could very well be in grave danger."

*   *   *

"I told you it would be bleeding cold down here," Gertie said, doing her best to keep her teeth from chattering.

Ross McBride grinned. "I can think of warmer places to meet. I dinna suppose you'd reconsider and come up to my room?"

"If it gets much bloody colder, I might be tempted. We could catch bloody pneumonia down here."

"I'm sorry, Gertie. I just wanted to take you out for a quiet drink and a chat somewhere. I didna want to be responsible for making you ill."

"Oh, I'll be all right." She smiled at him, resisting the urge to wipe her chilled nose with the back of her hand. "I'm bleeding tougher than I look. Anyhow, we can still have that drink if you like. It will probably do us good . . . keep out the bloody cold, like."

"You brought some with you?" He looked at her as if she'd created a miracle.

"Nah, I didn't have to, did I. These cupboards are full of bleeding booze. Here, have a look for yourself." She took the ring of keys from her pocket and unlocked the small cabinet.

Ross whistled in appreciation when he saw the rows of wines and spirits. "I dinna believe it. That's a good bottle of scotch there, right enough."

"You want some?" She took out the bottle and selected a bottle of brandy for herself. "If Michel can drink the stuff, then I'm going to."

"You won't get into trouble for this?"

"Course not. You're a guest in the hotel, ain't you? The stuff's bleeding there for the guests to drink, ain't it?"

Ross laughed, giving her that warm feeling again. She took out two glasses and stood them on the table. "You do it. I'm not very good at pouring drinks."

Ross took hold of the brandy and poured a generous measure. "Here, lassie, drink that down. It'll warm the cockles of your heart, right enough."

She watched him pour out his scotch. Lifting the glass, he gave her a wink. "Bottoms up," he said, and drained the glass without so much as a blink of his eye.

"Cor, how do you do that?" Gertie said, impressed. "I thought you didn't drink."

"I didna say that. I said I didn't like going down the pub with the other pipers. I prefer to be on my own. That's unless I have the opportunity to spend some time with a pretty lass like you."

Gertie tossed her head. "Go on with you. I bet you say that to all the girls."

"No, Gertie, I don't." His face growing serious, Ross put down his glass and reached for her hand. "You are the first woman I've looked at since my wife and bairns died in that fire. I swear it, Gertie."

The warm touch of his hand on hers made her forget the cold. She tried very hard not to let his words go to her head. Men were all bloody alike, weren't they? No one should bleeding know that better than her.

Then why did Ross McBride seem so much nicer than any man she'd ever met before? Why did he make her feel all squishy inside, in a way that Ian had never made her feel?

She pulled her hand away, suddenly afraid. "Here, pour yourself another drink," she said, hoping to change what appeared to be a dangerous turn to the conversation.

"You've hardly touched yours yet."

He was looking at her with such an intense look in his eyes, she felt uncomfortable. "I don't drink that much," she said lamely.

"A little sip or two can't hurt you. It will make you feel warmer."

It couldn't make her feel any bleeding warmer than she was already, Gertie thought nervously. Nevertheless, she picked up the glass and took a tiny sip. The liquid burned her throat all the way down to her stomach.

She did her best not to shudder, but couldn't prevent her face from screwing up.

Ross laughed. "By the third sip you won't even feel it going down," he said.

"Blimey, I drink this lot I'll be on my bleeding back." She took another sip, and this time it didn't seem to burn quite as much. It certainly did make her feel warmer inside. In fact, she felt as if her stomach was on fire.

Ross poured himself another glass, but merely sipped the scotch before putting the glass down again. "I have something to ask you, lass," he said, his face all serious again. "I don't want you to answer me now, but I want you to think about it long and hard."

She felt that sudden quiver of fear again. Hoping that another mouthful of brandy might help, she drank it down too fast. Her throat felt as if it had exploded. Coughing and choking, she put the glass down and held onto the table until the spasms had passed.

Ross looked on anxiously, but made no attempt to touch her.

Finally she croaked, "What is it, then? What do you want to ask me?"

He looked at her as if he was afraid to speak. Then, to her utter amazement, he said the last words in the world she expected to hear.

"I want to take you and the bairns back to Scotland with me," he said. "I know we don't know each other very well, but we don't have time to spare to get acquainted. I'm asking you to be my wife, lass."

CHAPTER

✺ 19 ✺

"If I may say so, madam, this is not one of your most prudent ideas."

Cecily took a careful breath. Nevertheless, the smell made her feel quite queasy. The frigid air was unpleasantly damp, and the darkness wasn't quite heavy enough to hide the shapes of dead animals hanging all around them.

"I'm sorry, Baxter, I know the cellar of a butcher's shop is not the most comfortable place to spend an evening, but I really had no choice. I had to move quickly."

"It must be past midnight."

She nodded, though she knew he couldn't see her. He stood several paces away, hidden behind a stack of wooden crates. She had chosen to stand behind the sacks of sawdust stacked in the corner. "Well past, I should say," she said agreeably.

"And the smell is quite appalling."

"Nauseating, in fact."

"We have been here for the best part of an hour, if I'm judging correctly."

"Yes, Baxter, I would say that's about right."

"And there is no sign of an intruder."

"Not as yet, no."

"Might I suggest that perhaps your plan is not working, madam?"

"You can suggest whatever you like, Baxter. I, however, am convinced it will work."

"How—?"

Whatever question Baxter had intended to pose died on his lips, as a slight sound from the floor above silenced him. "Did you hear that?" he whispered.

"Yes, I most certainly did." She paused, her head tilted on one side as she heard the unmistakable sound of the street door opening.

Holding her breath, she prayed that Baxter wouldn't speak again, or that the potential sneeze tickling her nose would not suddenly explode. The door above quietly closed. There was a long pause, followed by the slight creaking of floorboards.

Cecily let out her breath carefully as the tickle in her nose subsided.

Whoever it was had reached the top of the stairs, and was now coming down them, one cautious step at a time. Light from an oil lamp washed over the floor, and she shrank back, flattening herself against the wall.

Each one of the steps creaked as weight was put on them, and Cecily counted off the squeaks. The intruder was almost at the bottom when she heard a slight thud, followed by a soft curse.

At that moment, Baxter said loudly, "Now, madam?"

"Yes, now, Baxter."

They stepped out together, into the light from the lamp. At first Cecily could see little above the bony knees and the kilt. Then the intruder raised the lamp to get a better look at who faced him.

"Damn you to hell," Alec McPherson said.

"Good evening, Mr. McPherson," Cecily said pleasantly. "Or should I say good morning? I'm so glad Phoebe gave you my message."

"I should have known it was a trick. I should never have listened to that ridiculous woman."

Out of the corner of her eye, Cecily saw Baxter edge closer to her. "I had to be sure I had the right man," she said. "Tell me, what was it that Peter Stewart knew about you that could ban you from the contest?"

"I don't have the slightest idea what you are talking about." The Scotsman twisted his head around as if making sure there was no one else skulking in the shadows.

"Come now, Mr. McPherson. We all know you murdered Peter Stewart. I'm just curious to know why."

The piper's eyes rested on her face, coldly calculating. "If you must know, Stewart worked with me in the mines a few years back. He knew me when I got arrested. Three years in jail for nothing more than a fistfight. That was all it was."

Alec McPherson stood the lamp on the floor at his feet and sat down on the steps. "I used a broken bottle to defend myself. The bugger would have killed me if I hadn't. The judge said it was my fault for starting the fight. He said I'd disfigured the man for life."

The Scotsman shook his head, his harsh features made cruel by the shadows. "Disfigured. It was me who was disfigured. My entire life ruined, because some nosy bastard couldna mind his own business."

He looked up at Cecily, his eyes glittering in the lamplight. "I couldna get a job after that. Except for digging a ditch now and again, or lending a hand in the fields at harvesting. I practically starved to death at times."

"So Peter Stewart was going to tell the organizers about your prison term?"

"Ay, he was. He knew he didna stand a chance in the contest unless he got rid of me. I'm the best piper o' the lot, and he knew it. This contest was my chance to start a new life. I'd changed my name, hoping the judges wouldn't find out about my prison term. But then Stewart recognized me. He picked a fight and got the worst of it. Then he told me he was going to report me."

"So you followed him back here."

"Ay, I did." Slowly the husky Scotsman got to his feet. "I saw my chance and I grabbed it. It was easy enough to knock him out cold. I hung him up on the rack and I slit his damn throat. I knew the butcher would most likely get the blame. Especially since I'd heard that Stewart had been fooling around with his wife."

"It seems that Peter Stewart made more than one mistake," Cecily said quietly.

"You are the one who made a mistake, Mrs. Sinclair. You and your friend here." He took a step forward.

Before Cecily could move, Baxter stepped in front of her. "I would not try that if I were you, sir."

Alec McPherson uttered an unpleasant laugh. "And who is going to stop me? Not you, I think."

Baxter threw up his hands. "I might not be much of a brawler, Mr. McPherson, but I assure you I can give a very good account of myself."

"There'll be no need for that," a gruff voice said at the top of the stairs.

The Scotsman swung around as P.C. Northcott lumbered down the steps, followed by two wide-eyed pipers.

"I'm sorry I'm late, Mrs. Sinclair," the constable said, puffing slightly as he reached the floor. "I thought it wise to stop by and recruit some reinforcement, so to speak."

Cecily smiled. "Very wise," she agreed.

"I could have handled it quite well on my own," Baxter muttered in an aggrieved tone.

Fortunately the constable didn't hear him. He was too busy issuing orders to the pipers to hold on to their colleague while he snapped on the handcuffs.

Announcing that he was arresting the Scotsman for the murder of Peter Stewart, P.C. Northcott led him up the stairs. Cecily watched the pipers follow him up, then turned to her manager. "Thank you, Baxter. I am most impressed by your eagerness to protect me from that villain."

"I was merely doing my duty, madam."

She reached for the lamp that Alec McPherson had left behind. "You disappoint me. I was rather hoping you were prepared to fight for my life out of your concern for my safety."

"I am always prepared to do that, madam."

Sadly she nodded. The wonderful, intimate, romantic bond that had so entranced her while dancing with him a few short hours earlier appeared to have vanished. Now she had only the memory of a very special moment, in the arms of a very special man.

Cecily found it difficult to arise with her usual vigor the following morning. Had it not been for the twins' christening, due to take place at noon that day, she might have indulged in the rare luxury of sleeping late.

She was, however, thankful that she had arisen at her normal hour, as shortly after she had eaten breakfast she received another visit from Elsie Abbittson.

Tom, it seemed, had been released earlier that morning and was now enjoying a rest at home.

"I can't tell you how grateful I am for all your help, Mrs. Sinclair," Elsie said as she sat on the edge of her seat on the velvet armchair. "I don't know what I would have done without you, honest I don't. Tom was that scared, and so was I, I don't mind telling you. I thought he was heading for prison, I really did."

Cecily leaned forward to pour coffee into a tiny china cup. "I'm just so happy that the right man was arrested for the crime. I must admit, for a while there I was worried that I might not be able to help."

"Well, my Tom is very grateful as well. He said to tell you that he will see you all right for meat from now on. He'll be putting some good bargains your way, you'll see."

Cecily smiled. "That's really very generous of him, Elsie, but it's not necessary. I would have done the same for anyone in Tom's position. I have a horror of injustice in any form."

She handed the woman the steaming cup and saucer. "I hope that your unfortunate association with Peter Stewart can remain a secret now."

Elsie took the cup with a rueful smile. "Oh, Tom knows about it, Mrs. Sinclair. He knew all along. That's what they were fighting about, as you suggested the other day. Of course, I didn't know that until today, when Tom came home and told me the whole story."

She tasted her coffee, then put the cup down. "I think Peter must have been coming back the night he was murdered to warn me that Tom knew about us. I can just imagine the temper Tom was in. I'm surprised he didn't kill Peter in the pub himself."

"Oh, dear," Cecily murmured. "I hope he wasn't too angry with you when he got home?"

Nibbling on her nail through her glove, Elsie shook her head. "We got it all talked out, we did. I told him as how I was so lonely, and that I missed him when he went down the pub every night like that. He's promised he won't do that no more. Not as often, anyhow."

She pulled her hand down and tucked it into her lap. "And when he does go down there, he says, he'll take me with him. I can sit in the saloon bar with the other ladies while he's playing darts in the public."

"You still won't be with him," Cecily pointed out.

Elsie shrugged. "It'll be a darn sight better than sitting at home on me own."

"Well, I'm so glad everything has worked out so well for

you both." Cecily picked up her coffee. She was anxious
now to put an end to the meeting. It would soon be time to
leave for the christening, and she had no wish to hold up the
proceedings.

Elsie, it seemed, wasn't quite ready to leave yet. Ignoring
her coffee, which was growing cool, she said brightly,
"Speaking of the pub, Mrs. Sinclair, Tom tells me it's being
sold again. Is your son leaving Badgers End, then?"

Very carefully, Cecily put down her cup and saucer.
"Michael did mention to me that he thought he would return
to Africa. His wife is having a difficult time adjusting to the
English climate."

"Black, isn't she," Elsie said, on a note of sympathy.
"They have a hard time of it here, I daresay. We don't get
the sun like they get it out there. That's why they have that
black skin, you know."

Cecily made an effort to hold her tongue. There would be
nothing to gain by jumping to Simani's defense. "You say
the George and Dragon is on the market?"

"So my Tom told me. He heard about it that last night he
was down there." Elsie's eyes narrowed. Leaning forward,
she said in a voice tinged with pity, "Don't tell me you
didn't know, Mrs. Sinclair? Oh, I am sorry—"

"Not at all, Elsie." Cecily swallowed hard. "Of course I
knew. I just wasn't sure when Michael was going to put the
inn up for sale."

Elsie went on chattering, but she barely heard the woman.
Michael had to have known when she was down there,
Cecily thought, feeling herself sink into a sea of misery. For
some reason he hadn't wanted to tell her it was definite . . .
and imminent.

Quite suddenly she felt a desperate urge to talk to Baxter.
She waited for an appropriate pause, then said quickly, "I'm
sorry, Elsie. Would you please excuse me? One of my
housemaids is having her babies christened at noon, and I
have a few things to do before I leave for the church."

Elsie's eyes widened. "You are going to a christening for your housemaid's babies?"

"Yes, I am. As a matter of fact, I'm the godmother." Cecily rose, indicating she expected the woman to leave. "Thank you so much for coming by."

"I think that's very generous of you, Mrs. Sinclair." Elsie got up hurriedly from her chair. "Not too many women in your position would want to be seen dead attending their servant's gatherings, leave alone be a part of it."

"Not too many women in my position," Cecily said firmly as she ushered Elsie Abbittson to the door, "are fortunate enough to be blessed with servants such as the staff of the Pennyfoot Hotel."

Looking a trifle flustered, Elsie nodded. "Oh, indeed, indeed. Give credit where it's due, that's what I always say."

Closing the door after her, Cecily leaned against it for a moment. Michael was going back to Africa. She would miss him dearly, but then she really hadn't seen that much of him since he'd come back to Badgers End. Part of that was her fault, she knew. If she had been more tolerant . . .

She shook her head, trying to ease the ache in her heart. There was no point in regretting past mistakes. She would just have to put a good face on it, and be as pleasant as she could manage about the whole affair.

Right now, however, what she needed was a good cigar. Not to mention the comforting presence of Baxter. Without wasting another moment, she left the room and headed for the stairs.

"For heaven's sake, girl, whatever are you staring at out of that window?" Mrs. Chubb demanded, her piercing voice making Gertie jump out of her skin.

"Ow! You don't have to blinking yell like that, do you?" Gertie hastily finished polishing the pane of glass she was supposed to be working on. "I'm not bleeding deaf, you know."

"You will be, my girl, if I have to box your ears for being saucy."

"Sorry." Gertie pinched her mouth closed and began soaping the next pane of glass.

"Well, aren't you going to tell me what you were staring at?"

Gertie winced as a dresser drawer slammed shut behind her. "I wasn't staring at nothing. I was thinking, that's all."

"Well, you'd better get thinking about finishing that work, that's what I say, or you'll be late for that christening. Where's that Daisy, anyway? She should be finished with the rooms by now."

Gertie didn't answer, her mind busy with her problem.

"Are you listening to me, Gertie Brown? Don't know what's got into you, I don't. You're not worrying about the christening, are you? You've no need to, you know. The vicar will do all the talking. Just be sure those babies are wrapped up nice and warm in their blankets. Never mind about everyone seeing those beautiful christening gowns. That church is much too damp and draughty to—"

Gertie raised her eyes toward the ceiling as Mrs. Chubb broke off.

"Oh, there you are, Daisy," the housekeeper said as the door swung open. "Or are you Doris?"

"I'm Daisy, Mrs. Chubb."

"Well, where have you been, Daisy? The silverware has still got to be polished, and Gertie can't do it because she's got to be in the church."

"Yes, Mrs. Chubb, I know." Daisy sounded as if she had the weight of the world on her shoulders.

"Before you do that, take these candles in to Doris in the dining room. The candlesticks need changing."

"Yes, Mrs. Chubb."

Now, Gertie decided, was a good time to tell the twins what she'd decided. She waited until the door had closed behind Daisy, then wrung out her chamois leather and draped it over the side of the bucket.

"I'm just going to the dining room for a minute," she told Mrs. Chubb. "I'll be back in a tick."

Before the housekeeper could utter the protest hovering on her lips, Gertie fled from the kitchen.

She caught up with Daisy just as she reached the doors to the dining room. Following the girl inside, Gertie saw Doris setting up glasses on a table.

"I want to talk to the both of you," Gertie announced as Daisy carried the candles over to her sister.

Both girls turned a wary eye on her. "Yes, Miss Brown?" Doris said nervously, while Daisy merely looked guilty.

"I've got something to ask you two." Gertie tried to look indifferent. "I don't mind if you don't want to, but I thought I'd bloody ask anyway. Just tell me if you don't want to, all right?"

"If we don't want to what, Miss Brown?" Doris asked in her meek little voice.

Daisy just stood there, looking belligerent now.

"Well," Gertie said casually, "it's like this. My twins being born without a father, so to speak, and me not having any parents, well, except for me father, but he's no bleeding good . . . anyway, what I'm saying is, Lilly and James don't have no aunts or uncles, like so I was wondering . . ." She paused, then finished in a rush, " . . . if you two would like to be aunts to me twins. I mean, I know it won't be official like, but they could call you auntie, and they'd have twin aunts like they're twins, you see, and . . . well, I reckon that being twins you'd understand better what it's like to be twins—" Aware that she wasn't making much sense, she shut her mouth.

Doris had gone pink in the face, though Gertie wasn't sure if that was because she was pleased or not. Then she looked at Daisy, and her own face started to get warm. Because, right there in front of her, Daisy was smiling.

It wasn't a big smile, mind you, but it was a smile nevertheless.

"I'd like that very much, Miss Brown," Daisy said.

"Me, too, Miss Brown," Doris echoed.

Feeling as if she'd just jumped into a warm bath, Gertie hunched her shoulders. "All right, then. I'll see you after the christening. I wish you could have come, but someone had to stay here and look after the guests."

She left then, before she started bawling. Though why she felt like that now that she had two new members of her little family, she wasn't really sure.

Mrs. Chubb was waiting for her when she got back to the kitchen. The housekeeper was fairly buzzing with curiosity. "What was all that about, then?" she demanded as Gertie went back to polishing the windowpane.

"I just asked the twins if they wanted to be aunts to my babies, seeing as how they don't have any."

"Oh, Gertie, that was nice. What did they say?"

"They were happy about it." Gertie smiled. "Daisy even bleeding smiled."

"Go on! I don't think I've ever seen that girl smile."

"Nor'd I, not till now," Gertie said with smug satisfaction.

"It's nice for the babies to have someone they can call auntie. As long as the girls don't spoil them, that is."

"Well, I reckon James and Lilly will do all right now. What with the twins for aunts, and madam and Mr. Baxter for godparents, and you for grandma . . ."

"What!"

Gertie grinned and turned around to face the startled housekeeper. "Well, you've been a bleeding mum to me all this time, it's only right they think of you as their grandma. Besides, I've got to have someone stop us all spoiling the babies."

Mrs. Chubb clasped her hands together. "Oh, my, two more little grandchildren to love. I gave up waiting for my daughter to have another baby. Now I've got three little ones to love."

Well pleased with her morning's work, Gertie turned back to the windows. Now she had only one more problem to face, and that one wouldn't be near as easy. Her smile faded as she thought about Ross McBride.

She had promised to give him his answer that afternoon, after the christening. She had been awake most of the night, and she still wasn't sure what she wanted to do. She could only hope that by the time she met him in the conservatory, she would have made up her mind.

CHAPTER

❈ 20 ❈

The church seemed unnaturally quiet as Cecily stood at the font with Lillian in her arms. Gertie stood next to her, holding James, while Baxter watched the Reverend Algernon Carter-Holmes with apprehension on his face.

The little group was silent as the vicar began the ceremony. Gertie seemed ill at ease and kept glancing at Cecily as if for reassurance. Cecily did her best to comply with a warm smile.

It was good to feel the soft, warm weight of a baby in her arms again, she thought, as the vicar intoned the words of the service. Lillian stirred, her wide-eyed gaze on the light filtering through the colorful stained-glass windows.

Looking down at her, Cecily felt a moment of bittersweet anguish. Once she had held her own babies like this. How she had longed to hold her grandchildren. Now Michael was once more going somewhere beyond her reach.

Sensing his eyes upon her, she looked up at Baxter. He was watching her with a slight frown of concern. She hadn't been able to find him before they left for the church, and there had been no time then to tell him about Michael's imminent departure.

The vicar chose that moment to take James from his mother. The baby uttered a howl of protest, which escalated to a scream when Algie brushed the cold water across his forehead.

Lillian turned her head but remained quiet, much to Cecily's relief. Poor Gertie looked as if she were about to die of mortification when the vicar handed the screaming baby back to her. Cecily was impressed, and immensely thankful to say the least, when the bumbling vicar somehow managed the maneuver without mishap.

Now it was Lillian's turn. As Cecily handed her over, Baxter rolled his eyes heavenward, evidently expecting more screams to be added to the racket. To everyone's surprise, Lillian lay calmly in the crook of the vicar's elbow while he crossed her forehead with water.

"That just goes to show," Cecily told Baxter later, as they sipped champagne at the reception in the ballroom, "that women can withstand trauma more easily than men."

Baxter, looking uncomfortable in his uncustomary role of guest, raised his eyebrows. "To use one of your more endearing phrases, madam . . . piffle."

Cecily grinned. "I would not expect you to agree. You must admit, however, that Lillian was a little angel, while James, on the other hand, created quite a fuss."

"Merely exercising his right to protest, I would say."

"Ah, I see." Cecily nodded her head. "When men make a fuss, they are exercising their right. When women do, they are complaining."

"I did not make the rules, madam."

"Maybe not, but do you have to enjoy them quite so much?"

He was about to answer when a suave voice interrupted them. "Cecily, my dear! How good it is to see you again. May I say how utterly ravishing you look today?"

Cecily smiled up at the handsome face. "Why, thank you, Kevin. That is very gallant of you."

"If you will excuse me," Baxter said, putting his glass down on the table, "I have something that needs my attention." He gave the doctor a curt nod. "Prestwick."

"Mr. Baxter." The doctor clicked his heels and inclined his head. "And how are you, my dear chap? Well, I hope?"

"As well as can be expected." Baxter gave Cecily a cool look. "Please excuse me, madam."

"Of course, Baxter. I will speak with you later."

She watched him with a slight feeling of regret as he crossed the floor, his coattails flying behind him in his hurry.

"Cecily, my dear," Dr. Prestwick murmured, "I don't think there is a sight in this world more enchanting than watching a lovely woman hold a tiny infant in her arms."

Cecily lifted her chin. "Gertie did look quite wonderful, I agree."

"I was referring to you, my dear, as you well know."

How could she ever have thought herself attracted to this man? Cecily wondered. There were times when she found his effusive flattery quite irritating. Although she was quite sure that the rumors about his philandering were unfounded, she could quite see how they had arisen.

As for Baxter, it was painfully obvious to everyone except Kevin Prestwick that he thoroughly disliked the doctor. Cecily would have made her own excuses to leave at that moment, had not Dr. Prestwick added, "I saw your daughter-in-law a few days ago."

"Yes, Michael told me she had been ill. I really don't think she will feel better until she is back in her native country."

"Ah, so Michael did tell you," Prestwick said, nodding his head. "I wondered when he would get around to it. Simani seemed to think he was afraid to tell you they were returning to Africa. I suppose it's natural she would want her baby born in her native country."

Cecily stared for a long time at the glass in her hand, amazed that the sparkling champagne did not spill. "I'm sure she has her reasons," she said evenly. "I am happy for them both, of course, though I shall miss them when they return to Africa."

"I'm sure you will. I was only saying to her—"

"If you will excuse me, Doctor? I see Phoebe is about to leave, and I simply must have a word with her before she goes."

The doctor's shrewd eyes regarded her for a moment. "I'm sorry, Cecily, I thought—" He broke off, apparently reluctant to finish the sentence. Instead he took her hand and raised it to his lips. "If you need someone to talk to," he murmured as he let her go, "I am always happy to lend an ear."

For a brief moment she almost wished she cared enough for him to confide in him. Then she caught sight of Baxter across the room. He was talking to Gertie, actually smiling at her.

"Thank you, Kevin. I appreciate your concern, but I assure you, I am not in need of your services for now."

"In that case, I will take my leave. I have an appointment later this afternoon. I'm afraid a doctor can never count on a day's rest."

Feeling a little ashamed of her slight, Cecily murmured, "You provide a wonderful service to this village, Doctor. I really don't know what we would all do without you."

"I am more than happy to do what I can." His smile seemed a little strained as he bid her goodbye.

Cecily spared him no more than a passing thought as he left. Now she very badly needed a cigar. Actually, she needed more than that. She needed Baxter.

*   *   *

"Whoa, you dinna have to be in such a hurry," Ross McBride said when Gertie rushed into the conservatory an hour later. "I just got here myself a few minutes ago."

"The bloody reception went on forever," Gertie said, gasping for breath. "I couldn't bleeding get away until it was all over. Everyone wanted to talk about the babies."

"How did the bairns like being christened?"

Gertie gazed up at him. He was such a nice man. Not that she knew him all that well, it was true, but somehow she knew he would make a good father and a good husband. He was kind, and honest, and nice-looking. He'd told her he had a good job working for the railways. He was well able to provide for her and the twins.

"Lilly was all right, but James played up," she said, plonking herself down on the padded bench in front of the aspidistras. "Made a terrible noise, he did. Near on bleeding deafened me. He was making such a racket I couldn't hear what the bloody vicar was saying."

Ross chuckled as he came to sit down next to her. "I wish I could have been there."

"Yeah, it was too bloody bad you had to be in Wellercombe."

"Ay, but at least I'm registered for the contest. Though I didna think I was going to make it back here in time to meet you."

He seemed different today, somehow, Gertie thought, beginning to feel awkward now that she was alone with him again. He seemed older, more serious.

"Well, now," he said, taking hold of her hand, "it does a boy good now and again to air out his lungs."

"I suppose so." She looked down at their linked hands and wished she knew what to say next. There was plenty of words in her bloody head, they just didn't seem to want to come out.

"Have you given any thought to my proposal?" Ross said, squeezing her fingers just a little bit.

She'd been awake all bleeding night thinking about it. She couldn't tell him that, though. "I did think about it, yes." She could hear Doris singing somewhere down the hallway. For several moments that was all she could hear.

Then Ross prompted gently, "And?"

Her heart ached as she pulled her hand from his. Plucking at her skirt, she mumbled, "I can't come to Scotland with you, Ross. I'm very sorry."

She squeezed her lips together hard as the seconds ticked by.

After a long pause, Ross said heavily, "I see. Well, I thought it was too good to be true. I had hoped . . . oh, never mind what I had hoped. I couldna expect a lass like you to love an old man like me."

"You're not old." Tears sprang to her eyes, and she dashed them away with the back of her hand. "It's nothing like that, honest. I do like you a lot, I really do. It's just that this is me bleeding home, and now that I've got the babies, I need to be with people I know. I never had much of a family, like, and now I've got one, sort of. I can't go and leave them now. I just can't."

Determined not to cry, she clamped her lips together as tight as she could get them.

Ross uttered a soft curse and put his arm around her. The weight of it felt good . . . sort of comforting. "There, there, lass, dinna take on. I know I've rushed ye, and I'm sorry for that. It's just that I didna have much time before I left."

"I know." Gertie swallowed down the lump in her throat. "I'm really sorry, Ross. I've never been to Scotland, you see, and it's such a bleeding long way away. I feel safe here in Badgers End. What with two babies to take care of . . ."

"I understand, lass." He squeezed her shoulders.

They sat in silence for a long time while she wondered if she was being a bloody fool for turning him down.

Then he said tentatively, "Would ye mind if I wrote to

you when I get back? Just a little note now and again to see how you and the bairns are getting along?"

She smiled up at him with blurry eyes. "Ooh, I'd really like that, I would."

"You'd write back to me?"

She sniffed and wiped her nose on her sleeve. "Yes, I will, I promise. I'm not too good at writing, but Mrs. Chubb can help me."

"Ay, then I'll have to be satisfied with that for now." He put his finger under her chin and lifted it. "I'll wait for you, Gertie. For as long as you need. Just try not to make me wait too long, all right?"

She would have nodded, except he was kissing her, and she was enjoying it too much to pull away.

"I thought the entire proceedings went very well," Cecily remarked as she gazed around at the cluttered tables in the deserted ballroom. "I hope Gertie enjoyed the reception."

"She left in rather a hurry, I thought," Baxter said, reaching down to pick up a fallen serviette from the door.

"Leave that," Cecily said, moving over to sit down on a chair. "The housemaids will take care of it later." She felt tired now. Weary, and uncommonly dispirited.

"Are you feeling all right, madam?" Baxter said, watching her from a few feet away.

"What? Oh, yes, thank you, Baxter. Though I would dearly love a cigar. Do you happen to have some with you?"

For once he made no comment as he lit up a cigar for her. Drawing in the smoke, Cecily closed her eyes for a moment.

"I hope that doctor chap didn't say something to upset you," Baxter said a trifle sharply.

"Not at all." She watched the thin, gray spiral float up toward the ceiling. "At least, not in the way you mean."

Baxter edged a step closer. "In what way, then, might I ask?"

She managed a faint smile. "Don't sound so belligerent, Baxter. The good doctor merely advised me that my daughter-in-law is expecting my first grandchild. I was left to wonder why my son felt it imprudent to inform me of the fact."

She wasn't looking at him, but she sensed his immediate concern.

"I'm so sorry," he said after a short pause.

"So am I."

"Cecily—"

She silenced him with a lift of her hand. "It's all right, Baxter. It's no more than I deserve. I'm afraid I have rather bungled things with Michael. I hope someday he will forgive me."

"Oh, I'm sure . . ." His voice trailed off, as if he had no idea what to say next.

What could he say, she thought sadly. There were no words to comfort the ache. Only time would heal, as she well knew. Deciding it was time to change the subject, she said firmly, "I saw Elsie this morning. She is very happy that things turned out so well for Tom. I hope they will have a better marriage now. It's an ill wind, as they say."

"It is indeed." Taking his cue from her, he asked, "There is one thing I would like to know. How were you so certain that Alec McPherson was the culprit?"

Cecily leaned forward to tap the end of her cigar into an ashtray. "I was quite certain the murderer was one of the pipers. Elsie said that when she looked out of the window that night she thought she saw Peter Stewart walking away from the shop. At the time I was preoccupied with all the rumors about ghosts, so I didn't put too much significance on her statement."

"But it wasn't Stewart, of course."

"No, it couldn't have been. The poor man was already dead. What Elsie saw was a man wearing a kilt."

"But it could have been any one of the pipers."

"True." Cecily watched the end of her cigar glow as she drew on it. Breathing out the smoke, she added, "I decided it was much too late at night for any of the Wellercombe men to be in Badgers End, which meant the suspect had to be someone staying here at the hotel. Actually, it was Colonel Fortescue who gave me the clue."

Baxter rolled his eyes. "By accident, no doubt."

This time she managed a genuine smile. "Naturally. He told me that he saw two of the pipers fighting at the George and Dragon, apparently because they recognized each other. It occurred to me that since the contestants needed an impeccable background in order to qualify, that incident could suggest a motive for murder, given the grandeur of the prize."

"So you decided that the murderer and the victim must have known each other before."

"I thought it possible, yes. I admit it was a wild guess, but one worth pursuing, given the absence of motive."

"I see." Baxter frowned. "I still don't understand how you knew McPherson and Stewart knew each other."

"Well, I must admit, I had a bad moment when I ran into Gertie last night." Cecily smiled at the memory. "Gertie happened to mention that the man she had met earlier, Ross McBride, also knew Peter Stewart before the contest." Cecily looked up at her manager. "Did you know he proposed to Gertie?"

Baxter looked shocked. "Stewart?"

"No, Ross McBride." Cecily frowned. "She was supposed to meet him this afternoon to give him her answer. I wonder what she told him."

"I certainly hope she refused. I should hate to lose such a good worker."

Looking up at him, Cecily asked softly, "Or someone you care about? Such as the mother of your godchildren?"

Baxter's face turned a pale shade of pink. "Perhaps I do feel somewhat responsible for that young lady and her children. She has, after all, been under my employ for several years—"

"Relax, Baxter, I do understand. I feel the same way myself."

He sighed. "You were explaining how you knew McPherson had known Stewart before the contest."

"Simple deduction, as always." Cecily leaned back in her chair with a sigh of satisfaction. "You see, Elsie told me that Peter Stewart had missed the first day of practice. That's how she met him. Phoebe had also told me that Alec McPherson had missed the second day of practice to work with her girls. Since Peter Stewart was killed that night, the men could not have practiced together. Yet Alec McPherson had assured Phoebe that Peter Stewart was tone-deaf, judging by his performance on the pipes."

Baxter nodded, looking impressed. "So therefore McPherson must have known Stewart at some time before the contest."

"That's what I surmised. There was one way to find out." Cecily paused long enough to take another draw on the cigar. "I told Phoebe that Elsie had found new evidence on the floor of the cellar. I said that Elsie would leave it there until the police could examine it the next morning. In which case, it was likely the pipers could be forced to stay in town until after the investigation, thereby missing the contest."

"Very cunning, if I might say so."

Cecily shrugged modestly, though rather pleased with the compliment. "I was reasonably certain that Phoebe would immediately pass on the news to Alec McPherson. If, for some reason, I was mistaken, there still remained the chance that he would pass on the news to the rest of his group. I hoped the guilty person would do exactly as our murderer did, rush to remove the evidence before the police could see it."

"You never fail to amaze me, madam."

"Thank you, Baxter." She smiled rather wistfully, wishing she could recapture the magic of the night before.

It seemed as if he had read her mind, for he said, with feigned indifference, "It was a pity our dance had to be interrupted yesterday."

Assuming a matching air of nonchalance, Cecily nodded.

"It was indeed. I was rather enjoying myself. It has been such a long time since I've danced, I had almost forgotten how very pleasurable it can be."

Baxter cleared his throat. "We could possibly conclude the dance now, since there is no one here to interrupt us."

"We could, I suppose." She held her serious expression as she looked at him. "Except for one thing. There's no orchestra to play for us."

He stared down at her, and she felt a flutter of excitement at the determined look on his face. "Maybe not, but I do believe we could manage without it."

Quickly she stubbed out her cigar. "I would like that very much, Baxter. Just as long as you don't expect me to sing. I am like that poor man, I find it impossible to hold a tune."

She rose and allowed him to take her hand. Following him onto the dance floor, she marveled at this welcome change in him. Even though she cautioned herself against depending too much on hope, she couldn't help wondering if at long last, Baxter was beginning to bend to the pressures of modern society.

It didn't seem possible, and yet . . . it was very difficult not to hope. She looked up at him as he turned to her and placed his hand above her waist.

They took two or three awkward steps, and then they were off, gliding in perfect unison around the floor.

"I cannot help wondering," Baxter murmured after a period of pleasurable silence, "why McPherson would have gone to all that trouble to assist Mrs. Carter-Holmes with her dance troupe. It was a thankless task, at best."

"I think he was merely attempting to create an image . . . the portrait, if you will, of a Good Samaritan, offering his expertise to a helpless woman in need of his advice."

"I think you may be right." Baxter expertly whirled her around in a tight spin.

She was catching her breath when a slight movement on the balcony above her took her breath away again. "Baxter," she whispered urgently. "Look up there, behind you."

With a startled expression, Baxter paused and looked over his shoulder.

Together they watched the hazy figure of the piper in full dress walk slowly along the balcony. He reached the door, paused for a moment, then simply vanished through it.

"By God, I don't believe it," Baxter whispered hoarsely.

"Neither do I," Cecily echoed, her voice unsteady. "But there it was, right in front of our eyes."

"It has to be one of our guests," Baxter insisted. "Though what he would be doing on the balcony now I have no idea."

"Particularly," Cecily said quietly, "since every one of the pipers left this morning for Wellercombe. They had to report by midday for the contest. Of course, they could have returned, I suppose, but I sincerely doubt it. And if Ross McBride came back to visit Gertie, I can't imagine why he would need to walk the balcony. Or how he was able to walk right through the door."

Baxter seemed unable to answer, and she gave him a moment or two to recover before adding, "It would seem that the Pennyfoot has acquired a ghost. I shall have to consult Madeline as to the best way to deal with it. We can't let our guests be frightened away by its presence."

"Indeed no." Apparently recovering his composure, Baxter turned back to her and once more placed his hand above her waist. "Neither will I let it interrupt our dance."

Cecily happily agreed.

"As for the ghost," Baxter remarked, "all I have to say is that I sincerely hope that it isn't your late husband's ghost roaming the balcony. Now that would make me most uncomfortable indeed." Holding her a shade closer, he swept her across the floor.

Peeking up at him, she could tell nothing from his bland expression. She could perceive a tiny gleam in his eye, however, that left her pondering on the delicious implications of that remark.

Welcome to Hemlock Falls...
a quiet town in upstate New York
where you can find a cozy bed at the Inn,
a tasty home-cooked meal—and murder
where you least expect it...

THE HEMLOCK FALLS MYSTERY SERIES

CLAUDIA BISHOP

with an original recipe in each mystery

__A PINCH OF POISON   0-425-15104-2/$4.99

When a nosy newspaperman goes sniffing around the local
mini-mall project, Sarah and Meg Quilliam smell something
rotten in Hemlock Falls. It's worse than corruption—it's
murder. And the newsman is facing his final deadline...

__A DASH OF DEATH   0-425-14638-3/$4.99

After a group of women from Hemlock Falls win a design
contest, one disappears and another dies. Just how far
would television host and town snob Helena Houndswood
go to avoid mixing with the déclassé of the neighborhood?

__A TASTE FOR MURDER   0-425-14350-3/$4.50

The History Days festival is the highlight of the year in
Hemlock Falls, with the reenactment of the 17th-century
witch trials. But a mock execution becomes all too real
when a woman staying at the Inn is crushed under a pile of
stones and the killer is still on the loose...